CHEKHOV'S CUT

ROBERT BELL

First paperback edition September 2023

Back cover photograph by Alessia C_Jpg

CHEKHOV'S CUT

Every swing of the old wooden door cost his heart a beat.

This time it was a couple. Middle-aged, with faded clothes and fleshy faces. They seemed normal enough. Probably an accountant and a nurse, something like that. Happy for a night out, even just the local pub. Probably one of them would say as such soon. They shook the rainfall off their clothes. The woman looked around as the man headed to the bar.

Blondeau turned back to his table. Andrea hadn't taken her eyes off him. She drilled her cigarette into the ashtray and immediately lit another.

He smiled awkwardly. "I was thinking tomorrow we could try The Golden Eagle, up in Ashwell. Bob Starkey from *The Times* was raving about it the other day."

She said nothing, just kept staring at him. His forehead felt like it was burning.

A crack of thunder hushed the room. At the bar the accountant ordered a gin and tonic and a pint of Carling. Normal enough. A dog, sat with a lone drunk, gave a low growl. The students by the window huddled together conspiratorially.

Blondeau tried again: "Or there's The Clarendon Inn at Amersham? We've been talking about that one for a while, what better time to–"

"I am not," Andrea grit her teeth, "spending another single

night in some pub in the middle of nowhere. While you... pretend everything's fine, all the while you're glancing over at the front door every ten seconds and thinking I won't notice."

He sighed. *So she'd noticed.* "I never said things were fine, OK? I'm just saying we should try and make the best of a bad situation."

She leant forward, her words barely more than a whisper, "And I'm just saying, that you need to go home and get those men out of our house." She scowled. "How many chances did you have to walk away from this? How many times did I tell you that some things were best left in the past? But you had to keep scratching away, didn't you?"

Blondeau held his hands up in protest. "How could I have possibly known things would end up like *this*?"

She moved closer to him still, he could smell the nicotine and red wine on her breath. "Tomorrow morning," she nodded as she said it. "Tomorrow morning, you are going to go home and get those men out of my house."

Blondeau grimaced but said nothing. In his periphery the door swung open again, but, for once, he held her gaze.

"Fine," he said at last. He finished off his IPA and slammed the glass down. "Fine."

The rain pattered on the windows. The thunder rumbled. The dog howled.

THREE MONTHS EARLIER…

One
The Star

The bus was running so late that it turned up early. A little luck at last.

Stephen Blondeau staggered on and squirmed his way down the aisle.

A voice called his name. It was Turnbull from down the road, a spare seat beside him. Blondeau took it gratefully, pretending not to have noticed the elderly woman struggling along behind him.

Turnbull looked at him with concern. "Everything OK, Stephen? Your eye–"

"It's fine," Blondeau said, winking frantically. "It's just- I fell asleep with my contact lenses in and now it feels a bit uncomfortable. It'll sort itself out soon."

"Blimey."

"I was watching the cricket," Blondeau explained. "It wasn't supposed to happen – I should never have lain down." The bus hit a speed bump and he felt his stomach churn. *Of course, the wine hadn't helped much either.*

Ahead of them an old man in a wheelchair and a woman with a pram eyed each other across the aisle. The tension was palpable. Those contraptions were so damn big these days, Blondeau thought with unease. If another baby turned up they were all going to have a problem.

"Can't you take the lens out?" Turnbull asked him.

"No time. I've got to interview Chase Ashley at The Dorchester in fifteen minutes."

A few heads twitched at that, a few mouths turned sceptically.

Turnbull chuckled. "I saw the trailer for his new one the other night. Not my type of thing, I must confess. I suppose I might be pleasantly surprised, though."

"I wouldn't have thought so," Blondeau said grimly. He was giving it two stars on Friday, the worst of all ratings. At least one out of five inspired a morbid curiosity.

"Shame," Turnbull commiserated. "You'd think he'd be too old to keep making those kind of films. Surely he has enough money by now?"

"I'll ask him for you," Blondeau smiled. "Though I'm not sure the word 'enough' has entered the Hollywood lexicon."

As if on cue they passed a billboard of Ashley's new film. Hollywood's golden boy was abseiling a building, his co-star Lisa Caspian held in his free arm. They faced the camera with very serious and seductive expressions. A couple of birds were perched on top of the billboard, pecking at their rope.

Turnbull kept chuckling. "Far too old," he repeated to himself.

Blondeau checked his watch. Twenty to five. They had given him the last slot of the day and he was still going to miss it. He caught his reflection in the glass as the bus ducked under the bridge by Edgware Road station. His right eye was red raw, he padded it gently with his palm. His hair was a greasy, ragged mess and there was a stain of unknown origin on his shirt collar. Thank God this was only a newspaper interview.

"You know, Stephen," Turnbull began, "I'm never quite sure whether I envy your life or not. It must make for good dinner party talk, but it seems to bring a great deal of stress as well."

Blondeau gestured dismissively. "It's not as glamorous as it sounds. These press junkets, the actors sit in a hotel suite all day and we trudge through one by one for our ten minutes like Soviets queueing for bread. Everyone asks the same questions, and we get a few bland answers to take back home."

Turnbull made a disappointed little noise.

"When I first started," Blondeau continued, "I used to try and massage something more interesting out of the actors, but now I think it works better if we all just go through the motions. There's an efficiency to it that way."

The bus approached Marble Arch and slumped into a wall of traffic.

"Oh, come on," Blondeau groaned.

"That's rush hour for you," Turnbull said, wincing. "Plus half the roads around the City are closed for a demonstration. Anti-capitalists or anti-globalists or some such. Anti-something, anyway."

Blondeau shook his head with disapproval. "It would never happen in North Korea, you know."

"It's the millennium," Turnbull explained matter-of-factly. "Y2K, or whatever you want to call it. It's driving everyone loopy." He grimaced. "I feel it myself sometimes. Like a tension, you know? I'm sat at home watching *Antiques Roadshow* and suddenly it's there, in my neck and my shoulders."

"Andrea's friends with a chiropractor," Blondeau muttered. "I'll get you his number."

He leant forward for a better view. Traffic had slowed to a tectonic crawl. He checked his watch. Quarter to five.

There was only one thing to do.

He stood, took a breath, got off the bus and ran.

No movie star ever looked more a movie star than Chase Ashley. He had Paul Newman's vivid blue eyes, the golden mane of Achilles and cheeks that could wear down cliffs. If not a god himself, he was at least an argument for intelligent design.

Ashley sat in what had to be The Dorchester's most opulent hotel suite, one leg folded over the other, slightly slouched, in a vintage leather armchair.

He swatted away the PR boy's protestations like a cobweb.

"But Mr. Ashley, the premiere is–"

"Not going anywhere. This man has come all the way across town to talk to me and he deserves his opportunity, late or not." He turned to Blondeau. "Stephen, how's the family?"

Chase Ashley knew how to butter you up.

Blondeau could tell he was blushing. "Great, thanks. And thanks again for being so understanding with the–"

"London traffic," Ashley winked. "I get it."

"Just throw me a couple of bones and you can be on your way."

Ashley made a pitching motion and flashed his picture-perfect, shiny-white teeth. Though Blondeau noticed that despite his pretences, Ashley wasn't quite his usual self. His hair was a little frazzled, there were faint circles under his eyes. Blondeau had noted a table stacked with dirty coffee mugs outside the suite when he'd hurried in. The strain of the press junket wore on even the mightiest of beasts.

He drew a breath. "So, um–"

"I gotta stop you there, Stephen." Ashley grew serious. "What's going on with your eye? It's freaking me out a little."

"It's- it's nothing. Bad contact lens." He could feel his eye flickering like a basement light bulb, tears were starting to well. "I fell asleep during the cricket," he explained stupidly.

Ashley looked perplexed. "I could have you seen by my doctor? He travels with me everywhere. There's no one better."

"Thanks, but it's really not necessary."

"Mr. Ashley," the PR boy interjected. "We really need to make progress here."

Ashley turned on him with a look of such sudden, visceral hatred that both the boy and Blondeau recoiled.

Blondeau tried to distract him, "I was going to ask you what it was like working with Lisa Caspian again, after all these years?"

Ashley turned back to him and the darkness was gone. The smile that had launched a dozen blockbusters was there again. "Oh, she's a real sweetheart. When *Waiting for a Train* blew up it took us both by surprise. No one involved with that movie expected it to do much of anything."

Blondeau detected the note of roboticism in his voice. He must have ran through this spiel twenty times today.

"Lisa and I were both thrust into the burning lights of Hollywood," Ashley continued, "and we really supported each other the first few years in coping with all that. Late night phone calls, or letters, or whatever other way we could think of. On the rare occasions we were ever in the same town we'd sneak off from our people, go to the dirtiest, most run-down bar we could find and start hitting back the shots until we couldn't remember the names of our hotels. You know, if it hadn't been for Lisa, I might not have become the well-adjusted man I am today." His laughter was impossible not to share.

"Although your career paths have taken a somewhat different

path since?”

Ashley’s smile vanished. “You mean that Lisa’s got an Oscar and I haven’t?”

Blondeau felt a sting in his chest. *What did I say that for?* There were few species more fragile than the actor. He really didn’t want today to turn into a scene, especially after what had happened with Meg Ryan the previous month. “I was just–”

Ashley laughed again and slapped him on the shoulder. “You should see your face right now, Stephen. Relax! So Caspian’s got an Oscar. So do a lot of people I know. I’m on Japanese TV selling coffee machines, how many people can say that?”

“It’s a fair point,” Blondeau said, relieved.

The PR boy was ostentatiously checking his watch though Ashley took care not to notice him. Blondeau almost felt sorry for the poor bastard. One more question and they could all be on their way.

“I’m interested in the connection you felt to your character. As the father of young children yourself–”

“If I’m ever as self-absorbed as that guy, you can personally call up Child Welfare and have my kids taken away from me.”

“Is that how you see it?”

Ashley nodded. “Absolutely. Those two spend the whole movie squabbling over trinkets while their little boy sits at home with a cavalcade of babysitters. You think that kid’s going to turn out alright?”

“I suppose they learn their lesson by the end, though?”

“Of course they do,” Ashley sneered. “It’s Hollywood! You couldn’t possibly make it through a whole film without a lesson being learned. Because a single drop of light is enough to blot out the darkness, right?”

Blondeau shrugged. If Ashley wasn’t going to defend his film, he certainly wasn't about to either. "So, if it wasn't the character that drew you to the film, what did?"

Ashley rubbed his fingers together and smiled sadly. "It's what I do, right? '*A newlywed couple discover they both moonlight as jewel thieves.*' Come on! It was a Chase Ashley film before I'd ever even heard of it."

The PR boy was really starting to fret now. He dabbed his forehead with a handkerchief. Blondeau ignored him. Ashley was giving out some interesting stuff for once and no pimple-nosed little pen-pusher was going to get in his way.

"Is that really how you view your career, Chase?" he asked. "It seems a little... cynical."

Ashley blew out his cheeks. "How else could you view it? After all these years I'm a realist. It's not so bad. People know what they're going to get from me – two hours to leave their brains at home. Not everyone can be Daniel Day-Lewis."

"I can't imagine *The Family Jewels* working too well with him," Blondeau agreed.

Ashley slumped back in his chair and sighed. "The sad thing is, I really thought *Death of a Bachelor* would be the turning point. Man, what a film that was. My entrance to the world of *real* acting. If the mighty Paul Chekhov could see that potential in me, it was surely only a matter of time until everyone else did. Scorsese, Polanski, Bertolucci – they'd all be hammering my door down." He scowled. "But everyone around me treated the whole thing like it was just a phase I was going through. Like a midlife crisis. 'Let Chase get this acting business out of his system and he'll be all ready to sign on for another *No More Heroes* sequel.'

"Vic Roache was the worst of the lot," Ashley continued. "I remember how he put his arm around my shoulder when I signed the contract, how he told me he just knew I'd win an Oscar for *Bachelor*, that he'd personally make sure of it." He let out a short bitter laugh. "In the end I didn't even get a nomination."

Blondeau tried to show sympathy, though he didn't much feel it. Did Ashley really think he deserved an Oscar for sleepwalking through Chekhov's dirge? If so, he was, well, only about as deluded as everyone else in Hollywood. Victor Roache had worked some miracles with Oscar campaigns in his time, but getting Ashley's name in the envelope would have been like walking on water while turning it to wine.

Ashley ranted on: "I always secretly suspected that Silverlight didn't campaign as hard for me as they made out. Because the truth is Vic Roache wanted Chase Ashley, The Star; not Chase Ashley, The Actor. He could never tolerate me getting ideas above my station." His jaw clenched at the memory. "Still, at least he didn't screw me the way he did Chekhov."

The PR boy was approaching meltdown. "Mr. Ashley, we really have to–"

"What are you talking about?" Blondeau cut in. "What did Victor Roache do to Chekhov?"

Ashley hesitated. He looked at Blondeau as if truly seeing him for the first time. He measured his words: "You know the thing about Chekhov – that he always got final cut on his films? The guy wouldn't even negotiate without first having it guaranteed."

Blondeau nodded. *Everyone knew that.* Final cut – the right for a director to control the content of their film and release their approved edit to the public – was highly prized. In an era when the major studios were all part of even more powerful corporate conglomerates, there were few directors with the clout to negotiate it. The list was short, and Paul Chekhov had topped it.

"I attended a screening of *Bachelor* in New York," Ashley said. "Miranda and I both had it in our contracts that we were to see the final cut before release, so Chekhov had it flown over." He smirked. "Poor old Clara Davis probably had to prise the cans from his fingers. So anyway, I'm watching it, totally blown away. I never imagined that I could be a part of such... art."

Ashley ran his fingers down his face and dug them into his cheeks. "The night of that screening in New York was the same night Paul Chekhov died. I found out the next day and couldn't believe it. I just couldn't believe what he'd... done. I didn't see *Bachelor* again until months later at the premiere in L.A. But I remembered it, you know? When you shoot as many takes as Chekhov puts you through, you remember which ones make the final cut. It's like the furniture in your house. You can be away for weeks, or months, but if you come back and something's been moved around, or gone missing – no matter how small it is – you always notice."

"Are you saying," Blondeau narrowed his eyes, "Victor Roache recut *Death of a Bachelor*, after Chekhov's death?"

The PR boy was quivering, ashen-faced. A few more studio bodies had entered the room, carrying mobile phones and looks of dismay.

Ashley began to laugh, almost maniacally. No one joined in this time. He picked up a single red rose from a nearby vase and stared as he twirled it in his fingers. "I'm saying I watched a film in New York, and then months later I watched something else. It's funny, no one's ever been quite able to explain that to me. And every time I mention it, I get the distinct feeling that I shouldn't have.

"Now if you'll excuse me," he rose from his seat with a smile, "I have a premiere to attend."

Two
A Summer Evening

"I still don't get why this is such a big deal," James Raikes offered between drags of his cigarette. "Run it past me one more time, Stevie."

Blondeau grit his teeth. Raikes was his oldest friend. They had been thrown together in university halls and had remained that way long after the rest of their circle had drifted from orbit. He was the heir to a major manufacturer of chocolate biscuits and had dedicated most of his adult life to drinking and womanising. His body and face were long and thin, slicked-back blond hair accentuating a narrow nose and high, hollow cheeks. He dressed always in skinny jeans, leather jackets and shirts buttoned so low you could practically see his naval.

What James Raikes was not, despite Blondeau's best efforts, was an adept in the art of cinema.

Blondeau tried again: "If Paul Chekhov's final film was recut after his death – against the terms of his contract – it would be one of the biggest scandals in Hollywood history. Victor Roache has pulled some stunts in his time but this would be beyond the pale. His reputation might never recover."

"Right," Raikes nodded. He paused. "Why, though?"

Blondeau let out a groan of defeat. He slumped in his chair and gazed up at the setting sky. It had been a sweltering day but at last a stream of cool air was threading through his garden. The crickets chirped and the little rock fountain flowed – at that moment those were the only sounds he needed.

"It's not just about Roache either," he said after a while, thinking aloud. "If it turned out that Chekhov's version of *Death of a Bachelor* had never been released, it would instantly become the most sought-after treasure in cinema history. More so even than the original, full version of *Metropolis*, or Orson Welles' cut of *Touch of Evil*."

Andrea brought out a few more bottles of beer from the kitchen. "I can't remember if I've even seen this film," she said as she sat beside them.

"You've definitely seen it," Blondeau insisted. "I remember you were there when I reviewed the VHS release. As I recall, your dad rang up halfway through to tell you he couldn't find the TV remote, and we had to pause it to drive over."

She looked puzzled as she swigged her beer. "I'm not sure that narrows it down. Is it the one when he's never sure whether it's all a game or not? There's a scene where he drives into a river."

"Are you talking about *The Game*?" Blondeau replied. "With Michael Douglas?"

"Oh yeah, maybe."

"No, then. The clue's in the title."

Andrea rolled her eyes. "I'm *so* sorry. We can't all have your freakish memory for these things."

"I know the one he's on about," Raikes announced. "It's the one where the girl's after him, then he kills her, and then there's a play at the end."

Andrea made a sound of semi-comprehension.

"Didn't think much of it, though," Raikes added. "That bloody boat ride nearly sent me into a coma." He stubbed his cigarette out in the ashtray. "That what I don't get about you critics – it's like, the longer and more pretentious a film is, the more you all eat it up."

"If you'd have read my review at the time," Blondeau said crabbily, "you'd have known that I agreed with you, actually. I believe I said that it was 'ponderous and pointless' or something to that effect. But that's beside the point. It was Paul Chekhov's final film and there's a story here."

"Then why didn't you publish what Chase said in Friday's paper?"

Blondeau scowled. The memory was still raw. "The studio refused to release the audio of the interview, and kindly suggested to my editor that our silence on the matter would be remembered in a 'favourable light with regard to future opportunities.'"

"So... you chickened out?"

"I did not chicken out. I am merely biding my time."

Raikes smirked.

"I am! I need to verify things first, that's all. That's what proper journalism is. I heard from a few other people who talked to Ashley at the junket – apparently he'd been saying crazy stuff all day. Claiming he was getting screwed on pay or blocked from taking certain roles. I think they only let him carry on as they were scared he'd skip the premiere otherwise. Much less bother to enforce a code of silence after with carrots and sticks. The thing he said about Chekhov, though... I believed him. Why would he make it up?"

"Perhaps he was mistaken?" Andrea suggested. "He forgot what was in the film. I can barely remember any of it."

Blondeau sighed. "Maybe." He'd thought about it often in the days since the junket and he had to admit it was possible. He remembered a similar story one of his critic friends had told him from earlier in their career. The critic had attended a screening of a cult crime film in the northern English town in which it had been filmed years earlier. The writer of the screenplay, a local boy made good, had been present. When the credits rolled he turned to the critic with pent-up anger.

"What the hell did they do to my film?" he demanded.

"What do you mean?" the critic replied in confusion. "It seems fine to me?"

"Someone's messed around with it. It's all... different."

After much deliberation they realised the writer had been remembering his original screenplay and not the actual film itself. The scenes he had written were so vivid to him that he could picture them, regardless of whether they had been shot. His memory has swirled it all together like clothes in the wash.

And then there were the famous mass misremembrances. Nobody ever says, "Play it again, Sam" in *Casablanca*, nor does Darth Vader announce: "Luke, I am your father." The mind was a strange old thing.

But this business with Chase Ashley felt like something different entirely...

"That's precisely why I need to verify his story," Blondeau said. He picked up the book lying on the table and pointed at the picture on the inside cover. "This guy here – Anthony Hudgens – wrote the first biography of Chekhov published after his death. If any funny business happened with *Bachelor* then it can't be only Ashley that knows about it. And Hudgens could point me in the right direction. He was talking to the right people at the right time, he must have heard something. I've arranged to meet him next week."

Raikes raised his eyebrows. "You're serious about this."

"Of course I'm serious. If Ashley's story is true, I'll be the one to reveal it to the world, regardless of what the editor at the *Daily Herald* thinks. It'll be a much bigger deal than some poxy newspaper article anyway. I've been thinking about it: this could be my entrance into television."

Andrea got up and wandered back inside – she'd heard it all already.

"A documentary," Blondeau nodded as he said it. "Probably Channel 4. Half an hour to map out the whole story and then show the film afterwards."

Raikes scrunched his nose up. "*You* – on television?"

"What do you mean by that?!"

"Well, you're just not that... photogenic. I mean, no offence, mate. Would you get your hair cut shorter?"

Andrea called out from the kitchen: "He should get it cut anyway!"

Blondeau swept the hair from his eyes. "It's not like I'm the bloody Elephant Man, is it? I'm just talking about a film show, you don't need to be George Clooney for that. There's a gap in the market, you know. Barry Norman's sodded off to Sky, and Jonathan Ross isn't even a proper critic."

He stared off into the distance. "I see a set of programmes – *Hollywood's Greatest Secrets*. We start off with this Chekhov business, then we can do something about the Black Dahlia, the curse of *The Exorcist* – I mean that one's obviously a load of rubbish, but you get the idea. There's enough content for a series. And when the BBC decide they want to employ a proper film critic again, I'll be ready to swoop in." He clasped his hands together and smiled.

Raikes mulled it over. "Could work, I guess."

"I'll have spent fifteen years at the *Herald* in October,"

Blondeau said, jaw tightening. "I write film reviews for a paper read by those too old to go to the cinema. A two-page spread a week, plus the occasional interview, where, if anyone ever tells me anything of actual interest, my editor's too much of a coward to let me run with it." He tapped his beer bottle on the metal frame of the table. *Clink, clink, clink*. "It's a waste of me."

At that moment a creature resembling a dirty mop on legs came bounding out into the garden. Every time Blondeau saw his dog, for a brief moment it was like seeing him for the first time. He was a Komondor, a Hungarian sheepdog breed known for their long, dreaded coat. Andrea had bought him following a break-in at a neighbour's a few years back. Quite why she couldn't have bought a German shepherd, Blondeau had never fully understood, but he had soon grown to love the great slobbering beast. Marley had a habit of scaring off his wife's most irritating friends and that was worth his exorbitant purchase cost alone. He ruffled the dog's head as it came close.

Raikes tipped his beer bottle as if to pour some out for the creature.

"Can you please not do that?"

"Why? It's only Heineken."

"Because I'm pretty sure he'd make a mean drunk." Blondeau grinned. "One of our neighbours came over earlier to get a phone number off Andrea. Marley nearly had the poor bastard's throat out. I can't imagine it would have been much of a fight, anyway."

The dog snorted agreement.

The aroma of next door's barbeque clawed at Blondeau's stomach. His mind was homing in on the pizzas in his freezer when he noticed his friend's face had lit up.

"I've got it!" Raikes exclaimed.

"What?"

"I've just solved your little mystery, or at least how to solve it."

"Go on, then..."

"It's simple – get a copy of the script. If it matches up to the film as it is now, then Chase must have been making it up."

Blondeau looked at him with surprise. He hadn't actually solved it, but it wasn't the worst effort. "Won't work, I'm afraid. You can track down original screenplays easy enough, but they rarely match up to what's released. Especially with Paul Chekhov. Hudgens has a fascinating bit on his filmmaking process in the book. Chekhov would develop his understanding of the film during the shoot itself, as if feeling his way into it, writing new scenes or even completely new characters. Even with the scenes he kept from the screenplay, he would spend days improvising with the actors before starting to film, and then each scene would be shot thirty, forty, fifty times, all from different angles and with different moods. It could be an exhausting experience for the actors. Quite a few have talked about nearly suffering nervous breakdowns while working for him.

"Then, once filming was finished, Chekhov would take everything he had shot and try and make sense of it in the editing room – he was his own editor for most of his career. He thought of the act of making a film as more like piecing together a montage than a simple linear process. It's why his films took so long to make. He had Chase Ashley – the biggest movie star in the world – in London for a whole year shooting *Bachelor*, no one else could have got away with it."

Raikes rewarded this lesson with glazed-over eyes and a sizable yawn. "Hang on, I thought that film was set in New

York?"

"It is set in New York. But it was actually filmed on a studio set just outside London."

"What did he do that for?"

"Chekhov was basically a recluse for the last thirty years of his life. He was walled up in his manor, just outside Maidenhead. In the 1970s he didn't make a single movie. There were all sorts of rumours about what he was up to. He made a comeback in the eighties but still refused to film far from his home. Which basically meant London and the home counties. The monastery in *High Upon the Hill*, the hospital in *The Night Sessions* – everything was filmed not much more than an hour away from where we sit right now.

"You see, it's not just the incredible films he made, it's all these little quirks and idiosyncrasies. The man had become a near-mythical figure in the years prior to his death, refusing all interviews and maintaining complete secrecy on his sets. Which is why, if it does turn out that Victor Roache recut his final film, Roache would find himself in the deepest of all shit."

"Are you sure you want to piss this Roache guy off? From the way you've described him he sounds a bit... terrifying."

Blondeau shrugged. "He's terrifying alright. The common joke is that they'll have the words, 'You'll never work in this town again' inscribed on his tombstone. But that town is Hollywood, and this"–he gestured around–"is Hampstead. He can't touch me."

Raikes gave him a look that suggested he was not entirely convinced. Blondeau was starting to get tired of those kind of looks.

Andrea called from inside the house: "Stephen, you should see this."

Blondeau swore under his breath. "If that damn dog has chewed up another cushion..."

He headed through to the living room and was relieved to see no obvious signs of damage. Andrea was in front of the television, watching what must have been the *News at Nine*.

On screen were images of Chase Ashley at the premiere of his latest film, from the day Blondeau had interviewed him. He was grinning from ear to ear, signing autographs, posing for pictures with gawking fans.

The banner at the bottom of the screen read: "HOLLYWOOD STAR ENTERS REHAB".

Three
A Little Deeper

Blondeau spent the morning watching press screenings at the Odeon in Leicester Square: first an American rom-com so syrupy it nearly made him retch, then a Japanese gorefest that probably should have, but which he instead enjoyed thoroughly.

He had arranged to meet Anthony Hudgens for lunch nearby at The Ivy. Having a half hour to spare, he ordered a Carlsberg at the little pub next to the cinema and took a seat outside.

It was another sweltering day. Gangs of teenagers drifted through the gardens, tourists ate lunch on the benches, children played by the fountains flanking Shakespeare's statue in the middle of the square.

Blondeau flipped through Hudgens' biography of Chekhov one more time. The chapter on the last years of Chekhov's life was briefer the others, owing both to the lack of available information, and to Hudgens having written most of the book before Chekhov's death, presumably rush-releasing it shortly after to beat the crowd.

He fell upon the pages containing Hudgens' summary of *Death of a Bachelor* and began to read:

The film's protagonist, Sam (Ashley), is a professor of literature at a prestigious, unnamed New York university. We open with Sam at a glitzy party for the city's elite. The camera pulls focus from Sam in the foreground to Lindsay (Silver), a young waitress serving drinks in the back of the shot. She notices Sam and watches him with an ambiguous expression.

Days later Lindsay approaches Sam in his office, claiming they'd had an affair years earlier while Lindsay was a student of his, until Sam abruptly ended the relationship. Flustered, Sam denies any knowledge of Lindsay or her story.

Over the following weeks Lindsay continues to invade Sam's life, repeatedly appearing at his work, phoning his home and eventually contacting Katherine (Hamilton), Sam's wife. Katherine, a renowned psychologist, appears to believe Sam, suggesting Lindsay's behaviour is a form of delusional disorder. Despite this, their marriage becomes increasingly strained.

After Lindsay appears at the school of Sam and Katherine's son, Sam angrily confronts her at her run-down apartment. Their argument becomes violent and Sam slams Lindsay into a wall. He leaves her lying on the floor, bleeding from a wound to the back of the head.

The next day Sam is confronted by Joshua (Jacobs), a friend of Lindsay's, who accuses him of having caused Lindsay's death. Sam, unnerved, denies it. The audience is also left unclear as Lindsay was clearly alive when Sam left her apartment.

At the midpoint the film undergoes a dramatic shift. Sam receives a mysterious invitation which takes him by boat to a small island, where a theatre group, the House of the Damned, perform an interactive, free-roaming version of *Hamlet*. Sam and the other passengers serve as the audience. Among the performers, unseen by Sam, is Joshua.

As the performance progresses, the audience, a selection of the worst of New York high society, mock and mistreat the performers. Sam stumbles upon one of the theatre group stealing from a drunken, slumbering audience member. In the film's moment of highest tension, the audience member discovers the theft and, under pressure, Sam identifies the culprit. The thief confronts Sam, who is shaken by the turn in events.

Sam leaves the island on the boat, unsure how much of what he had seen was real, and what was part of the production. He returns to find his home empty.

The final scene sees Sam and Katherine attending their daughter's graduation, their relationship seemingly healthy once more. At one point they are served drinks by one of the

> performers from the island. Sam does not appear to recognise her.

Hudgens offered his own analysis:

> Given Joshua's presence in the House of the Damned, the common reading of the final act views the theft sequence as staged, a manufactured moral quandary to test Sam's conscience. Colin Flannery of *The New York Times* is one of many viewing the entire film from a class-war perspective: Sam's relationship to the troubled and near-destitute Lindsay mirrored by the obnoxiously upper-class audience's treatment of the theatre performers.
>
> There are problems with this reading, however. The nature of Sam's prior relationship to Lindsay (if any) and her death are never made explicitly clear. Throughout the film Sam is portrayed sympathetically. Lindsay is the interloper who assails his comfortable life. This is amplified with the casting of Ashley, a whiter-than-white superstar only ever known for playing the valiant hero. If the final act is intended as Sam's trial, it is unlikely to be one the audience would feel is deserved.
>
> As such, the true intent of Chekhov's final film remains as murky as the water in which that ramshackle old boat sails.

Blondeau felt Hudgens was tiptoeing around the real issue. Having rewatched it the previous night, he held the same view as he had upon its release three years ago: the film was a mess. Clocking in at just under three hours, its plodding pace made the lack of any clear resolution all the more frustrating. Blondeau was not a critic impressed by deliberate ambiguity.

His sentiments had been shared by many at the time. Given the publicity surrounding the legendary director's posthumously released film, much of the initial reaction had been that of crushing disappointment. *Bachelor* was no *Journey Beyond* or *Fear*. He knew, however, that the film held a certain cult following in some circles.

As for Ashley's story, Blondeau's rewatch had sparked differing emotions. The released version of *Bachelor* did feel like a film that had something missing. It wasn't just the unresolved plot points, there was something about it that just felt off. He couldn't put his finger on it.

He glanced over at the statue of William Shakespeare in the middle of the Leicester Square Gardens. Early in his career, Blondeau had worked as both film and theatre critic for a local newspaper. Although it was *Hamlet* that was performed in the film's final act, something about *Bachelor* instead reminded Blondeau of another Shakespearean tragedy, *Timon of Athens*, a play with no record of having ever been performed in Shakespeare's lifetime, and whose only surviving copies felt oddly disjointed. He remembered reading speculation that Shakespeare's work had been revised by the playwright Thomas Middleton, giving the play its uneven quality. Had similar happened with *Death of a Bachelor*, Victor Roache having taken it upon himself to become Chekhov's Middleton?

There was just one problem with that theory. If *Death of a*

Bachelor didn't quite feel like the film Chekhov had intended, nor did it feel like one Roache had got his grubby mitts on.

Victor Roache was the most fearsome studio boss in Hollywood. An obese, foul-mouthed, fouler-mannered brawler from Queens, Roache had built Silverlight Pictures from the ground up on the basis of buying up arthouse films for cheap and massaging them into something that could fill seats in a multiplex. To Roache that meant one thing more than all others – cutting. Anything that didn't fulfil the immediate needs of the plot would be left on the editing floor. Anything that might make Middle America yawn or check their watches likewise. He once cut a four-hour Italian picture down to ninety minutes in such a fashion. They didn't call him "The Demon Barber of Los Angeles" for nothing.

But *Death of a Bachelor* did not fit the profile of a film that had been given Roache's usual "treatment." It was far too long, full of incidental scenes and drawn-out sequences. It wasn't just a matter of audience response either. Simply put, the longer a film was, the less screenings could be crammed into a single day. And that meant less money for Victor Roache. It was hard to imagine him being happy with that.

Blondeau thought back to his interview with Chase Ashley and the story he had told. He had the sense the actor had only seen half the picture.

He finished his beer and wandered over to Shakespeare's towering monument. The Bard was leaning on a plinth in a somewhat unnatural pose. In one hand he held a scroll with a quotation from *Twelfth Night*.

It read: "THERE IS NO DARKNESS BUT IGNORANCE".

***

Anthony Hudgens was ordering the most expensive items off the menu with the air of a man who did not expect to be paying for them.

Blondeau gnawed his lip thinking about it. What was the protocol here? He had been the one to initiate contact, but it was Hudgens who had gleefully suggested The Ivy. It felt like a grey area.

"So, tell me about your article," Hudgens said, smiling as he tucked his napkin into his collar. He looked exactly as his picture – a portly bald man with a bushy moustache and a bow tie. He seemed friendly enough, if a touch pompous. His mannerisms reminded Blondeau of a little woodland creature; he could picture him living in a neat and cosy burrow in the middle of the forest, dusting the shelves, sweeping the floor, prepping a full larder for winter.

Hudgens pulled up the sleeves of his pink cardigan and began tucking into his Dover sole *à la meunière.*

Blondeau paused, knowing he had to get the next few moments exactly right. He had already decided not to tell Hudgens the whole story. The last thing he needed was another writer sniffing out the scandal, perhaps even beating him to the punch. This was his moment, his opportunity. And so, to protect it, he had brought along some well-crafted bullshit...

"I do the occasional piece for *Total Film*," he began. That much was true at least. "It's the only real chance I get for long-form writing these days. My idea is to explore the final films of the great directors. I'll cover the famous ones: Hitchcock, Kurosawa and, of course, Chekhov."

"A worthy topic," Hudgens declared merrily.

"His case is an especially interesting one," Blondeau added, "what with his death coming before *Bachelor*'s release."

"You can certainly say that again," Hudgens chuckled. "I was already writing the book, as you may know. There was a lot of discussion at the time that *Death of a Bachelor* would be his last film. He had never made any comment to suggest as such, of course, but he was nearly seventy, and every additional film seemed to take longer to complete than the last. It seemed a reasonable assumption." He sipped his glass of Meursault white and gave a sigh of approval. "But his death? Now that came as a great surprise to everyone."

"Why do you think he...?"

Hudgens gave a solemn shrug. "There wasn't a note. Anything else is speculation, really. I try, as a journalist, not to dabble in it."

"But you wrote an entire book about him?" Blondeau said. "You must have some idea–"

"Sometimes the more you learn about a subject, the less you understand it."

Blondeau grinned. "That's why I stopped reading about Israel–Palestine."

He looked around the restaurant. It was a busy lunchtime. Cutlery clinked and clattered, waiters crossed with trolleys and trays. The Ivy was well known as a haunt for the elite of the entertainment world due to its proximity to the West End and its theatres. Among the diners he noted famous actors, producers and television presenters. *Television presenters.* The ones in attendance didn't look all that special without their makeup artists and their professional lighting. Blondeau thought he would fit right in, to hell with what James Raikes had to say about the matter.

"I talked to anyone who would return my calls about Chekhov," Hudgens said. "The picture they painted was complex. He was clearly a man capable of great affection and kindness, in particular for his wife and his brother's family. But there's no doubt that on a film set he could be an utter bastard. Some of the mind games he would play with his actors you wouldn't believe."

Hudgens grimaced. "Psychological warfare might be a more appropriate term. Calling them onto set and then telling them they weren't needed, turning the camera on without their knowledge, being full of praise one day and screaming in their face the next. And those were the more benign examples. Had I included every tale I heard, I imagine most readers would have ended up despising the man. And I haven't even mentioned all the takes he would put them through."

"Yes, what was that all about?" Blondeau asked. "Was it just perfectionism?"

"There was an element of that, no doubt. He had a meticulous side that was bordering on obsessive. Like with the sets, for example. He would spend days adjusting every minute detail, down to the specific food brands in the cupboards and the exact arrangement of books on the shelves. For *Bachelor*, when he couldn't find the specific type of painting he wanted to decorate Sam and Katherine's living room, he had one commissioned. It cost thousands of pounds, set back filming a week and didn't even make an appearance in the final film." He swilled the dregs of his glass. "I'm not convinced that was all it was about with the actors, though."

"No?"

Hudgens leant forward conspiratorially. "I heard this from a couple of people close to him. Chekhov would say that he did not want acting, he wanted *truth*. If anything he felt that formal acting experience created barriers to accessing that truth. For smaller parts that meant he would often use non-actors. Several of the townspeople in *Eternal Fire* were 'discovered' by Chekhov while shooting on location in Georgia. Similarly, much of the supporting cast in both *Hearts of Stone* and *High Upon the Hill* had military experience. But he couldn't get away with that for the main roles. So he'd shoot take after take after take, to peel away their defensive layers."

Blondeau narrowed his eyes. "Are you saying he shot all those takes and only ever had the intention of using the last ones?"

"I suppose that's one way of looking at it, yes. He thought actors could only give their best, truest performances when they had reached their breaking point, mentally. Until that moment there would always be a built-in resistance to his instructions. Hence all the mind games, hence all the takes. He wanted to batter them into submission."

Hudgens held up his hands. "It's a theory, anyway. I heard it from a few people. Others denied it. But Chekhov certainly had a keen interest in the extremes of the human mind. He said multiple times in interviews – back when he gave them – that the only other career he could have imagined for himself would have been as a psychologist." He signalled to the waiter to bring another bottle of the Meursault.

Blondeau winced, mentally totting up the damage. Though perhaps getting the little man drunk wasn't the worst idea. The conversation had thus far felt like negotiating a labyrinth, slowing probing deeper, trying to reach the golden knowledge at the centre without sparking off the sentries in Hudgens' head. It might be easier if those sentries were a little soused. He simply had to think of it as an investment.

He asked, "Did you hear anything about Chekhov's state of mind while filming *Bachelor*? Your book doesn't delve too much into that period."

Hudgens had begun to hiccup. "Well, my deadline was moved up a couple of months following his death, hence the need for brevity in some parts. As a man with a weekly column, I'm sure you can sympathise." He rapped his chest with his knuckles and poured a glass of water. "Regardless, by all accounts *Bachelor* was an unusual shoot. It lasted an entire year, of course – one of the longest continuous shoots in film history. Part of that was Chekhov's usual eccentricities, but even for Chekhov, his behaviour was said to be... erratic. He dealt with fewer and fewer people on a personal level. Everything would be done through a few long-term assistants, Clara Davis in particular. Sometimes entire days of filming would be cancelled at short notice, no explanation given."

"What was he up to?" Blondeau asked.

"I just think he had lost his ability to deal with people. All those years cooped up in that manor in Berkshire, it probably exacerbated his worst behaviours."

Blondeau nodded. "That's another part of his life you don't spend too much time on?"

"Are you a literary critic as well now, Stephen?" Hudgens chuckled. "I am guilty of all charges, I confess it. My book is a front-loaded affair by necessity. In the sixties our hero was a public figure in all senses of the word. He could never resist offering up a choice quote to a journalist, and ran in powerful circles.

"The turning point was *Heart's Desire*, as far as most people tell it. In the aftermath of that debacle came the permanent move to England, the self-imposed exile. And with that, the end of any public statements, and fewer and fewer connections to the outside world. In terms of the content available to a biographer, it was like going from rich farmland to arid desert."

The conversation at the table next to them was increasingly animated; Blondeau couldn't help listen in. A long-haired man with tattoos was attempting to secure funding for a theatre production based on *The Tibetan Book of the Dead*. Blondeau had never read it, and was fairly sure the long-haired man hadn't either. Perhaps at every table in The Ivy there sat a bullshitter clawing for a career boost. It felt like that kind of place.

The waiter came to take their plates and Hudgens gleefully ordered a sticky toffee pudding. Blondeau checked his watch as he waved the waiter away. He was due back at the Odeon for the afternoon screenings shortly. It was time to stop wandering the labyrinth and bore straight through the walls...

He said: "Did you ever hear anything... I mean- what with *Bachelor* being released posthumously... is it- is it certain that the released version was what Chekhov had intended?"

Hudgens studied him for a while. "What makes you say that?"

"Nothing, really. I just- I watched it again the other day. It just doesn't feel quite right. I can't even explain it."

"Hmm, interesting." Hudgens seemed unsure whether to continue. "You're not the first one to say that, you know. There *were* rumours at the time."

"Rumours?" Blondeau repeated in as innocent a voice as he could muster.

"That somehow *Death of a Bachelor* had been altered after Chekhov's death. By the studio, I presume. I suppose that kind of speculation was natural, given the circumstances." He gave a sad smile. "But I'm afraid I have to disappoint you. It would have been out of the question. Chekhov had final cut guaranteed in the contract he signed with Silverlight. He had announced the film was complete and even sent the final version to New York for the actors and executives to view."

"But, I mean, what with him being dead–"

"His side of the agreement passed on to his estate, headed by Constance, his only surviving relative." Hudgens leant in closer. "Let me tell you, in that family, obstinacy runs in the blood. Chekhov's niece is just as headstrong when she needs to be. She would certainly not have been intimidated by the likes of Victor Roache. The released version of *Bachelor* is Chekhov's intended one, like it or not."

Hudgens paused, watching him. "Though I feel that I have not entirely convinced you, Stephen," he added. "Perhaps you are more of a conspiracy theorist than I had realised."

Blondeau bristled. "I am not a conspiracy theorist."

"Would any consider themselves as such? Nonetheless, the subject is clearly of interest to you. If you think I am judging then you could not be further from the truth!" He rubbed his mouth with his napkin and searched around the room for his dessert. "Look, I attend a monthly get-together with a group of Chekhov's more dedicated fans. Among them are a few who feel strongly about this very issue. They have their ideas. I couldn't possibly do them justice, they are a little... out there for me." He gave up looking for the waiter and turned back to Blondeau. "Why don't you come along next time?"

Another chance to bankroll one of your dinners, Blondeau thought sourly. He was beginning to wonder who the real bullshitter at their table was.

"Thanks for the invite," he said, smiling. "I'd love to."

Four
Chekhov's Club

The Zebra was hidden away down a gloomy narrow lane in the heart of Whitechapel. It took Blondeau twenty minutes to track down from the tube. The place didn't even have a sign, just a small painted animal from which the pub took its name on one boarded-up window. A scrawny-looking cat sniffed around an overflowing dustbin near the front door.

Blondeau paused just before entering. It most certainly did not seem like Anthony Hudgens' kind of place.

The inside did nothing to allay his doubts. The lighting was as dim as to be non-existent, the clientele old men drinking alone at the bar, a few couples in the corners. The pub smelled of stale beer, stale smoke and stale dog. The sole barman gave him a sour look and went back to watching the evening's football match on a handheld television.

An altogether welcoming place.

Blondeau ordered a pint of Chiswick Bitter and asked for the snug. The barman gave him a strange look and then gestured, barely, to a set of winding stairs by the toilets.

Hudgens' pink cardigan and bow tie came into view before his face, in a small room at the top of the stairs. There were four others, all sat around a low table in battered leather sofas and armchairs. The walls were decorated with photos of old boxing matches from London's East End. The lighting was as low as downstairs, though here it felt warmer, cosy even. It wasn't really a snug, but considering what he'd come from, Blondeau wasn't going to complain.

"Stephen!" Hudgens exclaimed. "We were starting to wonder if you were going to turn up."

"It's not the easiest place to find," Blondeau replied, taking a seat on one of the sofas.

"Yes, we like to have somewhere quiet to talk. Let me introduce you to everyone..." and then he did.

There was Barbara Zaniolo, a glamorous olive-skinned woman who looked in her forties.

Adam Woodford, a nervy pallid man who immediately informed Blondeau that he worked for a rival paper.

Nancy Sheldrake, an older woman with long, unkempt hair and horn-rimmed glasses.

And Cain Xavier, a slick-looking American who Blondeau suspected was using a name other than the one on his birth certificate.

"And together we make up the premier fan club of Paul Chekhov in London." Hudgens beamed with pride.

Blondeau nodded, not knowing quite what to say. He couldn't imagine how such a variety of people had come together in the first place. Personal ads for lonely Chekhov fans, perhaps.

They were talking about *Obsession*, Chekhov's feature-length debut, which he had been so embarrassed by in the years that followed he had attempted to have all traces of it scoured from the earth. Blondeau argued that it wasn't bad for an early effort and Hudgens agreed, adding that Chekhov was his own worst critic. Nancy Sheldrake suggested that Chekhov's attempts to remove the film from circulation were more about his desire to create a mystique than any feelings towards the film in particular.

Then they talked about the aborted sequel to Chekhov's sci-fi masterpiece *Journey Beyond*, and who was responsible for its failure. Nancy, who Blondeau was beginning to suspect didn't even particularly like Chekhov, argued that it was the director's tendency to juggle multiple projects at once that had led to its inevitable collapse. Hudgens and Cain Xavier were more generous, blaming studio interference and the poor quality of the various screenplays respectively.

Then they talked about which of the new generation of directors were best-equipped to assume Chekhov's mantle. Hudgens suggested David Fincher, while Blondeau mentioned a young director named Darren Aronofsky who was currently receiving a lot of hype. Xavier announced that he had seen *The Blair Witch Project* the last time he had been in America, and that the two directors responsible for it were destined for the top.

Then, an hour after Blondeau had first sat down, the conversation angled around to *Death of a Bachelor*. Blondeau mentioned his fictional article for *Total Film*, realising as he said it that the more he talked about it, the more likely he was going to end up having to write the damn thing just to cover his tracks.

"So, as I was saying to Anthony," he said, "something about the film doesn't sit right with me. I wondered if the studio had made any alterations after Chekhov's death?"

He caught the glint in the eyes of Adam Woodford, Barbara Zaniolo and Cain Xavier. Nancy Sheldrake rolled hers.

"It's a bit of a hot topic here," Woodford said. "Well, it has been at least; it's been three years now. I almost feel like we've talked it to death."

"Surely my presence tonight can resurrect it?" Blondeau smiled.

"The evidence suggests that a part of the film was, indeed, removed," Cain Xavier stated with authority. He had a rich, confident Californian accent. "One of the studio executives reported to *Variety* a 174-minute running time, from the New York screening. The released version, however, clocks in at 165 minutes. So, somewhere, we have lost nine minutes. *Variety*, of course, now claim the initial report was made in error."

"Mistakes can happen to the best of us," Hudgens offered weakly.

"Yeah, and if you believe that, I've got a bridge in Brooklyn to sell ya," Xavier replied.

"Nine minutes is more than enough time for the murder scene," Woodford said with a hint of excitement.

Xavier scoffed as he stood up. "If he's going to start with that again, I'm off to take a whiz."

"What murder scene?" Blondeau asked in what he hoped was a mild tone. He sensed he was finally about to get somewhere with the whole business.

Adam Woodford clasped his hands together and smiled. "How much do you know about the death of Karl Hennigan?"

"Karl Hennigan..." Blondeau repeated, trawling his memory. "The stuntman, right?"

Woodford nodded eagerly. "He 'fell' out of a window at the wrap party for Chekhov's *Zenobia*, in 1960. It's said that the first person seen in the room after it happened was the film's leading man, a certain Leonard Blake."

"I know this story," Blondeau said. "The rumour is that Blake pushed him out, killed his own stuntman. All over a woman, wasn't it?"

"Then you likely would have also heard how the studio helped to cover it all up?" Woodford asked. "Blake was one of cinema's biggest names at the time."

"And I suppose you're saying Chekhov was also involved? That he helped with the cover-up?"

Woodford raised his eyebrows. "It's hard to imagine a control freak like Paul Chekhov not, at the least, having some knowledge of what was happening on his production."

"Interesting," Blondeau said. "But I don't see what this has to do with *Death of a Bachelor*?"

"Have you ever seen a picture of Karl Hennigan?"

"Can't say I have."

Woodford opened his wallet and pulled out a newspaper clipping. He was so excited he nearly fumbled it. He brought the photo into Blondeau's view. "Look familiar?"

Blondeau scrutinised it for a few seconds, then his smile grew wider, until finally he was grinning from ear to ear. "Ha! Now *that* certainly is interesting."

Karl Hennigan, stuntman on Chekhov's desert epic *Zenobia*, bore a striking resemblance to the character of Joshua, Lindsay's friend, in *Death of a Bachelor*. The same sandy-blond hair, the same heart-shaped face. The same button nose, the same dimpled chin. The actor from *Bachelor* could have been Hennigan's son.

Woodford explained: "Joshua first appears in the film when he confronts Sam, shortly after Lindsay's death. The antagonistic relationship is established. It is implied he is the one behind Sam's invitation to the House of the Damned and he is clearly shown as part of the theatre group. Yet no final confrontation ever occurs. The characters never cross paths after their initial encounter."

"Except... in your theory they do, right?" Blondeau said. "Sam kills Joshua."

"Perhaps even via defenestration." Woodford motioned a push.

"And then... what? The studio cut out the scene–"

"It would have been obvious to everyone, wouldn't it?" Woodford said, bouncing in his seat. "Paul Chekhov's leading man kills a character with a striking resemblance to a stuntman killed by another of Chekhov's leading men some forty years ago. And both over a woman, no less. It's virtually a witness testimony.

"Leonard Blake may be retired but he has sired one of the greatest acting dynasties in Hollywood. His sons, his daughter-in-law, his grandchildren. Several of whom are currently in multi-film contracts with Silverlight Pictures, I might add. All their reputations would be in jeopardy if the truth were to out."

A silence filled the little room.

"I like you, Adam," Blondeau said honestly. "What is it you said you write about in *The Times* again?"

Woodford blushed and looked down at his beer. "I set the crosswords." He shrugged. "Always had a keen interest in true crime, though. Especially cold cases. Karl Hennigan's family never accepted that his death was accidental."

"You're basing an awful lot on a simple resemblance though," Blondeau said. "I mean, I like it as a theory, I really do. I love it. But it feels a bit like conjecture..."

"I have more!" Woodford squeaked. "In the novel *Bachelor* is based on, the role of Joshua is a female character, Julia. Admittedly, like many of Chekhov's films, it's only a loose adaptation, and normally I'd argue against reading too much into such a change. But this is the only role in the entire film that Chekhov switched the genders for. Even the initial screenplay still has it as a female. Chekhov specifically required this character to be male. And it also explains the title."

"The title?"

"Death of a Bachelor," Woodford said, as if it was the most obvious thing in the world. "Haven't you ever wondered what it actually means?"

Blondeau ran his fingers through his hair as he considered it. He had heard the film's name so many times he had almost forgotten it was supposed to have a meaning. His brain simply processed it as a succession of sounds. And now that he properly thought about it, it was a strange title...

"I suppose I always assumed it referred to Lindsay," he said eventually. "Hers is the only death in the film, after all. And... she is a bachelor, in the sense of being a college graduate, right?"

Woodford shook his head. "Maybe so, but the more commonly used meaning of the word 'bachelor' is an unmarried young man. There's only one character in the film that fits the bill – Sam is married to Katherine, all his well-to-do friends appear to be that way as well. Of the other, named characters with speaking parts, it can only be Joshua."

Woodford spread his hands theatrically. "Joshua is the bachelor, and his death was cut by the studio to protect the Blake acting dynasty."

It was certainly a good story, Blondeau thought. Worthy of the career boost its uncovering would bring. *If it was true.* Adam Woodford wore an expression of such wide-eyed hope that he almost wanted to accept it right there and then. But he had the sense things wouldn't be quite so simple.

Meanwhile, Cain Xavier had returned from downstairs with

a tray of vodka shots. Blondeau wasn't sure he trusted any clear liquids coming from the bar below, but peer pressure was a powerful thing...

"It's funny we're talking about this right now," Xavier said, "what with our friend Chase in rehab."

Blondeau felt his chest tighten, and it wasn't just the vodka.

Chase Ashley had been all over the news in the time since the story had broken. It was a sudden and shocking downfall for Hollywood's golden boy. Sleeping pills were the official story, though speculation was rife of stronger stuff. None of it approached Blondeau's nagging suspicion about the whole matter, though: that Chase Ashley had been put away to keep his mouth shut.

Hudgens shook his head sadly. "I can only sympathise. People do not fully understand the strain leading actors carry."

Xavier smirked. "You really do believe everything you're told, Tony, don't ya?"

"What do you mean?"

"Are you telling me you haven't heard the rumours?" Xavier asked. "Chase Ashley got sent to the Betty Ford because he mouthed off to a journalist the truth about *Bachelor*."

"Where did you hear that?" Blondeau stammered.

"I have my sources."

"You mean you read it on the internet, dear boy?" Nancy Sheldrake sneered. "It's hardly steered you well in the past, has it?"

Xavier and Nancy began to bicker but Blondeau was barely listening. How could Xavier have known about Ashley and him? It seemed impossible that the story could have slipped out of that hotel suite into unwanted ears.

He could sense the walls closing in. He stole a glance at

Anthony Hudgens and noted a slight tensing of the little man's face. Was he putting it together?

He tried to steer the conversation away from Ashley before his cover was blown: "I'm still interested in this Karl Hennigan businesses. Did–"

"I cannot bear to hear another word," Barbara Zaniolo interrupted.

"You don't believe it?" Blondeau asked her.

"*Pfft*. I am supposed to accept that the great Paul Chekhov titled his final film after a minor character, one who does not even appear until an hour and a half in?"

"He wouldn't be a minor character if the key scene hadn't been removed," Woodford replied. "Joshua's death would have been the true payoff to the second half of the film."

Blondeau had the feeling they had run the circuit of this argument many times before, their claims and counters little more than muscle memory. But at least it was better than the Ashley talk. He could feel his heart returning to its usual rhythm.

"I saw your face light up when I first mentioned this, Barbara," he said. "What's your opinion?"

Barbara Zaniolo smiled as she lit a cigarette. She tossed her dark curly hair back from her shoulders. Her moment had come. "The bachelor is Lindsay, as you correctly surmised. Of course it is – it is Lindsay who drives the entire story. Without her there is no film. The use of the word 'bachelor' in the title is a straightforward reference to Lindsay's history as Sam's student, nothing more.

"Now, Adam is correct to say that the crucial scenes have been removed. However, it is not the death of Joshua, but the murder of Lindsay, that is, in fact, missing from the film."

Blondeau finished off his beer as he let her last words sink in. "I'm all ears..."

Barbara explained: "It is the one moment that everyone who watches the film highlights as particularly jarring. Sam argues with Lindsay at her apartment, throws her into a wall. He leaves, and the next day is informed of her death. So what happened? She was not injured enough from their confrontation to have died. As a narrative it is incoherent, disconnected. The only possible explanation is that part of that narrative was removed."

She crossed her legs, revealing a pair of knee-high boots. "I theorise that Sam returns to Lindsay's apartment and kills her. The scene has been removed, however, not because of the murder itself, but because it reveals the true nature of Sam's relationship with Lindsay."

"Which is?"

"Consider the film as we see it. Lindsay is framed as the villain, an archetypical 'bunny boiler' who tries to destroy Sam's happy family life. But that is because we accept Sam's explanation of their prior relationship: that it did not happen, it is a delusion in Lindsay's mind. Based on everything we see in the film, our sympathies lie with Sam.

"The crucial, missing scenes do not just contain Sam's murder of Lindsay, but his confession. He did have a relationship with Lindsay when she was a student of his. Lindsay is not the villain of the film, she is the victim."

Blondeau's first thought was that he preferred Adam Woodford's explanation. "OK, I can see how that works, but... why would such a scene be removed by the studio? With Adam's version of events there's a justification, but here... if anything it would have made for a better film."

Barbara took a long drag of her cigarette. She was as sedate with her story as Adam Woodford was animated. "When I say there was a relationship between them, it is perhaps not as you imagine it. The relationship was not consensual. Even without the missing scenes, Lindsay shows clear signs of having suffered traumatic abuse. I believe she is a victim of an upper-class sexual abuse ring, of which Sam is a participant."

Blondeau scrunched his face up. "Hang on, what? I don't see signs of that at all. She claims they had a normal relationship?"

"That is because the nature of her experiences have led to the development of false memories. It is an established mechanism of the brain for dealing with overwhelming trauma."

"How convenient," Blondeau smiled.

Barbara carried on undeterred, "Consider the first scene. Lindsay recognises Sam from across the room at the party, and the entire story begins. But if she had reason to be angry with him, why not confront him at an earlier point? Why only after recognising him at the party? The only explanation is that the presence of Sam at the party triggered a part of her memory that had been long buried. But although she now remembers Sam, she misremembers the true nature of their relationship, believing it to have been consensual.

"As part of my work I have spoken to women who have suffered similar experiences and have, as a result, developed false memories, even alternate personalities in some circumstances. I recognise many of their behaviours in the character of Lindsay."

Blondeau tried to make sense of it. "And you're saying Paul Chekhov was involved with this kind of thing?"

"He was certainly part of the upper echelons of American society at an earlier point in his life. In fact, from my work, I have been able to trace direct connections from Chekhov to many alleged members of such rings. So why not? It could be he was involved, or possibly only aware. Either way he fled America in 1969, never to return, no explanation ever given. Perhaps the guilt took its toll on him, and he used his final film to reveal the truth to the world."

"Only for the studio to make sure that truth stayed hidden?"

Barbara nodded. "The missing scenes would reveal the extent of sexual abuse and trafficking at the highest levels of American society. It would have been the smoking gun people such as myself have been after for years. And many, many powerful people would want that to remain hidden." She stubbed her cigarette out in a manner suggesting the matter was beyond dispute.

For Blondeau, if felt far from. Things were starting to get complicated.

Meanwhile, Adam Woodford had come up with another round of vodka shots. *Peer pressure, etc.*

Blondeau took his dose and slumped back on the sofa. "My head is spinning. What does everyone else think about this sex ring stuff?"

"It is obviously preposterous," Nancy Sheldrake declared immediately. "Barbara is allowing her own interests to cloud her judgement."

Barbara scowled at the older woman. "It is true I have spoken to many victims of such abuses. You consider this a weakness to my argument, Nancy? I know better than most the reality of such experiences, and I can therefore recognise it where others are unable to."

"That's the problem, my dear girl. You recognise it everywhere." Nancy smiled acidly. "There isn't a famous man in the world you don't believe a rapist and an abuser. It's a funny form of feminism you've developed."

Anthony Hudgens shifted in his seat, clearly uncomfortable with such talk. "I told you my view about all of this at The Ivy, Stephen. Whether it's Adam's theory or Barbara's, the idea that anything was removed from the film after Chekhov's death is a myth. Constance Chekhov would never have allowed it to happen."

"Unless she didn't know about it?" Adam Woodford countered. "When Paul Chekhov died, the film was in New York, remember, for the screening. Victor Roache, or anyone else from Silverlight, could have made the changes before Constance even saw it. She would never have known the film was any different."

"The timeframe you're talking about here," Hudgens was growing exasperated, "a matter of days, hours even. It's just not realistic."

"It could easily have been done," Barbara retorted. "As Adam says, the film was already in Silverlight's possession. Victor Roache made the cuts before Constance came into the picture. It wouldn't have taken long."

"Utterly preposterous," Nancy Sheldrake said to no one in particular.

They began to talk over each other, launching attacks and parries, of murders and sex rings, cover-ups and coincidences.

"You are, of course, all wrong," Cain Xavier then announced. His voice cut through; he had been silent throughout Barbara's pitch.

Blondeau turned to him. "Am I about to get another explanation?"

"It's only fair that you learn the truth."

"I think I need another shot first."

He went and got them. They dealt with it.

The room fell silent, waiting for Xavier...

"Aliens."

"Oh, for fuck's sake."

Xavier smirked. "You asked for it."

"Aliens? Come on..."

Xavier was unfazed. "Neither of the explanations you have heard address one of the key mysteries of Paul Chekhov's life: what was he doing in the 1970s? He moves to England, hides away in a manor house and doesn't make a single film the entire decade."

"He suffered a breakdown," Hudgens interrupted, unable to hide his frustration. "It's well known. Caused by his experiences filming *Heart's Desire*."

Xavier scoffed. "A cover story. And an obvious one at that. Stephen, let me first tell you a little about myself. I am one of the world's leading researchers in the field of extraterrestrial visitations."

"UFOs?"

"Bingo. Throughout my life I have built an enormous web of sources and contacts. A story has been relayed to me multiple times detailing Paul Chekhov's involvement in a U.S. government programme in the 1970s. Its purpose was to assess the veracity of video footage claimed to be of alien technology."

"Seriously?!"

"What's so crazy about it?" Xavier said. "You've seen *Journey Beyond*, right? Chekhov's techniques for filming the alien spacecraft were so far ahead of their time that even other directors didn't understand how he had accomplished it. You must have heard the story about what President Johnson said to him at the White House screening: 'This is more realistic than you could ever imagine.'"

Blondeau laughed. "That's just an old urban legend."

"It happened. And shortly after, Chekhov was approached by the U.S. government formally. Think about it: with the growth of the home camera market, the government was constantly obtaining footage of unidentified aircraft and phenomena. Who better to determine the legitimacy of such footage than the man who had produced the most realistic-looking footage of alien technology ever put to film? Chekhov would understand set production, effects, lighting, all better than anyone. If the footage was faked, he would be able to identify how it was done. And if he couldn't explain it..."

"But you're saying this was an American government project," Blondeau pointed out. "Chekhov was living in England in the 1970s. I've never seen anyone dispute that."

"I don't dispute it either," Xavier replied. "But he *was* living close to a U.S. aircraft base. I've talked to people in the village near his estate who were there at the time. Many claimed to have seen vehicles with blacked-out windows travelling to Chekhov's manor on a regular basis. They were secretly transporting him there and back."

Blondeau made a mental note to check up on the aircraft base. Xavier's sureness was disarming. It was obvious how he had become one of the premier voices in his field.

"What's the link then?" he asked. "Because I really don't remember anything whatsoever to do with aliens in *Death of a Bachelor.*"

"And that the exactly the point," Xavier smiled. "Chekhov made four films post-1970s, when his involvement in the UFO programme is believed to have ended. The first three films are full of UFO references. They are everywhere."

Blondeau tried to picture Chekhov's final films. It would

have been an easier task before the vodka shots. "I don't recall any?"

Xavier waved his hand dismissively. "I'm sure you would if you had been looking for them. Anyway, *Bachelor* has no such references, at least that our community have been able to identify. From watching it, you would assume Chekhov's interest in the subject suddenly ended."

"You think the references were removed?"

He nodded. "Moreover I believe that, although the references in his previous films were unspecific, in *Bachelor* he went further, explicitly referencing known UFO incidents whose footage he was unable to prove as fake. It would explain why action was taken over *Bachelor* but not any of the earlier films."

"Allow me to point out the obvious weakness in this theory," Nancy Sheldrake cut in. "Cain's entire argument for this being true, his entire backbone of evidence... is that there is no evidence. He draws this connection entirely on the basis of absence."

Xavier ignored her. "Prior to *Bachelor*," he said, "every single film Chekhov made since the seventies contains these references. It's clear that *Bachelor* was intended to continue that trend. Except that the powers that be got to it first."

Blondeau considered it. "So in your view, who is the titular bachelor? Lindsay, or Joshua, or..."

Xavier shrugged. "Who cares? It's not important, it never was. Don't worry about the plot. Chekhov always hid the interesting stuff in the background."

Blondeau's head was awash with so much new information he felt it had to be pushing out some of the old. Algebra, the Tudors, the periodic table – they were all at risk.

"Let me see if I've got everything." He drew a breath. "Paul

Chekhov used *Death of a Bachelor* to expose either a murder committed by one of Hollywood's most legendary actors, a sexual abuse ring at the heart of American high society, or the possible proof of alien life?"

"Why not all three?" Nancy Sheldrake mocked. "I mean, if you're going to believe part of this nonsense, why not go all the way?"

Adam Woodford was unselfish: "All three is fine with me," he said. "I don't see that they are mutually exclusive."

"I don't think my head can cope with combos," Blondeau said. "Death, sex or aliens. Death, sex or aliens. Nancy, do you have any other options?"

The older woman gave him a withering look. "Of course not. If any of this was accurate, how could it have possibly remained a secret? Film productions are not small affairs. It is true that few would have known what had made it into Chekhov's final edit, but the idea that all these additional scenes were filmed and no one has ever thought to mention them... it is patently absurd."

"I think they have a pretty good reason to stay quiet," Xavier replied. "Considering what happened to Chekhov."

The others eyed him uneasily.

Blondeau said, "You're not surely not claiming that he–"

Xavier responded without hesitation: "Chekhov was murdered. No doubt about it."

Hudgens laughed nervously. "That is simply not true, Cain. His death was a suicide, as ruled by the police and the coroner. There was never the slightest doubt. He shot himself with his own shotgun."

Even Adam Woodford seemed to agree.

Now it was Xavier's turn to laugh. "Here's the difference between me and the rest of you. I don't just take what I'm told by the authorities as fact. I do primary research. The police ruled out foul play, good for them. In the village of Ravenwood, close to Chekhov's estate, they tell a very different story.

"Paul Chekhov had called the police out three separate times in the weeks before his death, on each occasion claiming to have seen an intruder. He had even purchased a dog for protection. You all know as well as I do that Chekhov hated dogs, had done all his life. If a screenplay ever called for a family mutt, he would switch it to a cat wherever possible, just so he wouldn't have to be on set with one."

Hudgens nodded grudgingly.

"Chekhov was murdered," Cain Xavier repeated. "I mean, after everything we've talked about tonight, it could hardly be said there was a lack of motive, right?"

Five
The Long Weekend

It was Friday afternoon.

Barbara Zaniolo's apartment was a mess. The rooms were strewn with dirty clothes, used takeaway boxes and stacks of papers, books and binders. It wasn't one of those homes that looked in disarray but where the owner somehow knew where everything was either. Barbara had been rummaging around for ten minutes, her cat increasingly outraged each time its new resting spot was disturbed.

"Here!" she exclaimed at last. "Take a look at these."

She waved a series of photographs. Blondeau took and began to look through them. They appeared to have been taken from a party, though it was unlike any he had ever attended.

The guests were wearing expensive-looking dinner suits and evening gowns, combined with all manner of strange headgear. Deer antlers, elaborate bejewelled masks, one woman in a black dress had on what appeared to be a life-size bull's head. Most of the guests were middle-aged or older, but there were others, younger women in white robes. They did not seem to be enjoying themselves anywhere near as much as the others.

The pictures progressed from an opulent interior to the grounds outside. The final few showed the guests posing solemnly in a clearing in a wooded area. Behind them was an enormous stone statue. It had a human body and a bull's head. A large bonfire was lit beneath, the flames soaring above the guests' heads. Blondeau looked into the eyes of one of the young women in the final picture and felt a chill.

"What in God's name am I looking at?" he asked eventually.

"These are images I have obtained through one of the young women pictured," Barbara said. "I will not reveal her identity, for obvious reasons. The women in white are all victims of the group I have told you about. The older men and women include some of the most powerful people in America – financiers, politicians, leaders of business and media."

"Shouldn't you go to the police with this?"

She scoffed. "And tell them what? It's all on the record. An annual party hosted by one of America's richest banking families. They would be told the women worked the event as hostesses, case closed."

"But the police could try to contact the women and–"

"The few women who have had the courage to come forward with their stories have been dismissed as fantasists. By the police themselves, more often than not. The police are not on our side."

Our side? Blondeau wasn't sure he liked the sound of that.

Barbara asked: "Tell me if you see any similarity between these images and Paul Chekhov's final film?"

He looked through the photos again. He thought he understood her. The strange mix of gothic and surrealist imagery, the contrast of elegant splendour and primal nature – it was all of a similar style to how Chekhov had presented the production of *Hamlet* in the second half of *Death of a Bachelor*.

"You think he attended one of these things?" he asked. "Back in the day?"

"He certainly would have been in a position to receive such an invitation," Barbara said. "And remember – these are only the images that have escaped their clutches. The real horrors take place away from the cameras."

Blondeau shuddered. He preferred not to think about it.

"Did you ever question the significance of *Hamlet*?" Barbara asked him. "Why – of all plays – Chekhov chose that one for the theatre group to perform?"

"Just assumed he was forced to read it at school like the rest of us, I suppose."

Barbara looked unimpressed. "Think about the similarities. Like *Bachelor*, *Hamlet* contains another fictional work within it, in its case the play, *The Murder of Gonzago*. Hamlet stages that production in order to draw out the truth of his father's murder by his uncle, the new king. 'The plays the thing...'"

"'...Where I'll catch the conscience of a king'." Blondeau smiled.

"Exactly."

"You're saying Chekhov had the same intention? *Bachelor* was produced to expose a crime?"

She nodded. "*Hamlet* is the signal that there is something more at stake. And one final similarity: above all else *Hamlet* is a revenge play. Just like how *Death of a Bachelor* would be viewed, had the key scenes showing Lindsay's murder not been removed. Sam's ordeal on the island was depicted as such because Chekhov knew the audience would want him punished for what he had done to her."

Blondeau considered it. He wasn't sure it would have made for a better film than the one that was released, but he supposed it was plausible.

He looked again at the last few photos, the ones taken out in the woods under the giant stone statue. "What's the deal with the bull?"

"I believe it represents Moloch," Barbara said. "An ancient god associated with child sacrifice, through means of fire." She pointed at the bonfire in the images. "This conversation can take a darker turn, if you would like."

He grimaced. "It's dark enough already for me, thanks."

By the time he got home Andrea was rushing out the door with her suitcase. She was due to attend a work event in Barcelona. The Conference of European Medieval History, or some such combination of those words or similar. And James Raikes was sunning himself on a boat in St. Tropez. Blondeau had the whole bank holiday weekend to himself.

He ordered from the local Chinese restaurant and ate with a glass of Rioja while watching the Channel 4 news. There was an item on the upcoming World Trade Organisation conference in Seattle. Protest groups were said to be already organising in large numbers to confront the world's elite.

Blondeau watched the report with unease. The world felt like it was stretching at its seams lately. There was the usual anger, sure, but there was something more – a collective anxiety at the turning of the millennium. People from work had talked about heading out to their country pads for the big night itself. It wasn't that they really expected anything to happen, they all said. But why take the risk?

Two privately schooled children had done for Blondeau's dream of a country pad, and even leafy Hampstead seemed a little too close for comfort. He wasn't sure that a dog – even one as fiercely protective as theirs – would be enough to ward off an angry mob if it came to it.

As he pondered it, Marley stole a chicken wonton and carried it off.

After dinner Blondeau opened the envelope that had been lying on the console table in the hallway. He already knew it was from Adam Woodford. He had sent over photocopies of every piece of information he had regarding the death of the stuntman Karl Hennigan.

Blondeau took the bundle out onto his lap. The first clipping was from the 14th March 1960 edition of the *Los Angeles Times*:

> KARL HENNIGAN, STUNTMAN, DIES
> AT PARTY FOR BLAKE EPIC
> Associated Press
>
> Karl Hennigan, a movie stuntman, who was doubling for the actor Leonard Blake, died in Amman, Jordan after falling from a window at a party to celebrate the conclusion of filming of "Zenobia", local authorities say.
>
> Mr. Hennigan, about 40 years old, of Los Angeles, was pronounced dead at the scene. The movie, directed by Paul Chekhov, is expected to be released later in the year.

That was the lot of it. No further details, no picture. The whole thing could have been printed on a coaster.

As he progressed through the pages the story began to develop. Hennigan's family filed a wrongful death suit against the film studio, alleging an unsafe work environment. The legal wrangle dragged on for years. Eventually an even smaller item acknowledged the lawsuit being settled out of court, the terms undisclosed.

Throughout the assorted news and trade paper articles Leonard Blake's name would often appear, a little too much it seemed to Blondeau. It was as if the writers collectively knew something, but couldn't say it.

He reached the thickest object in Woodford's pack. It was a worn and water-damaged book, *BLOOD ON THE SANDS: THE SHOCKING TRUE STORY OF A HOLLYWOOD STUNTMAN'S DEATH*, written by someone called Roland Tatlock. It had been published in 1987. From Woodford's chronology, it seemed the first account to explicitly link Blake to Hennigan's death. Roland Tatlock was probably the reason that even the likes of Blondeau had heard the rumours.

The pages were covered in scrawled annotations, presumably Woodford's doing. He had also provided his own CliffsNotes summary with page references. Blondeau – a lazy man at the best of times and fully aware of it – was grateful. He read through Woodford's notes, switching to the relevant sections of Tatlock's book as he progressed, and began to build a narrative of the events.

Leonard Blake and Karl Hennigan were known to have been feuding over the affections of a young actress with a minor role in the film. It was probably the bravest thing Hennigan did the entire shoot, Blondeau thought with some admiration. The two men were involved in a heated argument in public just days before Hennigan's death. They had needed to be separated before coming to blows.

The film's wrap party took place on March 12th at a hotel in Amman, Jordan's capital. At roughly 1am Karl Hennigan fell from a fourth-floor window. Among his injuries were a broken back and neck; he was likely killed near instantly.

Although no one testified to having been present in the room at the time of Hennigan's fall, Tatlock's book included statements from several witnesses that Blake was the first person seen in the room, and that the actor appeared out-of-breath and flustered. There were also reports of raised voices coming from the room shortly before Hennigan's fall.

The Jordanian police arrived and conducted a suspiciously brief investigation. Blondeau noted here a particularly interesting account from a cameraman, who told Tatlock he had seen Paul Chekhov engaged in a long, intense conversation with the authorities.

Karl Hennigan's body was quickly removed to a local medical centre. The Jordanian autopsy stated Hennigan had a high blood-alcohol level, but the stuntman was a known teetotaller, and no one on the night could point to having seen him as otherwise.

Once Hennigan's body was returned to the United States, his mother insisted on a fresh autopsy. Skin cells were found under Hennigan's fingernails, a clear sign of self-defence. It was noted by Tatlock here that the skin samples taken from the second autopsy had since disappeared.

The rest of the book covered the long legal fight between Hennigan's family and the movie studio, but Blondeau had read enough of that. He checked the index for any more references to Chekhov, but they were few, minor and incidental.

He left the book on the coffee table and took Marley for a quick walk round the block. It was a cooler evening than recent ones. The air felt crisp and vibrant. A few couples strolled arm in arm, late commuters staggered to their sofas, garden sprinklers spun like figure skaters.

Blondeau's head was alive with visions of an Arabian night

four decades earlier. From the way Roland Tatlock wrote of the various witness testimonies, it seemed many had only been willing to come forward in later years. Time had loosened tongues, as it always did. Was it the same with Paul Chekhov, the great filmmaker waiting all those years, then deciding – from guilt, revenge, or whatever other reason – to reveal the truth to the world?

He had to admit the theory had something to it. The resemblance between Karl Hennigan and Tommy Jacobs, the actor who played Joshua in *Bachelor*, was uncanny. He had looked into the younger man's background earlier in the week. Chekhov had hired him as an unknown, and he hadn't made much of his career since – a return to independent films, the odd television part. Blondeau had attempted to contact Jacobs through his agents without luck. Jacobs apparently had no desire to talk about his highest-profile role. *Strange, that.*

It would, however, make Leonard Blake – icon of the silver screen – a murderer. Blondeau thought he could live with it. Blake was a star of Old Hollywood, his heyday the forties and fifties. It was before Blondeau's time, so he'd never developed much of a personal connection to the man. He'd been getting on a bit when Chekhov had persuaded him to don the purple toga for *Zenobia*, so God only knew what condition he was in now.

Once he returned home, Blondeau poured himself another glass of the Rioja and inserted the *Death of a Bachelor* VHS. It was time to get to the bottom of the Chekhov business, once and for all. Adam Woodford, Barbara Zaniolo and Cain Xavier were experts in their own fields, no doubt. But in the realm of cinema, they were no more than eager amateurs.

He thought back to the last time he had visited his parents, a few weeks prior. They had been half-watching, half-dozing through a detective programme on ITV. The main character was able to tell that the furniture in a house had been recently moved, solely by the marks on the floor and the contrast in the wear of the paint. And once he had that, the spots of blood, hidden by the newly-placed antique display cabinet, were only a short step away.

It was the same with *Bachelor*. Based on the timeline, Victor Roache, or whoever else, would only have had a short amount of time to make changes to the film before Chekhov's niece Constance assumed control of it. Any alterations could only have been simple, more butcher knife than scalpel. So if something had been removed, Blondeau felt sure there must be some clues as to exactly what left behind in the released version of the film.

It was a mystery that called for a film detective, and he supposed he was about as close as it came to that kind of thing.

With Adam Woodford's theory it was all a matter of space. Woodford contended that the removed scenes from *Bachelor* depicted Sam's murder of Joshua, a reconstruction of Karl Hennigan's death at the hands of Leonard Blake. But if that was the case, there was only a limited window of the film where such scenes could have been included. Joshua didn't even appear until halfway through, ruling out anything before that for starters. Blondeau fast-forwarded to his first appearance:

> Sam walks out of a jewellery store with a bag in hand. A young man approaches him in the street outside. He is breathing heavily. He stares at Sam, a look of barely-contained rage.
>
> "Do I know you?" Sam eventually asks him.

"You knew my friend," the man snarls. "She's dead now. You did it."

Some passers-by watch them cautiously, others don't seem to notice. Sam turns and walks off.

"You did it," the man calls out. "YOU DID IT!"

Sam turns back around and rushes towards him. He grabs him by his coat and backs him into a wall. "What the hell are you talking about?"

"Last night," the man says. "I know you were there. I know what you did."

"I didn't do a damn thing."

The man shakes off Sam's grip. "You killed her. You used her up and threw her away because that's what people like you do. Because you think you can't be touched." He spits in Sam's face.

Sam wipes it off. He moves as if to throw a punch but resists it. "You're crazy," he says. "Stay the hell away from me."

He walks away, weaving across the traffic-blocked road and down the street.

It was a scene that raised more questions than answers. Was Joshua (only named in the credits) accusing Sam of murder, or having driven Lindsay to her death otherwise? Was Sam's denial of either outcome genuine? Chekhov seemed to have tweaked every word, every moment to maximise the ambiguity.

Those were the only lines Joshua spoke in the entire film.

According to Woodford the two characters were to have clashed again; but from the brief dialogue they shared here, such an intention was far from clear. There was little to suggest Joshua was being built up for a more substantial role. Indeed, the film was full of such odd characters who appeared only fleetingly.

On the other hand, it had to be said that if Chekhov had hired young Tommy Jacobs purely for his acting skills, he had done a lousy job. Jacob's delivery was so wooden you could almost hear the termites.

More questions than answers...

Joshua was next seen at Lindsay's funeral, with Sam watching from a distance. He then appeared as one of the theatre performers of the House of the Damned. He seemed to have the role of one of Hamlet's old school friends, that odd pair Rosencrantz and Guildenstern. He and another, darker-featured man were dressed in maroon robes with matching caps.

Blondeau had been timing the film with a stopwatch. He began to note down each occasion that Joshua was visible on the screen: 2 hours, 6 minutes; 11 minutes; 13 minutes. Each new appearance further pushed back the window into which Chekhov could have placed his proposed death. 2 hours, 20 minutes; 26 minutes... and then perhaps once more, as Sam left the island on the boat at 2 hours, 29 minutes. There was a figure in the background, standing by a lamp post on the path up to the main house, that was either Joshua or the other, similarly costumed performer. The VHS copy was too blurry to make out the figure's face.

The film continued:

Sam sits at the rear of the boat, alone. Some of the other guests talk quietly amongst themselves. The atmosphere has dampened, the excitement of the first journey barely a memory. The moonlight flickers on the water as the boat lumbers on.

Sam returns to the warehouse where he had left his car. He gets in and drives away as the faint glow of dawn is visible in the sky.

He returns to Manhattan, parks up and walks blankly down the street, nearly crashing into a jogger. He barely seems to notice.

He arrives at his apartment and enters. He trudges from room to room, looking for Katherine. She cannot be found. At last he realises: his home is empty.

He opens a window and leans out, letting the morning air wash over his face. A flock of birds lift off the opposite rooftop...

The journey from the island to Sam's apartment took up five minutes of the film. Chekhov used editing to compress the, in reality, much longer journey. It was such a common technique one scarcely even thought about it. As Sam rounds the corner of one building, the camera cuts to him walking along another; as his car drives off the right of the screen, it enters the left at a different location. The use of continual motion created the sensation of a seamless journey, even when clearly not the case. And the gradual rise of the sun measured the passing of time. All basic stuff but perfectly done, as expected from Chekhov.

It also meant that from the moment Sam left the island to his arrival at his apartment, there was no real chance to have inserted any scenes that would have broken up the flow of the journey. The shots were clearly put together as one continuous sequence.

The window of opportunity closed further.

At this point, the film cuts from Sam, alone in his apartment, to the final scene at his daughter's graduation ceremony. The graduation scene was undoubtedly designed as the film's conclusion – the camera booms upwards and the credits roll over the New York skyline. But could Chekhov have included a scene between Sam's apartment and the graduation? Blondeau watched the transition between the two scenes again:

> He opens a window and leans out, letting the morning air wash over his face. A flock of birds lift off the opposite rooftop...
>
> ...as square academic caps launch into the air with cheers. Sam and Katherine applaud with the other guests, their daughter looks over at them and beams.

The method Chekhov used to transition between Sam's apartment and the graduation was known as a "match cut", where certain elements of a previous scene were harmonised with the next. It could be done by matching movement, visuals, sound – anything a creative mind could conceive. The blood flowing down the circular drain in *Psycho*, slowing dissolving to a close-up of Marion Crane's lifeless eye. Dustin Hoffman rising for the swimming pool float in *The Graduate* and landing in bed with Mrs. Robinson. The helicopter blades and the ceiling fan in *Apocalypse Now*. Just about anything could be matched.

Blondeau considered it. Match cuts were a way of building

connections and smoothing transitions. Paul Chekhov, however, had used them previously – famously – to imply the passing of significant time. At the beginning of *Journey Beyond* the main character, as a child, rides a bike down a road in suburban America. A close-up of the spinning spoke cuts to the similarly designed spaceship *Abeona*, journeying past Mars and captained by the same character as an adult. In *Heart's Desire*, an explorer is served a steak at an expensive restaurant in Lima. As he slices into the meat and the juices flow, the camera cuts to the same character hacking his way through the Peruvian jungle with a machete.

The transition Chekhov used for the final two scenes in *Bachelor*, where the movement of the soaring birds was paired with the throwing of the square academic caps, fit perfectly alongside his earlier work. It could only have been his doing; a quick studio reedit would never have been able to transition so masterfully.

The final two scenes were designed to be seen alongside each other.

The window of opportunity was almost closed. There was only one more possibility: back on the island. Blondeau checked his notebook. The last confirmed sighting of Joshua was at 2 hours, 26 minutes. He was then possibly seen in the background, as Sam's boat left the island three minutes later. If that figure was Joshua, then Woodford's theory was dead in the proverbial water. All the following scenes were edited together so seamlessly that the possibility of an additional sequence, taking the plot in a dramatically different direction, was virtually zero.

The figure might have been the other, similarly-dressed performer, though. Rosencrantz to Joshua's Guildenstern, or

Guildenstern to his Rosencrantz... whatever the hell it was. If that was the case, and if Joshua hadn't been present as Sam left the island... the murder scene could have taken place before he left.

Blondeau rewound to the crucial moment and peered into his television. It was no use. He just couldn't make out the identity of the figure in the background for certain.

He checked his watch, it was nearly midnight. Where had the time gone? He needed a clearer image of that one, crucial shot. He wouldn't get it tonight.

He crashed through his front door at lunchtime the next day, carrying in both arms a large metal canister. A supermarket sandwich rested precariously on top. He grunted and groaned as he hauled the thing upstairs. Marley followed him the whole way as if it was all a great game.

As Blondeau made his way up the winding staircase that led to the attic, the canister slipped in his arms and he almost dropped it. The sandwich slipped off and fell to the floor. The dog ran off with it. Blondeau swore like a Scorsese mobster, but kept going.

He opened the door at the top of the stairs and entered.

In the middle of the attic were two sofas with recliner seats. They faced the wall at the far end, which was covered with a large projection screen. Piles of bean bags, cushions and blankets lined the sides of the room. It was the little walled-off area to the left where the real magic happened, though. A 35mm projector peered out through a small window.

Paradise.

Blondeau had begun work on the room shortly after they had bought the house. Having moved to the place he fully expected to die in, he saw no point in waiting around. They'd been lucky to have found a house with such a large attic, though he wasn't sure Andrea saw it that way.

It took him the best part of a year and several thousand pounds. He had claimed it was for the kids, but no one really believed it. And although it had been popular for sleepovers when the boys were teenagers, nowadays he was usually the only one who made the journey up.

In reality, the 35mm projector soon proved impractical for such a space. It was too loud, the motor got too hot, and the hassle of having to continually change reels was far too much effort unless he was hosting a crowd. It hadn't taken him long to ensure the whole system was rigged up to handle VHS as well.

Indeed, the first thing he had done that morning was to head up and try out the *Bachelor* tape. But it was as he had expected. Although the screen in the attic was larger, the VHS was just as blurry. That face in the background, the man in the maroon robe, could not be deciphered. He needed a clearer, sharper version of the film itself.

He opened the metal canister. Inside were three reels of film. They had come from The Palomino, a small cinema in Camberwell that had run a season of Chekhov's films a few months earlier. He vaguely knew the manager, and it was now summer blockbuster season, so it hadn't been that difficult persuading him to part with them for a few days.

The three reels in the canister covered roughly the final third of *Death of a Bachelor*. Blondeau reached for the one in the middle.

His hands were shaking as he began to slowly thread the film through the machine, sending it on its journey along and between all manner of arcane cogs, sprockets, and gears.

Blondeau had the utmost respect for projectionists. It was an art form all of itself, one which, even with his own machine, he had gained only a surface-level understanding. There was much talk about the future of the industry, where projection would be managed automatically with computers and so forth. Blondeau didn't like the sound of it one bit. He didn't think that Paul Chekhov, known for delivering precise and exacting instructions, often in person, to projectionists on how to correctly show his films, would have liked it much either.

At last everything was in place, primed and proven. Blondeau engaged the motor and the screen came alive:

> Sam walks slowly down to the dock alongside the other guests. He waits for his turn, then clambers onto the boat and finds a seat. He shivers and pulls up his coat collar.
>
> The boat departs in silence. As it angles away from the island Sam turns for one last look

Blondeau dashed to the other end of the room. The figure came into shot, standing by the lamp post on the path up to the main house. He could see him clearly now. The same sandy-blond hair, the same heart-shaped face. It was him. Tommy Jacobs. Joshua.

He watched it back a second time just to make sure, but there was no longer really any doubt.

He fell back onto one of the sofas as he took it all in. So Joshua was still alive when Sam left the island, and that meant...

He felt a little bad for Adam Woodford. Of the three theories, Woodford's was the one he'd actually wanted to be true. It was a classic Hollywood scandal, steeped with sex and jealousy and, above all, power. People would have eaten it right up. The eventual reveal of the truth might even have brought a little closure to the remaining members of the Hennigan family.

He supposed that nothing he had uncovered explicitly ruled out Leonard Blake having murdered Karl Hennigan, or any subsequent cover-up. It just wasn't what Chekhov had intended for his final film. His hiring of the lookalike actor must have been a coincidence, or perhaps some trick of the subconscious.

One down, two to go.

But first, whatever happened to that sandwich?

He'd been thinking about it over lunch. There was a quote from the man himself, in Hudgen's biography, that was half-sunken in the depths of his memory. He took his copy and skimmed through until he came to the part in question.

Chekhov was talking about *Fortune's Kiss*, a hard-boiled heist film he had made in the 1950s. The film had a plot twist two thirds of the way through, when the gang were betrayed by one of their leaders. About this, Chekhov said to an interviewer:

> "I look at a good plot twist like [he taps his nose and chuckles]. You know what I'm saying? It's there all the time, right in front of you, but you can only see it if you know where to focus. Most of the twists I see these days, it's like they dreamt it up on a napkin the night before shooting. There's no logic, no consistency. That's not a narrative, that's an amusement park ride."

It was typical Chekhov, eloquent in his own strange way, effortless in cutting down his peers. The message was clear – Chekhov would never have introduced a plot twist without foreshadowing it.

Barbara Zaniolo argued *Death of a Bachelor* was a film missing its twist. That halfway through, the roles of Sam and Lindsay as victim and villain were to have been inverted. It was the crux of her entire theory linking Sam's supposed abuse of Lindsay to such real-world horrors.

But if that was the case, such a twist must have been foreshadowed in the treatment of the two characters beforehand. Blondeau just had to find it.

He made a coffee, inserted the *Bachelor* VHS and sat back on the sofa. The production logos appeared. By now Blondeau thought he could probably sketch them from memory.

The film opened at a party hosted by one of Sam's wealthy friends:

> Sam takes a glass of champagne from the tray. He stands in a group with three other men. Others slowly circulate around them.
>
> "I should introduce you to my shucker," one of his friends says.
>
> "Your shucker?" Sam grins.
>
> The man nods. "Finest oysters around. It's perfect for a dinner party. My guy will come to your house, you can watch him live in action. He'll tell you all about the history of oysters in New York."
>
> Another friend laughs. "It's all I hear about from this guy recently."

> “Have you bought up an oyster company you’re not telling us about?”
>
> “I wish! Oysters are a huge part of this city’s history, let me tell you. When Henry Hudson first arrived...”
>
> As the man goes on, a young women appears in the crowd behind Sam. She carries a tray of drinks. She turns and sees Sam, her expression changes. She watches him, without his knowing, from a distance.
>
> Eventually another server speaks to her and her attention is diverted. She walks away.
>
> Moments later, Sam turns around. She is already gone.

Blondeau thought back to what he had learnt about shot composition and framing in the early years of his career. At the time, he had immersed himself in the world of academic film theory, sponging up as much information as he could, through any books he got his hands on.

The placement and positioning of different elements within a camera shot was one of the fundamental building blocks of filmmaking. If done well, it could tell a story all by itself: progressing plot points; revealing character, relationships and power dynamics; and creating emotion. Kay watches Michael Corleone hold court through a doorway at the end of *The Godfather*, illustrating the new distance in their relationship, as he accepts his role in a world she has no place in. Charles Foster “*Citizen*” Kane frequently towers over other characters, reflecting a man who has mastered his world. The tilted “Dutch” angles of *The Third Man* evoke the main character’s disorientation in an unfamiliar, confounding city. It wasn't simply a matter of pointing a camera at whoever was talking, one had to *compose* an image.

Nowadays, much of the knowledge Blondeau had on the subject was rarely put to use. When your reviews are required to be little more than the length of a haiku, detailed analysis goes by the wayside. The thirty-year-old Stephen Blondeau would probably have had this whole thing solved by now, he thought wryly. Unfortunately, the version nearly twenty years his senior would have to do...

As the opening scene of *Bachelor* began, Sam was filmed in the bottom half of the screen, while Lindsay entered from the top right and walked across. Movement from right to left on screen was often used to instil a negative emotional response in the audience. It felt unnatural to Western eyes, used to thinking of progression in left-to-right terms.

The example he best remembered was the beginning of Hitchcock's *Strangers on a Train*. There, the camera focused on two sets of shoes, one walking from left to right and one from right to left. They belonged to the protagonist and antagonist of the film, respectively. The opening shots were a way of subconsciously establishing those roles, and the two characters' imminent collision.

Lindsay's first appearance, moving from right to left on the screen, unseen by Sam in the foreground, was similar. It created a sense of anxiety, an immediate negative response towards her as a character.

Additionally, the framing of Lindsay as above Sam in the shot suggested she had the dominant role in the relationship. Though in reality she was several metres in the background, it felt as if she was standing over him, as if she held all the power. This was at odds with Barbara Zaniolo's theory of Lindsay as the film's victim.

As the film progressed, and Lindsay reappeared time and time again, the same conventions held. She arrived at Sam's office, looking through the window in the top of the screen, as Sam obliviously worked away at his desk in the bottom half. Later, she approached the school of Sam and Katherine's son, walking down the street from right to left as the camera remained static.

Blondeau had noticed something else as well. When Sam spoke he was virtually always shot from the front, the audience could see his every expression and emotion. In contrast, Lindsay was often shot from side profile, or with her back to the camera.

The implication was clear: Sam was honest, with nothing to hide from the audience. As they could always see his emotions they could more easily emphasise with him. Lindsay was the opposite. Her face was often hidden from view, suggesting she was hiding something, that she was evasive and untrustworthy. The audience was always kept at a distance from her.

The film had reached the point of Lindsay's final scene in the film:

> The door opens. Sam pushes past Lindsay into her apartment.
>
> "Who the hell do you think you are?" he snarls. "Turning up at my son's school? I should fucking kill you."
>
> She sighs like an adolescent, turns and walks away from him.
>
> He follows her through her apartment, looking around as he goes. The place is a dump. Litter, dirty clothes and plates are everywhere;

the walls are stained and cracked. The ceiling is spotted with patches of damp.

"Did you even hear me?" he asks her as they enter the tiny, filthy kitchen.

She turns back to him and scowls.

"I'm telling you one last time," he says. "Stay away from my family. Stay out of my life altogether."

"Or what?" she spits. She lets out a bitter laugh. "There's nothing you can do to me more than you've done already."

Sam shakes his head and run his fingers through his hair. "Unbelievable," he says to himself. "You really are a crazy bitch, you know that? I've done nothing to you, I don't even remember you. I've tried to be nice about this, I've offered you money to get the help you need, and you throw it all back in my face. So now I'm telling you: leave me and my family alone."

She walks towards him. "I'm going nowhere. You ruined my life; I intend to return the favour. Now get out of here."

She tries to push him away but he grabs her. They struggle around the kitchen table as she claws at him. Eventually he shoves her backwards, hard into a wall. Her head cracks against the surface and she falls to the floor.

She sits slumped against the wall. She touches the back of her head, her fingers come back stained crimson.

Sam stands over her, open-mouthed. "Are you–"

"Get out," she says between heavy breaths. "Get out."

He leaves.

Blondeau had been mentally working through his list as the scene progressed. Lindsay walks through her apartment from right to left – *check*. Lindsay is framed above Sam in shot – *check*. Sam is shot from the front, Lindsay from side profile or with her back to the camera – *check*.

Every aspect of the way Chekhov presented Lindsay established her as the villain of the piece, an almost sinister presence who controls the film throughout its first half. Rather than sympathising with her, the audience, who would come to dread her appearances and the trauma they wrought, would likely be glad when she was finally out of the way.

Blondeau rewound the tape and watched the whole thing through again, but there was nothing that changed his mind. There was simply nothing whatsoever to foreshadow any potential plot twist inverting Sam and Lindsay's roles later in the film.

He stopped the tape and began to prepare some dinner.

He'd been expecting a call from Andrea during the day, but nothing had come. It was par for the course with those type of conferences, time always slipped. Still, it would have been good to talk to someone. He'd spent more time with Sam and Lindsay that weekend than any real person.

As his curry simmered away, he tried the two boys. Neither picked up, hardly surprising for a Saturday night. More of a shock came with his parents, barely able to spare him two words on their way out for a party. Septuagenarians with Saturday night plans? It was hard not to take that personally.

He ate in front of the television, mindlessly watching the lottery balls roll by.

That evening, he settled down on the sofa with a scotch and soda and inserted his VHS copy of *Fortune's Kiss*, the heist film Chekhov had made early in his career. Strangely, it was one of the few Chekhov films he owned, despite being one of his lesser-known works.

Blondeau always found it fascinating watching the early years of the great filmmakers, films such as Spielberg's *Duel* or George Lucas's *THX 1138*. Their methods weren't yet perfected, their budgets often infinitesimal, but there was usually raw promise, and hints of the genius to come.

Rather than bursting into the cinematic consciousness like a Jean-Luc Godard or a David Lynch, Paul Chekhov's early career had been a relative slow burner. Each of his first four feature-length films steadily gained more attention, but it was only with his fifth, the desert epic *Zenobia*, that he finally tasted both box office success and widespread critical acclaim. *Fortune's Kiss* was the third of what were now known as the "Early Chekhovs." It had definite rough edges, but he was getting there.

But that wasn't why Blondeau had picked it for the night's viewing. Watching *Fortune's Kiss* gave him the final confirmation he needed.

The main plot twist, where the gang were betrayed by one of their leaders, was foreshadowed by Chekhov with subtle visual clues throughout. The man in question was often filmed on one half of the screen, away from the rest of the gang, signalling the divergence in their intentions. When he spoke he was frequently shot from profile or with his back to the camera – like Lindsay –

indicating he had something to hide. When the gang discussed the possibility of a betrayal, he looked away from them. He didn't appear in certain scenes, where his presence would have broken the logic of his future actions.

In terms of telegraphing a plot twist, *Fortune's Kiss* was everything *Death of a Bachelor* was not. Like Chekhov said, you could see it coming if you knew where to look.

He wasn't sure his analysis would convince Barbara Zaniolo, but he suspected there wasn't much that would ever do that. Like the older woman, Nancy Sheldrake, had said, Barbara seemed to have allowed her own work to cloud her judgement, grasping at connections which were often tenuous.

It was a relief to leave the whole business of sex abuse rings and strange rituals to someone else's concern. He didn't doubt their existence, just their relevance to Paul Chekhov and his final film.

He just hoped that one day those creepy photos would fade from his memory.

He finished off his scotch, stretched and yawned. Marley snored away beside him.

He crashed through his front door at lunchtime the next day, carrying in both arms a large metal canister. A supermarket sandwich rested precariously on top. He grunted and groaned as he hauled the thing upstairs. Marley followed him the whole way as if it was all a great game.

Then he went back to his car and did the whole thing again.

The owner of The Palomino had been a bit less understanding this time. He'd had to placate him with the promise of a mention in a future column. How he would manage to crowbar that in was a problem for another time.

The canisters contained the three films Chekhov had made since his 1970s hiatus, prior to *Death of a Bachelor*. After years of rumour, gossip and innuendo, Chekhov had made a sudden return in 1980 with *The Fox and the Henhouse*, a political satire in which the American president is exposed as a Soviet spy. He followed it up four years later with *The Night Sessions*, an adaptation of a horror novel set in a psychiatric hospital. And five years after that the world finally saw his long-gestated project *High Upon the Hill*, a World War II drama based on the Battle of Monte Cassino. All three had been rightly lauded upon release and ever since.

There were worse ways to spend a Sunday.

Eight hours later it was done. Blondeau peeled himself off the sofa and headed back down into the real world.

He ate his warmed-up curry as the last glint of sunlight dipped below the horizon. He felt worn out and grimy. His joints were stiff through lack of activity.

He took Marley for a quick walk round the block. The dog was as full of energy as Blondeau was lacking. He strained at his leash, growling at neighbours and other creatures alike. It was the last thing Blondeau needed.

He was relieved to be heading into the final stretch of his weekend's work. Tomorrow Andrea would be back, perhaps even in time to do something. These were the last days of summer, the twentieth century's final burst of warmth. Part of him felt guilty for not having taken advantage of it the past few days, but the truth was he hadn't been so invested in his work in years.

It was no longer solely about boosting his career. It wasn't obvious at first, but there was something deeply mysterious about Chekhov's final film. It had an almost otherworldly quality, as if the film knew it possessed some dark secret, and teased it with every line, every shot, every sound. It was sucking him in.

That evening, he sat down at the kitchen table with a sizable glass of pinot grigio, putting the notebook he had used earlier in the day on one side of the table, a selection of printed-out documents on the other.

The printouts came from a floppy disk provided by Cain Xavier. Though rather than deliver it like a normal human being, the American had somehow managed to slip the disk, unseen, into Blondeau's coat pocket as he was buying a coffee one morning earlier in the week.

It had taken Blondeau a few days to work up the courage to try the disk out. The first level contained two items – a password-protected folder and a plain text file with a short message:

> B,
> It's best for you if we limit public contact. There are certain forces monitoring my movements. The situation is growing more difficult.
> I've attached a dossier outlining the case for C.
> The password is the place where we first met.
> I am relying on you to use your expertise and connections to expose the truth. If you need to contact me tape a child's artwork in a bottom floor window. I'll reach you if I can.
> Your friend,
> X

It all seemed a little over the top to Blondeau, a most ostentatious attempt at secrecy. He wasn't sure he believed a word of it.

Inside the folder were scans of several documents, allegedly U.S. government in origin. They were convincing if only in the sense that most were utterly impenetrable. They were about something called the "Aerial Phenomenon Identification Program (APIP)", a self-explanatory title at least. The documents discussed its objectives and organisational structure in opaque terms, full of the usual governmental jargon and acronyms.

The programme was established in the late 1960s, which lined up with Paul Chekhov's absence from filmmaking the following decade. It also made sense in that Chekhov's sci-fi classic *Journey Beyond* had been released around the same time. If Uncle Sam had wanted to make use of a filmmaker's particular talents, Chekhov would have been the obvious choice.

But from the parts he could decipher, Blondeau didn't see anything particularly explosive. It was hardly surprising that the U.S. government would want to verify footage of aircraft in their skies. There were no references to aliens, nor to any involvement from Chekhov himself. He couldn't help feel a little disappointed.

Of more use were the files that contained Xavier's notes on Chekhov, in particular the UFO references he claimed were in the director's penultimate three films. In The Zebra, Xavier had argued that the absence of such references in *Death of a Bachelor* was proof in itself that they had been removed, given their prevalence in his previous work. It was a curious sort of logic.

Blondeau had previously started to read through Xavier's

notes, before reconsidering his approach. Xavier was highlighting imagery, audio, uses of certain terminology. But if Blondeau knew what to look for, he was bound to find it. He needed to watch the three films himself first, free of any cognitive bias. Then he'd know whether Xavier was actually onto something, or was no better than the loons who kept finding Jesus's face on tortillas.

Now, having spent the day doing just that, he was at last able to compare the notes he had made to the references Xavier had provided.

Some things were right there in plain sight, hard for even Blondeau to miss. Two soldiers discuss seeing strange lights in the sky in *High Upon the Hill*. A child wears a t-shirt with a cartoon alien in *The Night Sessions*.

Others, as Xavier had claimed was Chekhov's penchant, were hidden away in the background. A poster of a flying saucer pinned up in an office in *The Fox and the Henhouse*. Tins of Martian brand baking soda in the pantry in *The Night Sessions*. Blondeau caught some of these, but not all. Xavier had included snapshots of the relevant scenes, saving him any further trips up to the attic. Everything seemed to check out.

Then there were the blink-and-you'll-miss-it references, which Blondeau largely did. A snippet of Orson Welles' *The War of the Worlds* plays on a radio at the soldiers' camp in *High Upon the Hill*. A brief shot of a newspaper front page in *The Fox and the Henhouse*, containing a small item about a UFO incident. Blondeau noted that Xavier had omitted to mention an article in the same shot regarding a Bigfoot sighting. The whole paper was likely just someone screwing around.

There were the references that only those with knowledge of the UFO world would have caught, which Blondeau, of course, did not. A character with the surname Drake in *High Upon the Hill*, according to Xavier a reference to a scientist involved in the search for extraterrestrial life. The protagonist in *The Night Sessions* resides in Room 4.39, apparently the distance in light years to Alpha Centauri, the solar system's nearest neighbour. To Blondeau, these all felt like a stretch.

And then there were the ones Blondeau missed, and that he thought were plain batshit crazy. A cloud in the shape of a spacecraft in *High Upon the Hill*. Similar imagery in a carpet design in *The Night Sessions*. Blondeau, even squinting, could barely make out such resemblances.

In a similar manner, Xavier had highlighted a hidden, backmasked audio message in *The Fox and the Henhouse*, supposedly the phrase: "I know they are out there."

Blondeau was immediately sceptical. Ever since *The Exorcist*, people had been claiming to have uncovered reversed audio messages in just about every medium. Perhaps some were legitimate, but he didn't see why Chekhov would have gone to all that trouble to include such a vague statement.

Xavier had included an audio file of the supposed quote. When Blondeau finally mustered the effort to play it, it was just as muddy, ambiguous and unconvincing as he'd expected.

He finished off the wine, rubbed his eyes and ran his fingers through his hair. He'd reached the end of both their lists and wasn't sure he felt any the wiser. For every reference that seemed legitimate there was another that failed to convince. The evidence, taken in its totality when spread across the three films, did not feel overwhelming. Inspect any film for long enough and he thought you might turn up similar.

The fact that Cain Xavier was willing to throw in such absurdities as the shape of a cloud alongside perhaps more substantial stuff was enough to discredit him in Blondeau's eyes. Xavier was a Jesus-on-a-tortilla man, no doubt about it.

Blondeau couldn't hold it against him too much. Neither Xavier, nor Adam Woodford or Barbara Zaniolo for that matter, would have been the first to read meaning into a film that wasn't really there. There was a fairly popular belief amongst critics that *King Kong* was an allegory for the slave trade, for example, which had persisted despite its creators repeatedly denying such an intention. And he remembered reading a brilliant but surely mistaken essay arguing that *The Wizard of Oz* was, in fact, about American monetary policy in the late 1800s, with the Yellow Brick Road representing the gold standard.

Some critics argued that such interpretations were valid, even if they were not what the creators had consciously intended. That everyone involved in the production of a film brought their own experiences and beliefs into their work, creating a multitude of hidden meanings. Blondeau had never bought into such arguments, feeling it gave critics a licence to come up with any old drivel without needing to justify themselves.

He couldn't explicitly rule out Xavier's theory the way he believed he had with the others, but he felt comfortable enough putting the topic of UFOs to one side. It had always been a long shot.

There was just one thing he couldn't work out. What Xavier had said about the villagers near Chekhov's estate seeing vehicles with blacked-out windows. It was one of the few things he'd heard from any of them that couldn't be explained away as a coincidence. Xavier had argued that Chekhov was being transported to the U.S. aircraft base nearby. But if not that, what *was* Chekhov up to?

Blondeau yawned and slumped back in his seat. He supposed

it could have all been a misunderstanding, or a Cain Xavier embellishment.

He checked his watch, it was long past midnight.

That loose end could be tied another day.

It was lunchtime on bank holiday Monday.

Blondeau woke, groggy, to the sound of the phone ringing. It was Andrea. Her flight had been cancelled and she hadn't found another until the following day.

Ten minutes later James Raikes called. He was back from St. Tropez and fancied the pub.

"I still don't see how you can tell?" Raikes asked him.

"I just can," Blondeau replied irritably. He'd been trying in vain to explain his weekend's work for the past ten minutes. "It's just, whatever they think is there, it's not. They're all only seeing what they want to see."

Raikes looked disappointed. "So there was nothing to it, after all?"

"I wouldn't say that," Blondeau said. "There's still too much about it that doesn't add up. The missing nine minutes of the film. Chekhov's disappearance from public life in the seventies. Not to forget the whole story from Chase Ashley that kicked this all off in the first place." He finished off his pint of London Pride and placed the glass on the bar.

They were drinking in The Med, a pub of certain local disrepute in Bermondsey. From the outside, it looked to have been bodged together from a pair of semi-detached houses. The inside was packed, with shaved heads, tattoos and gold-coloured jewellery as far as the eye could see. The beers were cheap, the room was smoky and noisy, and Robbie Williams' "Let Me

Entertain You" was playing on the jukebox.

Blondeau didn't mind the place, but it would hardly have been his first choice. His friend somehow knew every pub in the city, and it seemed a few days on the French Riviera had made James Raikes hanker for a taste of stereotypically working-class London life.

"Then there's the film itself," Blondeau said. "Something's up with it, I just can't put my finger on it. It feels so... unnatural. The whole thing floats along like some half-remembered dream." He gave a guilty look. "I watched it again this afternoon, just to see if I could get anything more from it."

"And?"

He shook his head glumly. "Nothing."

"Sounds like you've squeezed that fruit for all its worth."

"Maybe."

Raikes raised an eyebrow. "Maybe?"

Blondeau sighed. "I've spent hours trying to contact people involved in the film's production. Actors, cameramen, production staff – you name it." He scowled. "I didn't get a single positive response. Aside from Ashley – before they shut him up – no one is willing to talk about this film, there's a total code of silence. Doesn't that seem funny to you?"

Raikes shrugged. He was eyeing a brunette down the other end of the bar. He often did that. "Perhaps your reputation precedes you?"

"None more so than with Victor Roache himself, apparently. I've called his office three times, without luck." He gnawed his lip. "Roache knows the truth of this. He has to. And if he won't come to me, perhaps I'll go to him."

Raikes's interest was piqued. "A little work trip, perhaps?"

"Perhaps. Next week is the Venice Film Festival. Roache will be there. He's always at those things, trying to buy up anything he can. I haven't been myself in years, but maybe it's time to change that."

"You're going to... confront him?"

"I just need to ask the question. Whatever he says, I'll be able to see the truth of it on his face."

Raikes nodded agreement. "You know the whole thing, where you ask someone suddenly, unexpectedly, so they don't have time to come up with a lie? You should do that."

Blondeau grinned. "Walk right up to him out of nowhere and be all, 'Heydidyoumakeanychangesto*DeathofaBachelor*afterChekhov'sdeath?'"

"He'll have to confess," Raikes laughed. "Remember Maddy? She did the same to me once when she'd found another girl's underwear in my drawer. I hesitated for like half a second tops, but that was all she needed. She threw me out in my boxer shorts. Of my bloody flat, no less!"

"Of course I remember," Blondeau said. "You were camped out in my garden when I got home from work."

They both laughed at that. Raikes ordered another round of beers from a tired-looking barmaid.

Suddenly a voice from the other side of the room called out: "Oi!"

At first they ignored it. People were always *oi*-ing in these type of places.

Then the shout repeated, closer this time. Blondeau – reluctantly – turned his head.

A great big ape was coming right for him. "Yeah, you!"

Not to worry. It must be a case of mistaken identity.

"You're him, aren't you?" the big ape asked. "Blondeau?"

Oh, shit.

Blondeau stammered, "I don't know if–"

"Don't give me that shit. I'd know your face anywhere. I've got a bone to pick with you."

Probably one of my vertebrae, from the look in his eyes. He tried to keep his voice as level as possible: "What can I do for you?"

"I read your review of *City Girls*. My Erica did the makeup for that film."

Oh, shit.

"What was it you said in your review? That the actresses looked like they'd had makeup blasted into their faces with a sawn-off shotgun?"

Blondeau laughed uneasily. *That sounded about right.* "Look, I write for the *Herald*, OK? I have to include that kind of stuff. The average reader is about seventy; they just want to hate things."

"Yeah, well, because of your review, my girl can't find work on another film. It had been her dream all her life to work in the film business."

"I'm sure your wife will find another–"

"My daughter, you French bastard. The apple of my eye."

"I'm not French!" Blondeau spluttered.

"Well, what have you got that poofter name for, then?"

"It came with the blanket and the milk bottle, I'm afraid."

The man was not amused. A vein bulged in the middle of his forehead. His face was the shade of cured meat; his great big gut shifted under his polo shirt.

"I want you to write a correction," he snarled. "In this week's paper."

"I can't do that," Blondeau said, exasperated. "It would be too obvious."

The man moved in closer to him. "Make it unobvious, then."

James Raikes had been watching the whole thing unfold with a mild curiosity. He finally spoke up: "Look, guys, there must be some kind of middle ground we can reach here."

The man turned on him. "Who asked you for your opinion, beanpole? I suppose you're another one of these critics, are you? Think you know everything, you lot."

Raikes flushed with anger. "*I* am not a critic."

"What are you, then? Obviously some kind of tosser, at least."

"I'll have you know," Raikes announced haughtily, "I happen to be the heir to one of the world's largest chocolate biscuit companies."

"Chocolate biscuits?" the man cackled. He gestured to another man, standing nearby. "Are you hearing this, Kenny?"

Kenny shook his head with disdain. "Unbelievable, Charlie. I can't decide which one of these wankers I want to see you kick in first."

"I'd like to see you try," Raikes declared, a mad look across his face.

Blondeau stared at his friend in disbelief. What the hell was he playing at? Neither of them could fight – they were going to be made mincemeat of.

"You want to take it outside, then?" Charlie dared them.

Raikes nodded. "Lead the way, buster."

Charlie and Kenny seemed as incredulous as Blondeau that such a man could be fronting up to them. With bemused looks, they finished off their pints and made their way out the front door.

Raikes started after them until Blondeau grabbed his jacket. "What are you doing?" he hissed. "We can't fight them, they'll batter us."

Raikes smiled. "I've got a plan. Trust me." He tapped his temple and followed the men out.

Blondeau, reluctantly, shuffled after him.

They made their way around to the pub's car park, passing arguing couples and next month's arguing couples on the way. Charlie and Kenny were in the middle of the car park, waiting for them.

"Here they come!" Kenny exclaimed. "Boy George and Elton."

"Now I'm going to give you boys one more chance," Charlie offered charitably. "Agree to write a correction in your ne–*Ow*!"

Blondeau could barely believe his eyes. Raikes had darted towards the man and flashed an arm.

"He hit me!" Charlie cried. "The bastard punched me in the bloody ear!"

Raikes turned to Blondeau and gave the order: "Run!"

They ran.

Out of the car park, down the road, then weaving through narrow residential streets. At least here they had the advantage – their pursuers were far too beer-bellied to put up much of a chase. The shouts and footsteps coming from behind them gradually faded.

Blondeau and Raikes came out onto a main road. The wind hit their faces as late-night traffic rushed past. They stopped and gathered themselves by a used car lot.

Blondeau swore between heavy breaths. "That was your plan?! Punch him and run away?"

Raikes nodded. He pulled out a cigarette and offered Blondeau one. "He deserved it. He called you French – I can't let a friend be abused like that. What's the problem?"

"But I could have..." He paused, lost for words. "I could have just told him that I'd make the correction and then not done it. Didn't you consider that?"

Raikes looked at him as if he'd suggested breaking into Buckingham Palace. "You don't want to lie to these boys, mate. Didn't you see the tattoo on the other bloke's arm, with the blue lion? *Millwall.* You know, as in, Millwall F.C.? I reckon they were in the firm."

"The firm?"

"You know, hooligans and all that business. Those boys don't mess around, let me tell you."

"Oh, brilliant," Blondeau groaned. "Fan-bloody-tastic. Now I've got football hooligans after me. That's exactly what I need." He paced back and forth, gesticulating to himself. "How do you even know any of this stuff, anyway?"

"I'm a man of the world," Raikes replied easily. "Actually, now I think of it, maybe I shouldn't have punched him. I've probably made things worse for both of us. Hmm."

"Even I could have told you that."

Raikes considered it between drags. "Yeah, I think you might be right. Maybe I should get out of town for a little while. Let this all blow over."

He turned to Blondeau with an inquiring look. "Where did you say this film festival was, again?"

Blondeau asked the taxi driver to drop him off a few streets from his house. Perhaps he was being paranoid, but after the evening's events, he didn't want anyone from that part of the city knowing precisely where he lived.

As he turned onto his street a man in a fedora crashed straight into him. Blondeau was nearly knocked off his feet. The man continued on without an apology. Blondeau started to say something but caught himself. He'd made enough enemies for one night.

The first sign that something was wrong came as he opened his front door. It was already unlocked. Blondeau never forgot that. He briefly wondered if Andrea had returned from Barcelona early.

Marley was waiting for him in the hall. He was pacing back and forth, growling and baring his teeth. His tail was beating like a windscreen wiper in a downpour.

There was something on the floor. Blondeau knelt and inspected it. It was a piece of torn fabric. He didn't recognise it.

"Andrea?" he called. There was no response.

Marley was urging him forwards. He followed the dog through the house. Nothing looked out of place, though he noticed the house felt cooler than recent nights.

The explanation came in the kitchen. The back door was ajar. The area around the handle looked damaged, as if it had been forced.

Blondeau felt his whole body tense. He went straight to the counter and pulled out the largest knife he could find. He took a few, deep breaths, summoning his courage. Then, knife in hand, he journeyed back through the house.

He searched from room to room, downstairs to up, even the attic. And then back down, out and through the garden.

There was nothing.

Other than the back door and the piece of fabric in the hallway, he saw no sign of any disturbance or damage. Nothing of value appeared to have been taken. The house was quiet, eerily so. He turned on the radio to block out the silence.

He poured a glass of cold water and drank in. He tried to

make sense of it. The intruder had come through the back door, that was sure enough. But Marley must have scared him off, taking a chunk of his clothing as he fled out the front. *Good boy.*

Suddenly it came to him. The man in the fedora. Rushing from the scene, just moments before Blondeau arrived. It had to have been him.

He rushed back into the hallway and picked up the piece of fabric. It was light brown. He felt certain now that the man had been wearing a trench coat of a similar colour.

The knowledge that Blondeau had likely passed his intruder in the street disturbed him. If the taxi driver had dropped him off closer to home, he would have caught him in the act. He wasn't sure if that was a good thing or not.

He took a seat at the kitchen table as his heartbeat steadied. He'd have to call the police, he supposed, though it could probably wait until the morning. Like they'd ever catch the guy anyway. A break-in, with nothing even taken? It would hardly be high on the Met's list of priorities.

Then he realised. He finally understood what was different. He'd left them right there on the kitchen table.

The documents.

Adam Woodford's notes on the Leonard Blake–Karl Hennigan saga.

The images of the creepy masked party, given to him by Barbara Zaniolo.

Cain Xavier's UFO papers.

They were all gone.

Six
City of Masks

The sunlight shimmered on the water and crept up narrow, shady lanes. Stately domes and towers peppered the skyline; a kaleidoscopic array of flowers in bloom perched on open window sills and balconies.

The gondolas passed by serenely, some spurred on, others drifting like autumn leaves. A water taxi, one of those splendid, 1950s-style wooden speed boats, cut through the channel, casting an icy-white trail in its wake.

Blondeau sat at small table, sipping a Bellini cocktail. The blend of peach and prosecco was sweet yet vibrant. His hotel bar looked out onto the Grand Canal, the city's main channel. Its murky green waters snaked through the heart of the city.

It was close to midday. The streets below were busy but tranquil, the soft splash of the gondola oars hypnotising. It was as if the city itself was yawning, contentedly.

And somewhere nearby Victor Roache was screaming in the face of some poor intern. Or threatening to ruin the career of a budding young director if they didn't cut their labour of love down to ninety minutes. Or frantically trying to outbid a rival studio, making all manner of promises and commitments he had no intention of keeping.

But where?

That was the question. Blondeau had spotted him several times already at screenings, but had yet to get within speaking distance. The problem was that Roache never stayed for the entirety of a film. He would arrive late, sink his sizable frame into the front row seat always reserved for him, then leave before the credits rolled. By the time Blondeau came out into the foyer, he was gone. Good or bad, Victor Roache did not need long to make his mind up.

Blondeau was never going to be able to confront Roache in such a setting. But Roache's other activities throughout the day were a mystery. He had to face reality – he was simply not important enough to get within Roache's vicinity.

At the table beside him a pair of blondes discussed whichever party they were due to attend that night. James Raikes would be kicking himself. Blondeau hadn't seen his friend since the previous afternoon. In truth, he'd barely seen him all week. Raikes had submerged himself fully into the bars and nightlife of the city. It was what he did, Blondeau didn't hold it against him. After all, it was Raikes who had insisted – at his own expense – on upgrading them from the near-youth hostel the *Herald* had provided, to their current, altogether pretty damn luxurious lodgings.

Blondeau finished off his cocktail and considered ordering another. He decided, instead, to go for a walk through the city.

He headed southwards, without any great purpose. Though the evenings were cool, the days were still warm enough for the tables outside restaurants to be packed. He caught the smell of fresh herbs – basil, rosemary and thyme – as he went by.

He stopped to look at a canal boat, loaded to burst with crates of fruit and vegetables. An old man with a tanned face and a great bushy beard stood in the centre, jetting back and forth to serve customers standing above him on the pavement. He had the look and mannerisms of a street preacher. Blondeau stood by, blankly, for so long, that the old man's attention eventually fell on him.

"And you, *signore*, what you are you looking for?" he rasped in a heavy accent.

A great-gutted, foul-mouthed American. He purchased a banana instead. "I'm actually looking for a friend," he said. "He's an American, balding. Big stomach, like this"–he spread his hands–"Have you seen anyone like that come past recently?"

The old man laughed. "Many big Americans this week." He went off to serve another customer.

Blondeau carried on. He turned up a cobbled alley so narrow two people could barely cross. Away from the main waterways were bakeries, clothes shops, small cafes for locals. He passed a shop selling expensive-looking Venetian masks and stopped to look in the window of a model boat shop called Falco.

He entered the shop and wandered around, inspecting some of the models. They came in all sizes, from flat-bottomed rowing boats that could rest in the palm of a hand, to a reconstruction of an ancient Greek galley that had to be at least a metre in length. The gondolas, in particular, were gorgeous, with staggeringly intricate woodwork.

A man was standing behind the counter. Falco himself, most likely. He was middle-aged, thin, with combovered hair and large rectangular glasses that sat too high on his nose. He offered Blondeau a respectful smile but said nothing.

Fearing the little models would never survive the brutes at baggage control, Blondeau settled instead on a do-it-yourself kit of a gondola. His father's birthday was coming up, and it seemed like something that might occupy the time of a man whose time desperately needed occupying.

"Are you here for the festival?" the man that was probably Falco asked him as he paid up. He had a small, precise voice.

Blondeau nodded. "I'm just a critic, though. Must be a busy time for you?"

"Honestly, it's quieter than recent weeks."

"Really?"

"*Sì*. We *Veneziani* love to complain about how the tourists are pushing out locals. How our sons and daughters cannot buy houses because of the prices. But on this week, the famous people push out the tourists. They pose for pictures and go to parties, then they leave. They don't buy anything."

"That's a shame," Blondeau said. "I was going to ask you if you'd seen a loud, fat American."

The man gave a sad smile. "Only on the television."

Bag in hand, Blondeau made his way to the door, and then stopped. "How about another English guy then – thin, with slicked-back hair? Maybe wearing a leather jacket?"

Falco raised his eyebrows. "*Sì*, I've heard about that one."

From the look on his face, Blondeau thought it best not to press the matter.

A few minutes later he came out onto the Piazza San Marco, the city's main public square. Long arcades, lined with shops and restaurants, ran along three sides; the other housed the opulent domed church, St. Mark's Basilica, and an enormous red-bricked bell tower which soared above the rest of the city like a sentinel. The bells were ringing for noon.

For a city full of labyrinthine passages and alleyways, entering the open space of the square felt like being able to stretch one's legs after a long car journey in the middle back seat. It was a stirring experience.

Blondeau wandered across the paved stone floor, which was covered in geometric patterns that felt strangely at odds with the Renaissance architecture surrounding it. Groups of people were outnumbered by the pigeons, swarming every step, ledge and open space for scraps of bread.

He looked around for the unmistakable figure of Victor Roache. It was an absurd thought, that Hollywood's most powerful studio boss would deign to bunch up with the little people, but he was fast running out of options. Tomorrow was the final day of the festival. That evening, the customary awards would be handed out at a ceremony, and then the stars would shoot off in their private jets, and whatever was considered normality would return to this floating city of stone.

Blondeau's best chance of getting to the truth of the Chekhov mystery was slipping through his fingers. He thought back to those days and nights he had spent cooped up inside his house, scouring every frame of *Death of a Bachelor* for clues. And how that strange weekend had concluded.

He had never ended up calling the police about the break-in. He hadn't even told Andrea, instead claiming it was he who had broken in through the back door, having locked himself out after a night of heavy drinking. She had seemed to accept his tale without suspicion or, for that matter, much interest whatsoever.

He wasn't entirely sure why he was lying to his wife about the matter. It wasn't something he did often. He supposed it was just simpler that way. Nothing of value had been taken, so why worry her?

Blondeau himself was unconcerned about the whole business. The simplest explanation was that the intruder, harried by Marley upon entry, had swiped whatever he could lay his hands on and fled. He would have no doubt later been utterly baffled by what he had landed upon.

The alternate explanation – that the intruder had, in fact, taken exactly what he had intended? That was the kind of thing that happened in films, not real life. Besides, he'd disproved the crackpot theories of Chekhov's Club, so what would have been the point?

He turned around and made his way back to the hotel. He was planning on attending a screening later in the afternoon, an American film called *Boys Don't Cry* which was being shown out-of-competition but receiving much hype. He thought he could probably squeeze in a quick nap beforehand. After all, they didn't call it *La Serenissima* without reason.

As he entered his hotel, he recognised a youngish man pacing back and forth in the lobby. He was short, with thick eyebrows and greasy shoulder-length black hair. At first Blondeau couldn't attach a name to the somewhat simian-looking figure.

The man responded before Blondeau could: "Hey, I know you, right?"

The New York accent triggered the connection. It was Billy Giudice, a filmmaker Blondeau had interviewed the previous year. They had spoken at the London Film Festival for Giudice's debut feature, a low-budget crime film called *Recoil*. Not only had it been Giudice's first press tour, as Blondeau recalled, it had been his first time outside the United States period, and he had been a bundle of raw energy throughout, talking a hundred miles a minute about a dozen different subjects at once.

Since then, *Recoil* had blown up, and Giudice was becoming a name. Though Blondeau noted it hadn't yet seemed to have changed his demeanour.

Blondeau shook his hand and reintroduced himself.

"Blondeau, yeah, I remember," Giudice said, semi-convincingly. "That was a crazy time in Europe last year, man. I pretty much blew all the money I made from *Recoil* on... shit, I can't even remember. I doubt it was healthy, whatever it was."

"How are you enjoying Venice?" Blondeau asked him.

Giudice raised those great bushy eyebrows and exhaled. "It's been wild, man. I'd hoped to catch a few movies, like uh, the one about John Malkovich, but there's so much going on. Constant meetings with very important suits, you know? Times have changed, man. Back when we first met, no one knew my name. I couldn't even believe it when I heard that a critic from a big London newspaper wanted to interview me."

Blondeau laughed. "The truth is, Kate Winslet cancelled our interview that week. As much as I loved your film, I also had some column inches to fill."

"I'll always appreciate it none the less. Nowadays, I got people I never seen before telling me what a genius I am, but it's easy to say that once everyone else has."

"It's not the worst problem in the world."

"Shit, no! Don't get wrong – I ain't complaining. You should see the offers I'm getting. Warners want me to remake *Ocean's 11*, that old Rat Pack movie, for crying out loud. They're offering me a $70 million budget, say they'll get half the biggest names in Hollywood to star." He shook his head in disbelief. "Wasn't long ago I was having to beg my uncle for twenty thousand to shoot *Recoil*."

Blondeau smiled. Those on the other side of the business were rarely so free with such details. If Giudice didn't learn to hold his tongue, he was going to get a reputation. "Are you going to do it – the *Ocean's* film, I mean?"

"A goddamn Hollywood remake? Shit, no! I ain't no sellout,

man. Truth is I got this other script I've been trying to push all week. First thing I ever wrote, back in my early twenties. It's called *Brothers*. It's based on my dad and uncle, growing up in New York in the 1960s."

"It's... a coming-of-age tale?"

Giudice thought about it. "I guess you could call it that, yeah."

"Any interest?"

"A little, I guess." His face revealed the truth of it. "But mainly, it's like, 'OK, that sounds great, but first we'd like you to do this Ben Affleck picture,' or whatever. Screw that, man. Why can't they just let me be me?"

Blondeau shrugged. "Honestly, you might want to consider it. You know what they say – 'One for them, one for me.' If the Affleck thing, or the *Ocean's* remake is a hit, it'll give you more leverage to do whatever you want to do next."

"As if I haven't been told that by everyone already," Giudice grumbled. "So let me get this straight – I gotta make movies I don't wanna make, just to make movies I do wanna make? This business, man. I'd rather keep shooting scenes in my friends' apartments." He lit a cigarette and offered one to Blondeau. "My generation are too quick to play ball with all this studio bullshit. You never saw Francis Ford Coppola 'doing one' for a studio back in the seventies."

Blondeau grinned. "He just did a John Grisham film, though. They'll always get to you eventually." The truth was he'd interviewed enough young filmmakers in his time to have heard it all before. Giudice would likely either submit to the system or fade into obscurity. The guy had genuine talent, so he hoped it would be the former.

He noticed that Giudice kept glancing over at the hotel

staircase. "Anything wrong, Billy?"

The director looked at Blondeau as if sizing him up for the first time. "Maybe, yeah." He paused, scratching his lip, brows furrowed. "Look, maybe you can help me out with something, yeah? I brought my girl, Angie, to the festival. I just figured, you know, it's Venice and all, it would be romantic or some bullshit."

He sighed. "Problem is, I've been so caught up with meetings, I haven't had any chance to spend time with her. We're flying back out in a couple of days, so I promised her it would be this afternoon but... I just found out that Ed Norton wants to meet. You seen *Fight Club* this week? That movie is going to blow up, I'm telling you. And so will he. He'd be perfect to play my dad in *Brothers*. They even look alike, if you squint a little. If I can get him on board, maybe I won't have to make all these shitty movies the suits want me to."

Blondeau considered it. "Could work, I guess. I don't see where I come in, though?"

"If my girl is left alone again today, she'll flip out. She's pretty volatile at the best of times."

And there it is... "I'm not sure you're selling this all too well to me, Billy."

"Just give her a tour of the city, can't you?" He said it as if Blondeau was being the unreasonable one. "You're a critic, you must have been here before. Show her the uh... you know, the churches, or whatever the hell else is going on. Take her for a ride on one of those little boats. It'll only take a few hours. And I'll make it up to you in the future. Whatever you need – an interview, set report, whatever. You'll be first in line."

"Actually, I need something else," Blondeau said at once.

Giudice was taken aback. "Yeah?"

"Victor Roache."

Giudice scowled. "That bastard? He's the worst of the lot of them. What do you want him for?"

"I just need five minutes of his time. A personal matter, that's all."

"Yeah, well... I don't know if I can help you with that." He took a long drag on his cigarette, his features knotted. "I refused to sell him *Recoil* after I heard all the shit he's pulled. I don't know why everyone in Hollywood is so scared of the guy; in my neighbourhood he'd be dropped in a second. Anyway, he's already given me the usual spiel, how he'll personally see to it I never get another movie made, that I'll be stuck shooting dick pill ads, yadda yadda yadda. I can't say we're on the best terms."

Blondeau had to smile. He'd heard a few times recently that Roache's reputation was starting to precede him with newer filmmakers, and that it was becoming a problem for business. It couldn't have happened to a nicer guy.

"I don't need you to introduce us. I just need access to him. That's not an easy thing for a man of as little stature as myself."

Giudice scanned the foyer as if for a means of escape. "I don't know, man. I guess... there's the awards ceremony tomorrow, he'll definitely be there... but I can't get you into that, it's way too exclusive. I barely got tickets myself. Then I suppose there's the party afterwards–"

"Sounds perfect," Blondeau grinned. "I love a good party."

Giudice screwed his eyes shut. "Ah, come on, man. You sure you wouldn't prefer an exclusive interview when I'm the biggest director in the world? You know people are calling me the next Paul Chekhov, right?"

"I believe it," Blondeau replied. "And I'm happy for you to throw in an interview as well. But for now, I need Roache."

Giudice looked close to submission. "This is gonna take some serious stretch to get you in, you know that?"

"And if my wife finds out I've been floating around Venice with another woman, she'll mount my head in our living room."

Giudice muttered something to himself. It didn't sound PG. "You're a real asshole, you know that?"

Blondeau took it as agreement. "Only when I have to be."

Giudice gave him a long look that might just have been grudging respect. "What do you even need Roache for, anyway?"

For a moment Blondeau considered telling him everything. The tale from Chase Ashley, the days spent studying Chekhov's final film, the break-in. Perhaps a wunderkind director like Giudice would offer up a fresh perspective, or spot some clue he had thus far missed.

Then, he decided not to.

"It's complicated," he said.

Seven
The After Party and After

Blondeau scooped up a glass of champagne. *Just one, just to settle the nerves.*

James Raikes was already on this third.

"Can't you slow down?" Blondeau hissed at him. "Remember, we're here on business."

"*You* are," Raikes replied. "I'm here for a mooch, I already told you that. Plus, is that Salma Hayek I see over there? Perhaps I should introduce myself..."

"Please don't. If you're going to cause a scene, at least wait until I've spoken to Roache." He downed the glass in one. "Until then, we're Dutch, remember?"

There was always a hitch. True to his word, Billy Giudice had delivered them into the awards show after party, but he had done so using the tickets of two filmmakers from the Netherlands, nominated for the Best Short Film award. Blondeau didn't even want to know what the real nominees were up to that night. From the vague hints Giudice had offered, it seemed they were either ensconced in the city's best brothel, or tied up in Giudice's hotel room. He wouldn't put either possibility past him.

"*Ja, ja, ja,*" Raikes said dismissively. "Why don't you get off *mis ballens* already?" He headed over to the buffet table and began spreading a wad of caviar onto a canapé.

To Blondeau's ears, Raikes's Dutch accent sounded a lot like his impression of Arnold Schwarzenegger. Not that his own was likely to be any better. He just hoped that it wouldn't come to that.

He turned away from Raikes to take in the scene. All around him were extraordinarily beautiful people in extraordinarily expensive attire. Their skin shone, their jewellery sparkled, their fragrances spoke of distant and exotic lands.

There were others too, of course. Directors and screenwriters and producers. It had to be said – their roles were often behind the camera for a reason. Blondeau felt grateful for their presence. It meant he didn't stand out quite so much.

The chatter of the guests was backgrounded by a pianist rolling off soft jazz numbers in the corner of the room. He had the look of all musicians at such events – bored out of his brains.

The party was at the Excelsior, one of the most luxurious hotels in the city. Both the hotel and the entire film festival were taking place on the Lido, a resort island about a fifteen-minute boat ride from the main city.

The party itself was in a long, narrow ballroom, and the adjacent terrace. It looked out onto a small private beach and, beyond that, the dark shimmering waters of the Adriatic Sea. The hotel's combination of Belle Époque architecture and Moroccan design flourishes – arched entryways and latticed windows, polished wood floors and ornate chandeliers – created a sense of bygone charm and glamour. Blondeau half-expected to see the likes of Marlon Brando, Grace Kelly and Audrey Hepburn milling about, clinking glasses and sharing jokes. Instead, it was the new generation – Brad Pitt, Cameron Diaz and yes, Salma Hayek – that he spotted.

He remembered having interviewed a good portion of the guests, some on multiple occasions. He just hoped that none of them would remember him. To avoid suspicion he'd pulled his hair back into a loose ponytail, and was wearing a pair of thick-framed, entirely superfluous glasses that he had purchased, along with the tuxedo he wore, at a shop in the city that morning. Though he had cringed when first looking in a mirror, he had to admit they provided him the loftily pretentious air of a European auteur.

"There's my favourite Dutchie!" a coarse voice, as if on cue, announced from behind him.

Billy Giudice must have been the only person in the room more ill at ease in a tux than Blondeau. His looked about three sizes too big, for starters. Even stranger, he seemed to have on beneath one of those big frilly shirts commonly worn by silver-screen pirates. Blondeau wondered where on earth he had got such a get-up from.

"Perhaps you can help us figure this out," Giudice drawled, apparently oblivious to the impact his appearance was having on others. "What's the difference between Holland and the Netherlands? And then the people are called Dutch, which I don't really see what that has to do with anything. It's all too much for me, man."

The brunette on his arm rolled her eyes and wandered off to the buffet table. *Angie*. Of course. The hour Blondeau had spent floating around Venice with her already felt like some strange dream. He had tried his best, pointing out the few monuments he knew, and inventing stories about others when the silence became too unbearable. Throughout it all, she'd chewed bubble gum, smirked, sneered and scowled. Clearly, Blondeau was no fit replacement for her beloved.

And then, as they disembarked, they had bumped into James Raikes, and that's when things had really got complicated...

"Have you seen Roache here yet?" Blondeau asked Giudice. "The sooner I speak to him, the sooner I can get out of your hair."

Giudice shook his head. "Can't say I have. But you don't need to rush on my account. Enjoy yourself!" He raised his glass. "I gotta say, you really lived up to your side of the bargain. Angie couldn't stop talking about what a great time she had yesterday."

Blondeau felt his stomach churn. "Oh yeah?"

"I could barely believe it myself, pal. And taking her out at night – I didn't even ask you to do that. I tell you, if you were a few years younger, and few pounds lighter"–he gave Blondeau a tap on the gut–"I might have been a little suspicious."

Blondeau laughed uneasily. "Thank goodness for Father Time, then."

Giudice gave him a strange look. "...Sure."

"How was the meeting with Ed Norton?" Blondeau asked him, to change the subject more than of any genuine interest.

Giudice gestured as if he had almost forgotten about it. "It was cool. Cool guy, no doubt. Said he was looking to start up a production company, could be some interesting projects for me there. I kept trying to bring the conversation around to *Brothers*, but..."

"No luck?"

He groaned. "It's like, everyone in this business has their own pet project, which they think is special, and it's all they care about, and–"

Blondeau raised his eyebrows.

"–but mine *is* special, that's the difference! Only problem is these guys are all too self-involved to see it." He cast a scornful look around the room, shaking his head.

The champagne must have made Blondeau emboldened. "Go make *Ocean's 11*, Billy," he urged. "Maybe throw in *Ocean's 12* while you're at it. Everything will be easier for you after that."

Giudice eyed him with a hint of suspicion. "And I bet you'll massacre me in the reviews, right?"

Probably. "Who cares? You only get one life. You can either spend it fighting the system, or you can enjoy yourself. A guy with your talent deserves to be rewarded for it."

Giudice turned away from him and stared out at the sea. "Maybe you're right." He walked away, deep in thought.

James Raikes had reappeared at Blondeau's shoulder. "He seems like a nice guy," he said, as Giudice headed out onto the terrace.

"He does," Blondeau agreed readily. "Did you really have to sleep with his girlfriend?"

Raikes thought about it. "Probably not," he decided between mouthfuls of caviar. He waved at Angie across the room.

Meanwhile, a man and woman that Blondeau didn't recognise were coming straight for them. They looked like siblings, or one of those couples that looked like siblings, with tanned skin and straight, jet-black hair. A very tidy pair, all in all.

Blondeau didn't like the look of this one bit.

The man greeted them. "You are Timmermans and de Kock, yes?" he asked in accented English. "The makers of *De Verjaardag*?"

Blondeau nodded and smiled. That sounded about right.

"We must introduce ourselves," the man said. "We are the team behind *La Casa de Hielo*." He arched his chin proudly.

The revelation could not have meant less to Blondeau. "Ah, yes," he said in his own, woeful attempt at a Dutch accent.

"Congratulations."

"*Felicitaciones*," Raikes added, raising his glass.

"We must, of course, congratulate you as well," the woman smiled. "Truly, I felt that it was your work that most deserved to win."

Blondeau glanced at Raikes. *Did we win?* Or perhaps these two did. He couldn't quite work out whether they had come to gloat, commiserate or applaud them.

"It is as they say," Raikes said loftily. "The best team won."

The man and woman shared a puzzled look. "Yes, of course," the man said after a moment.

"But now," the woman added, "you can tell us the truth." Her smile had vanished.

"The truth?" Blondeau stammered. A sudden wave of heat came over him. It felt like all the air had been sucked out of the room.

"Yes, you know what we are talking about." She paused for dramatic effect. "Did you really shoot it all in one continuous take?"

"Ah! Of course," Blondeau tapped his nose. "I'm afraid that will have to remain our secret."

The man gave him a playful shove. "Come on, we are all colleagues here, are we not? Luisa thinks she found a cut, when the camera shifts behind the main character's head and over to his other shoulder, but I'm not so sure."

Raikes shoved the man back, a little less playfully. "We Dutch are very careful with our secrets," he warned. "I must ask you to respect our right to privacy."

Luisa and her partner exchanged another, bewildered look. "We quite understand," she said, gesturing in apology. "We did not mean to cause any offence."

"And yet," Raikes said gravely, "you have."

Blondeau nodded solemnly along. It was enough to get the two pests to back away and disappear into the crowd.

"I think that went about as well as could be hoped," Raikes said once they were out of earshot.

For once Blondeau agreed with him. He frowned. "I'm not sure this act has all that much of a shelf life, you know. We need to find Roache as soon as possible."

"I'll go check over there," Raikes said, eyeing a pair of leggy blondes across the room.

Blondeau made his way out onto the terrace. The open air was cool and sweet. He could hear the heave and hiss of the sea, only a hundred metres or so away. A paved path opened out to a tented patio with seating and a bar, and beyond that the hotel swimming pool. A wooden bridge had been erected over the pool, which was surely asking for trouble when the drinks were flowing as freely as they were that night.

Blondeau ordered a martini from the bar and looked around. There were as many stars under that tent as there were in the night sky; some shining bright, some burgeoning, others on the wane. Yet of Victor Roache there was still no sign. Where was he? The party was well underway by now.

Blondeau was starting to worry. Had all this effort been for nothing? He began to picture the worst. Perhaps a deal had gone awry, and Roache had stormed out of the festival in a fit of pique. Or perhaps the inevitable heart attack had finally taken place, leaving him bedded up in the city's most expensive hospital suite.

Then, as Blondeau made his way back inside, he saw him. Victor Roache was coming across the ballroom like a wrecking ball. Guests scampered out of his way, assistants trailed in his wake. His face was contorted with rage.

Blondeau tried to read his lips: "They screwed us," Roache seemed to be saying. "We had an agreement..." He stormed right past Blondeau, onto the terrace and down the path, without even looking at him.

Blondeau was frozen in place, open-mouthed. Just like that, Roache had come... and gone.

A moment later Raikes sidled up, a plate piled with *hors d'oeuvres* in hand. "Wasn't that your mate that just went past?" he asked.

For some reason his inane inquiry spurred Blondeau back to life. Perhaps it wasn't the best time to confront Roache, but he should at least keep him in eyeshot. For a large man, Victor Roache was surprisingly elusive. He followed him back outside, but his path was immediately blocked off by a woman.

And what a beauty.

Her eyes sparkled, green as emeralds; her cherry-red dress matched her lips. Her hair flowed free over her shoulders, light as clouds. And her skin, her skin glowed golden, like an Oscar. She lit up the night.

Blondeau was momentarily dazzled. Then he got a hold of himself. He knew who she was. Valentina Sanchez-Blake, the actress and wife of Noah Blake. Son of Leonard Blake, legendary actor, *possible murderer...*

Either this coming together was a mighty big coincidence, or Blondeau's extracurricular activities were about to come back and bite him. Perhaps literally, from the look in her eyes.

"People like you," she jabbed a finger at him, "you are vultures, you know that? Digging up ancient history. Threatening the reputations of good men."

"I don't know what–"

"You leave my family alone," she snarled. "You don't want problems with us, you vulture, you blood-sucking leech. We can make things very difficult for you."

A man hastily approached and steered her away with an arm on her shoulder. Blondeau barely had chance to register Noah Blake himself. Valentina's husband didn't even as much as glance at him as they departed.

Blondeau leant back against the outer wall of the hotel and let out a deep breath. He felt shell-shocked. He'd dealt with angry actors many times, it was a hazard of the job. But no one had ever looked upon him before with such pure, unadulterated hatred.

The brief confrontation had his head spinning. How had Valentina Sanchez-Blake known him? Of all the people there, he was certain he had never met her before. She had been a bit-part actress before marrying into the Blake dynasty, and had barely worked at all since, occupying her time instead with talk show appearances, cosmetic ads and vaguely defined humanitarian work.

Perhaps it was Noah who had recognised him. Leonard Blake's oldest son was certainly a big enough name in his own right for Blondeau to have interviewed him, though he couldn't remember having ever actually done so.

The matter of how they had known his true identify was hardly the most troubling part of it, though. How could they have possibly known of his investigation into the Chekhov business? And did Valentina's fury mean there was something to the old Leonard Blake–Karl Hennigan, blood-on-the-sands story, after all?

He rubbed his eyes and tried to steady himself. The night had been supposed to answer his questions, but instead, as seemed to be becoming the pattern, it had so far only created more. He felt punch-drunk. Or perhaps just normal drunk. That martini had a real kick to it.

Other guests were eyeing him warily now. The confrontation with Valentina Sanchez-Blake had taken place in full view of the rest of the party. Either his cover had been blown, or it was about to. He eyed brawny security guards circulating the perimeter.

He had only one thought – to get to Victor Roache. It was now or never.

He rushed back over to the swimming pool area but Roache was gone. He was about to curse his luck, when he turned and saw a figure, standing alone on the beach, silhouetted in the moonlight.

From the shape and size of the man it had to be Roache. But the way down to the beach was blocked off halfway by temporary walling, which looked to reach a foot or two above his head. There was a single gate, at the other end of the terrace, but it was manned by a security guard. Victor Roache might have been a big enough name to persuade the guard to let him out onto the beach, but Blondeau doubted that the Dutch nominee for Best Short Film would hold the same sway.

He edged down towards the wall as casually as he could. He sat on a sun lounger nearby and pretended to tie his shoes. He watched the security guard down the path. He had to pick the right moment. He would only have one shot.

A few moments later a man and woman approached the guard. They seemed to be asking to go out onto the beach. The guard turned his head to talk to them, just enough so that Blondeau was out of his eyeline.

He made his move.

He carried the sun lounger down a few stone steps towards the wall. It clinked off the floor loud enough for people close by to have heard, but he couldn't worry about that now. He pushed the sun lounger against the wall, stood on it and vaulted up. He struggled over the top of the wall, hearing a few amused cries in the background, and dropped to the other side.

He landed awkwardly with a grunt. He dusted himself off and looked over to the beach.

Victor Roache was still standing there, facing the water. He looked like he was talking on a mobile phone. He didn't seem to have noticed the commotion behind him.

Blondeau approached.

"Excuse me, Mr. Roache?" Blondeau's words carried a boyish squeak that he did not recognise.

Roache turned from the churning waters to face him. He peered at Blondeau in the moonlight. Then he nodded.

"So you're the son of a bitch who keeps calling my office."

Victor Roache was an enormous man. Six foot five and morbidly obese, word was he kept the McDonald's near his office in business all by himself. He was also enormously ugly. He had beady little eyes that didn't line up, at least three discernible chins and a nose that had never been completely set straight after being broken in a high school boxing match. Blondeau suspected Roache could have had the last one fixed at the least, but a constant reminder he was no stranger to violence didn't hurt his negotiating tactics.

Blondeau started to respond but Roache cut him off: "I should drown you in the ocean, you know that? I could do it, pal, believe me. Drag you over there and put your head under, keep it there while you squirm for life. I could leave your body limp on the sand and go back to that party, and no one would do a damn thing about it." He said the whole thing as casually as if he were remarking on the canapés.

"I'd really rather you didn't," was all that Blondeau could think to say.

Roache smirked. "You're a resourceful bastard, I'll give you that. How did you even get into this thing?"

"It's probably best you don't know." He thought he owed it to Billy Giudice not to move him any higher up Roache's shitlist.

"You protect your friends at least, then," Roache said. "I can respect that. You know, I looked you up. Stephen Blondeau, huh? I read one of your reviews, the one you wrote for *The Hands That Built America*."

Oh shit. Blondeau had a sinking sense of déjà vu. Of all the, mostly glowing, reviews of films from Roache's studio he had written, that was the one that Roache had looked up? What luck he had. Why must the things he had said so consistently come back to haunt him?

"You said it was an hour too long, right?" Roache turned the screw. "That it should have ended after the battle at the church?"

"I just thought that it might have worked better as a straightforward revenge film. All the other historical stuff felt a bit crowbarred in." He winced. "I said I loved the production design, at least."

Roache barely seemed to hear him. He bent down to pick up a beer bottle, set in the sand. He held it up, studying it, as if picturing the best way to introduce it to Blondeau's skull.

Then, incredibly, he offered the bottle to Blondeau instead.

"Have a drink. Don't worry, I haven't pissed in it." He blew out air from his nose. "You know, I thought the exact same as you about that film, right? I argued it over and over with that arrogant son-of-a-bitch director, but he wouldn't listen. He rabbled-roused the entire cast, had them threatening not to make any more movies with Silverlight in the future if I forced the matter. So I had to back down."

Roache spat on the ground. "It won't surprise you to learn that I don't much like having to back down. And you know what? I was right, after all. That film was too damn long; the audience scores were brutal. We lost a lot of money. And your review was about the only one I ever read that dared to call it for what it was, to tell the emperor his ass was showing.

"I guess what I'm saying is, in a different world, me and you might get along, might even be able to work together." He shrugged. "But we're in this world, where you're bugging me about Paul Chekhov, and I'm *still* thinking about drowning you."

Blondeau couldn't help glance back over to the crashing waves of the Adriatic. Couldn't help imagine his bloated body drifting back and forth in the shallows. "All I need is two minutes of your time," he said, his voice steady. "After that, I'll never hassle you again, I promise. I just need to know."

"Need to know what – whether I cut that Chekhov film after he kicked the bucket? Where the hell where you three years ago? You think I didn't get asked that a thousand times at the time?"

Blondeau had to admit he had no good answer. He hadn't even known of the story until hearing it from Chase Ashley. It was hardly the best mark of his credentials as a film critic. "A lot of people still have questions," he said, not feeling it necessary to mention that many of them appeared to be lunatics. "What's the harm in clearing a few things up?"

Roache gave him an inscrutable look which seemed to draw out across minutes. Each crash of the waves came louder as they stood together on the beach. The world shrunk to just the two of them.

At last Roache answered: "I never did a thing to that movie, OK? Boy, I wish I had, though. What a piece of shit. Three hours of fucking nothing. To this day, I couldn't tell you what it was about."

Blondeau hadn't come all that way to give up so easily: "There are other changes you might have made, not just about improving the film. Clues to Chekhov's past. Things that some people would like to keep hidden."

Roache smirked. "So you're one of those conspiracy theorists, are you? You disappoint me."

Blondeau grit his teeth. Victor Roache was the second person to have called him that in recent weeks. How many would it take before it could be considered, objectively, true?

"Let me spell this out to you," Roache said. "There was no way I could have recut that film. The only way I could get the mighty Paul Chekhov to sign the contract on the picture was to give him final cut. No studio guys on the set, no deadline, unlimited creative control. And to think that stubborn old bastard repaid me with that piece of garbage."

"You could have made changes after Chekhov had died, though?"

"No, I couldn't. The deal passed to Chekhov's estate, and his bitch niece. I tried and tried to convince her that the movie needed work, but she wouldn't listen. Nothing could get in the way of her uncle's precious 'artistic legacy.'"

Blondeau thought he had him, he could almost sense that the dynamic was about to shift. "Perhaps not, but I know for a fact that when Paul Chekhov died, his cut of *Bachelor* was in New York, with your studio guys. You could have made changes before Constance Chekhov ever saw her uncle's version of the film. She would never have known it was any different."

He waited for the look of guilt to come across Roache's face, the one he had been picturing in his mind for days. The sudden realisation that he had underestimated that pesky film critic from London.

Instead, Roache let out a long, rasping laugh. "You really don't have a clue, do you? You got yourself all worked up like you're Woodward and Bernstein, you made all that effort to sneak in here, and you never even got the story straight."

Blondeau stared blankly at him.

"The film *was* in New York," Roache said. "And it was with my guys. They were supposed to report back to me exactly what I had gotten myself into. Hell, I was meant to be there myself, but I was having a few... marital troubles at the time. Chekhov's assistant, Carla... Carla something, she flew out with it from London for the screening, on his orders... and then she flew right back with it the same night.

"Do you understand what I'm saying? I never got my hands on it, and neither did anyone else from my studio. The next time we saw anything of it – and we're talking weeks later – that bitch Constance Chekhov already had it in her possession, and she held it at arm's length from us all the way till its release. We dealt with the sound mix, the colour correction, but that was it. That was all she allowed us to touch, on the film that *I* financed, the things she couldn't sort herself."

He scowled at the memory. "People like her, and her uncle, will never appreciate what I do. Do you think everything that comes out of an artist's brain is pure gold, polished diamond?

Give me a break, man. I was put on this earth to take their work and make it better. And I'm damn good at it, too. The best."

Blondeau wasn't foolish enough to debate the merits of artistic freedom with the Demon Barber of L.A. Besides, it was what Roache had said about the screening in New York that really mattered. If it was true, if the film had been flown back to London the same night, then the whole theory of Roache's involvement was sunk.

He thought hard, desperate to land a blow. "What about Chase Ashley, then? Are you seriously going to tell me his trip to rehab had nothing to do with our interview?"

"That, and a thousand other things," Roache spat. "You have no idea what we've been going through with that guy. So yeah, your little interview was the straw that broke the camel's back. We packed him off for a few months to get his shit together, to remember how to be a team player. But that doesn't make what he told you true. If the guy on the street corner, ranting about the end of the world, finally gets packed off to the nuthouse, it don't mean the Rapture's coming."

"Then why did he say it?"

Roache's lip curled with contempt. "He must have picked the story up from somewhere and got it screwed up in his head, convinced himself that he'd seen something. Or maybe not, maybe he just wanted to make trouble for me. If so, mission accomplished. After everything I've done for him, too. You know how many Chase Ashley's there are waiting tables in L.A.?" He didn't wait for an answer. "Thousands. There's only one me, though."

Small mercies.

"How do I know you're telling the truth about all of this?" Blondeau asked.

Roache shrugged. "I thought you were a journalist? Go do some fucking journalism, that's how. Just leave me out of it." He started to walk back up the beach to the party.

"Just one more thing," Blondeau said gingerly. He knew he was pushing his luck now. "Earlier at the party I, well... Valentina Sanchez-Blake sort of, harangued me about all of this. But what I don't understand is, how she even knew–"

Roache came at him with incredible speed for a man his size. He grabbed Blondeau by the lapels of his tux and lifted him, nearly off his feet.

"You leave that family alone, you hear me? And I'm not saying that because I like them. They're worth a lot of money to me. Noah Blake can open a movie, and even his talentless brothers can fill out a supporting cast off the family name alone. I've answered your questions, but if you're going to start to threaten my investments, my friendly nature is going to be sorely tested."

He threw Blondeau to the ground. The bottle slipped from his hand as he landed and the remaining dregs of beer began to seep into the sand.

Roache loomed over him. "It's been real fun, pal, but I don't ever want to see you again."

Blondeau didn't return to the party, instead making his way along the beach and then taking a *vaporetto* water bus back to the main city. There were few other passengers at that time of night. Some wore tuxedos and evening dresses. He felt their eyes on him the entire journey.

He briefly remembered having left James Raikes behind. It wasn't a problem, he could handle himself. Besides, Raikes had abandoned him enough times on nights out to chase after women, to not have too much room for complaint.

As the boat traversed the open water the rain began to fall. It soon became torrential, it hammered on the metal roof of the boat like a barrage from the heavens. Blondeau pictured the guests at the party rushing back inside, or under the tent, desperately trying to protect their perfect hair and makeup. *Oh, well.*

It was close to midnight when they reached the main city. Gradually the other passengers got off until only Blondeau and the captain remained. At the next stop the boat waited for minutes with the engine off. Blondeau eventually asked the captain what was going on. The man barked incomprehensible Italian at him. Blondeau smiled and nodded as any true Englishman should.

He supposed he was near enough to his hotel to be able to walk the rest of the way, and so disembarked. Thinking he had some vague idea of his location, he took a shortcut up a narrow alley and was lost within minutes. *Bloody fool.* The rain was already drenching him through. He tried to retrace his steps, back to the vaporetto, but that didn't seem to work either. It was as if the walls of the city had shifted in position around him.

He kept walking, without much idea of where. It wasn't a big problem. The city was small, it could only be a matter of time until he came out onto the Grand Canal, the main waterway. And from there it was a straightforward journey to his hotel.

With such thoughts in mind, he travelled down countless alleys and passages, over bridges and under arches and a crisscross of clothes lines, past imposing churches strangely hidden away or hemmed in by other buildings. The shops, cafes and restaurants were darkened, or had metal doors drawn down, many tagged with graffiti. Residential windows towered above his head, but virtually all were shuttered. The only illumination came from the yellow glow of the street lights, which at times were so infrequent that entire areas were in total darkness.

The city seemed so much older at night. Without the bustle of tourists and locals and the constant drift of the gondolas, what instead caught the eye was the peeling and faded paint, the cracks in the walls and the crumbling and water-damaged bricks, stones and pillars. It was a city in slow decay.

Blondeau started to think about all the secrets hidden behind those doors through the city's history. All the plots and intrigues. What in daytime was charming and quaint, in the shadow of darkness suddenly felt oppressive, sinister even. Perhaps it was the stillness, from the total absence of people that did it, or perhaps it was having watched *Don't Look Now* a half-dozen times, but he had to admit: he was getting spooked.

The rain was coming down so hard he scarcely heard his own footsteps. As he turned one corner in particular he could have sworn he saw, or felt, a flash of movement behind him.

He picked up the pace. He did not know why. Or perhaps he did, and that was the problem.

The same thing happened at the next turn. Definite movement, around the corner from which he had just come. Though this time it seemed closer, which didn't make sense at all. Unless...

He moved forward with more urgency still. This time when he turned the corner, he pressed his back against the wall and peered down the alley from which he had come. The far end was shrouded in darkness, he couldn't see a thing.

He waited in the downpour. He could feel his heart pumping, he could hear his breath.

He waited...

A figure stepped out of the darkness.

Blondeau ran.

Now he tore through the city. His senses became more primal – the rain beating down on him, the yellow glow of the street lights, the browns and greys of the rotting city.

Eventually he ran through an archway and an enormous red-bricked tower came into view. He emerged onto the Piazza San Marco, the square in which he had searched for Victor Roache amongst the crowds the previous day. Now it was completely deserted. The paved floor was slick, the rain bounced up to his knees.

Blondeau ran across the square in his drenched tuxedo. If he could pick out the route he had taken the previous day, he thought he would be able to get on the right path to his hotel.

As he reached the other side of the square, he turned around. A man walked out from the same archway. He was wearing a light brown trench coat and a fedora.

Blondeau couldn't see the man's face, but he was pretty confident they had crossed paths before.

They stood across the square from each other, both perfectly still. The bells sounded for midnight, clear even through the rain. *Clang! Clang! Clang!*

At the final strike, the man started to walk towards him.

Blondeau remained in place. He did not know why. Something about the vast openness of the square must have altered his fight-or-flight response.

"I think you have something that belongs to me," Blondeau called out.

The man in the trench coat said nothing. He continued to walk towards him, slowly and deliberately. His movements were entirely without character, almost robotic.

Blondeau tried again: "Strong and silent type, huh? Well, I can talk for the both of us. How did you like my dog, by the way? I should have warned you, he doesn't much care for strangers. I hope you were able to patch up that coat of yours."

There was no reply to any of it. By now they couldn't be more than fifty metres apart.

Blondeau studied the man as he approached. Up closer, he was about average height and build. He could just make out the bottom third of his face under the hat, he had the faintest sense of recognition, just for a moment, then the shadows shifted and it was gone, like it had never been there at all.

The man reached into his coat pocket and Blondeau thought he saw the glint of something metallic.

Suddenly he heard voices and laughter coming from behind them. Both their heads turned.

A group of young men and women rushed into the square. One of the men pretended to steal an umbrella from the women, they giggled, squealed and shrieked in protest. *Thank God for drunks.*

The group didn't even seem to notice Blondeau and the man in the trench coat. They strode across the square towards an exit; one that, now he looked at it, Blondeau felt certain offered the route back to his hotel.

He decided to take his chance. He followed shortly behind the group as they left. He watched the man in the trench coat, over his shoulder, the whole way.

This time, the man didn't follow.

Back at the hotel he took a shower then hung his sodden clothes out to dry. He was due to fly back to London the following morning; he didn't fancy their chances.

He wrapped up in a towel and put the heating on full. The rain was still hammering down. He watched the city being drowned from his window. It was a strangely cosy feeling, despite the events of the past hour.

I guess that break-in wasn't a coincidence, then. Now he knew for sure. He was dealing with dangerous people, one, at least.

But why? He still thought that the theories of the Chekhov obsessives were wide of the mark. And Victor Roache had denied any involvement in the whole business. The man lied by nature, but Blondeau wasn't sure he was lying about that.

It felt like he was dealing with two realities. One, where a bunch of crazy fans had dreamt up even crazier ideas, none of which passed any real scrutiny. Where the final film of a revered director was simply that and nothing more.

And then another, where his house was broken into, his papers stolen, and he was being stalked by a man who could have come straight from a Raymond Chandler novel.

He couldn't make sense of it.

The rain kept falling. It met the wide, winding canal and became one.

Eight
House of Birds

His flight landed in Los Angeles early in the evening. Straight away the humidity beat down on him, his shirt stuck to his skin, his neck glistened. The sky glowed orange, like something from *Apocalypse Now*.

He took a taxi, speeding past the blurry lights of heaving restaurants and bars to his hotel, a colourful Art Deco-style affair in Santa Monica.

At the hotel bar he shared some drinks with a businessman from Iowa and an old Swedish couple. They talked into the late hours of the night about John Wayne, *The Phantom Menace* and *The Seventh Seal*. The businessman kept mixing up Ingmar Bergman and Ingrid Bergman. Then they talked about the end of the world. The Swedes thought it was drawing close. Blondeau didn't disagree.

The California sunshine greeted him the next morning like a flashlight in the face. The paving stones were hot under his feet. Kids clutching skateboards and muscle-bound jocks with towels round their necks passed him by on their way to the beach.

Blondeau had seen more than enough of beaches lately. He walked down streets of boutique shops towards the rental place and picked up his partner for the day – a Chevrolet Corvette convertible. *Because why the hell not?* Soaring palms reflected on the red bonnet as he put the top down. Placing his map on the passenger seat, he started the engine and within seconds had slammed into an impenetrable wall of Los Angeles traffic. He'd barely had chance to feel the wind in his hair.

The front gates to the apartment block were open when he arrived. He wandered through to a courtyard, centred on a large olive tree. It was an idyllic spot, somehow secluded away in the heart of the searing city. There were koi fish and turtles swimming in a fountain, an outdoor fireplace, wooden benches tucked in the shade. And plants, all around. Wisterias crawling up the white stone walls and pillars, preened hedges hemming the sides, and pots of all sizes, packed with seasonal blooms, evergreens and succulents, seemingly arranged at random, jockeying for space, occasionally blocking his path.

There was not a person in sight. Blondeau went from door to door, searching for the number he had been given. He eventually found it, down a narrow stone pathway to the rear of the building, and knocked.

He heard muffled sounds and a female voice coming from beyond the door. It opened. An elderly woman stood there, looking up at him expectantly. Her face was lined and thin, her hair a natural grey, but there was a brightness in her eyes that belied her years.

"Ms. Davis?"

She answered in a gentle, scratchy voice, "Please, call me Clara. Come in, Mr. Blondeau."

That's when it began. Shouts, shrieks, whistles, laughter – all coming from a room down the hallway.

Blondeau felt his body tense. *There was always a catch.*

He followed her through to a sizable living room. In each

corner was a cage. Two were open, the inmates perching on top. There was an artificial tree by the window, made from old dead branches, with colourful little toys hanging off. There were extra perches coming out from the walls, all around them.

There were places for people as well. A few, at least.

"I shall have to introduce you," Clara Davis said. "They won't give us a minute if I don't." She went first to the bright-faced pair sat together on top of one of the cages. "These are my cockatiels, Roy and Betty."

"*Hello,*" either Roy or Betty squawked.

"Hi," Blondeau replied without thinking.

"And over here," Clara continued, "we have Conrad, a galah; and this is Mary, she's an African grey." She paused, drumming her fingers on her lips. "Now that just leaves... where on earth has he gotten to?" Her eyes eventually darted up the door they had just passed. "Ah, there he is! He loves to get up there. That little fellow is Adam." She furrowed her brow. "I think that's all of them, anyway."

"Quite the collection," Blondeau mumbled, trying to calculate the point in the room furthest from any of them. He was certain none of this had been mentioned when they had spoken over the phone. Clara gestured for him to take a seat on the sofa, seemingly oblivious to his discomfort. The seats and cushions were caked with down.

"Retirement can be a dreadfully dull business," she said, as way of explanation. "First came Roy, then I thought he could use some company of his own kind. I bought an extra cage for Betty, but they got on so well I never ended up needing it. Which left me with an extra cage. You can imagine how these things sort of spiral."

"I'll be honest, Clara, the only things I'm imagining right

now are Tippi Hedren and the climbing frame."

She waved a playfully dismissive hand at him. "Oh, they're perfectly harmless. To us, that is. To each other, well, that's when it gets complicated. Roy and Betty are like a house on fire, as you can see. And Adam up there, he's also quite friendly with them, hence why he's allowed out at the moment. However, Adam also gets on with Mary, who most certainly does not like Roy and Betty, so I portion out their free time. And as for Conrad... well, Conrad doesn't much get on with anyone."

"*I'm a good bird,*" Conrad insisted.

Clara shook her head. "He can only come out when all the others are in their cages. There's a strict timetable."

Blondeau watched as one of the cockatiels flew onto Clara's shoulder and began preening its feathers. He wondered why anyone would have subjected themselves to such a responsibility. Then again, Clara Davis must have been somewhat of a glutton for punishment to have worked with Chekhov all those years.

"Thanks for agreeing to talk to me," he said. "I'd almost given up trying to make contact with you."

"When I heard you were travelling here anyway, I thought why not. As I rule, I don't talk to journalists, but not too many have your sheer stubbornness. It's a quality I know well, of course." She gestured to a photo of Paul Chekhov on the mantelpiece, a rare smile on his face as he posed outside a large house. Blondeau thought he recognised the location. It must have been from one of his films, though he couldn't quite place it.

"And when will you be seeing Ms. Chekhov?" Clara asked him.

"This afternoon. Though I'm sure your own experiences are

just as interesting." He took a pen and notepad from his bag. "I'd just like to confirm a few details about yourself, for starters."

"Of course."

"So, your first..." he faltered. The cacophony of the birds was making it impossible to concentrate. Clara sat beside him patiently. It must have faded into the background for her long ago, now no different to the hum of the fridge. He grit his teeth and pinched his forehead. "You first worked with Chekhov on... *Fortune's Kiss*?"

Clara nodded. "1955, if I recall." She smiled wistfully. "So young, both of us were."

"What was it like? Being an assistant to the mighty Paul Chekhov?"

"It certainly kept you occupied," she said. "Scouting locations, running dialogue, keeping the studio people off the sets. I always felt the term 'assistant' didn't tell the half of it."

"And you worked with him outside of production as well?"

"That's correct. I dealt with all his correspondences, for example. When they discuss his frequent collaborators, they will talk about this actor, or that composer, but truly, I was his longest-term partner." The old woman said it without pride or bitterness; it was simply a statement of fact.

"I'm glad we have the opportunity to talk then," Blondeau said. "It feels like quite the coup."

"Actually, you're the first journalist to contact me since the days following his death."

Blondeau hesitated, chewing the top of his pen. It felt like the hint of an opening, but he had to be careful. "While we're on the subject, I hate to bring it all back for you, but there's a very minor detail that I'd appreciate clarification on." *Easy does it,*

Columbo... “Am I correct in thinking that you were the one who transported the final cut of the film to New York, for the actors and the studio executives to view–”

Clara gave a short, slight nod of the head.

“–and then, you travelled back with it to England, on the same night?”

The second cockatiel flew over and landed on her other shoulder. The pair stared at Blondeau with their cold, prehistoric eyes.

“That’s correct,” Clara said. “Straight there and straight back – those were the orders. Paul didn’t trust any studio people, especially those on the payroll of Victor Roache.” She shook her head sadly. “Of course, when I got back, it was a different scene I found.”

Blondeau’s mouth fell open. “You were the one who... discovered him?”

She looked away. “A lifetime in film has provided me some pretty grisly sights, but nothing can quite prepare you for *that*.”

Blondeau cursed inwardly at his carelessness. Had Anthony Hudgen’s biography neglected to mention that detail, or had he simply forgotten? Still, he had no choice now but to push on... “I’m sorry, truly, to bring this all back. But I do just have one final question about the journey of the film–”

She seemed to know what he was going to ask before he even got there. “Constance arrived the following day, once she had heard the news. I handed the film over to her and had no further involvement with it.” She studied him as he noted it down. “I’m not sure how these type of administrative concerns can help with your article?”

“I just like to have the details straight,” Blondeau replied, attempting an easy manner. “Otherwise, there’s always some bore who writes in with a complaint. And *Death of a Bachelor* is a tricky one, what with it being completed before Chekhov's death, but released after. It's a little difficult to nail the exact timeline down."

"That's if you believe it *was* completed, of course."

Blondeau raised his eyebrows.

Clara smiled mischievously. "I'm just teasing you now, I'm afraid. Of course, I've heard the rumours. But no, the film was complete. Paul would never have sent me with it to America had that not been the case. What you saw in the cinema was entirely as he intended."

Before he could respond, Blondeau heard the flutter of wings by his ear, and then something was digging into the top of his skull. His eyes darted around the room and he counted: one, two, three, four... *Oh god, no.*

"Oh dear," Clara said, although she didn't sound all that concerned. "He must have mistaken your hair for a nest. It's all messy and thick and–"

"What do I do?" Blondeau winced. He was frozen in place, his hands held out as if in surrender.

Clara pondered it. "Well... you could leave him there? It's not dangerous, just a little uncomfortable. Although they do have a tendency to–"

"Get it off me!"

Clara frowned. She seemed genuinely disappointed that Blondeau could not simply put up with it. "Of course, of course." She rose to her feet, the two cockatiels still on her shoulders, and wandered over to the open cage by the window. "Adam, come on, over here!"

"*Come here!*" one of the cockatiels joined her in urging. "*Over here!*"

Throughout it all, the notorious Conrad was frantically bobbing up and down in his cage, cackling like a Bond villain.

After a few minutes of Clara's cooing, Adam took note and launched off Blondeau's head back to his cage. Clara teased him inside and closed the door.

Blondeau sighed with relief as she sat back down. He couldn't get out of this madhouse quick enough. Danger came at you from all angles.

"Where was I?" he murmured. "Oh yes, what were your experiences like on the set of *Bachelor*? I've heard it was a difficult one."

Clara puffed her cheeks. "What Chekhov film wasn't? You must know the way of it. Endless takes, days lost tinkering around with the sets. Meticulousness to the point of madness."

"I heard that his behaviour was even more... erratic than normal. That he would cancel filming without explanation, he would only issue instructions through yourself and a few others, that he was distant from the rest of the cast and crew."

She thought about it as the pair of cockatiels, seemingly having lost interest in Blondeau, launched off her shoulders and returned to their cage. "There's probably some truth in that, yes. He had spent far too much time cooped up in that old house, hidden away from the world. Losing Diana must have made things even worse." She sniffed. "Or perhaps he was just getting old. It gives you less patience to suffer fools."

Blondeau didn't much like the sense that her last comment was directed at him. His questions thus far didn't seem to have done him much favour in Clara Davis's eyes. He decided to say something intelligent: "I wondered if it was reflected in how *Bachelor* ended up. It's an emotionally distant work. I'm not sure exactly who I'm supposed to be sympathising with."

Clara's laugh was almost a schoolgirl's giggle. "And why is it that you think you were supposed to be sympathising with anyone? I think Paul liked the idea of casting those two Hollywood stars as a pair of self-absorbed liberals, and duly tormenting them. He was always adamant about Ashley, in particular. It *had* to be him. I've never thought the boy could act worth a damn, frankly, but Paul would not be deterred."

"*He's a good boy*," one of the birds squawked, presumably in Chase Ashley's defence.

Blondeau glanced back at his notepad. *Now this could be interesting...* "Speaking of casting," he said, "I noticed the only character from the source novel that Chekhov switched genders for is Joshua. I'm interested to know if it had any deeper significance?"

"Joshua..." Clara repeated vaguely, scratching her head.

"Lindsay's friend? He confronts Sam shortly after her death, and then is seen later on the island."

"Ah yes, that's right. Please excuse my memory, I'm afraid my best days are behind me. Now I believe that role was changed to a male as Paul didn't want *Bachelor* to be seen as some kind of feminist revenge piece, with all the women tormenting Ashley, and so forth. Another man evened up the gender balance.

"As for the casting," Clara continued, "we did have a bit of trouble with that one. The first actor was in a car accident shortly before filming began, and his replacement claimed nervous exhaustion after only a few days of Paul's... methods. We were getting desperate, there was a risk it would further hold up filming." She clasped her hands together. "Goodness, I remember now. It was that boy, wasn't it? Jimmy, Jimmy..."

"Jacobs. Tommy Jacobs."

"That's it. I think he was the nephew of our costume

designer."

Blondeau stared at her. "You're saying the only reason Tommy Jacobs was hired into that role was because he was related to one of the production staff?"

Clara cringed. "Like I said, we were in a bit of a bind. Besides, he only had a few lines. It was hardly the worst piece of nepotism this industry has seen."

Blondeau allowed himself a wry smile. Adam Woodford, *The Times*'s crossword man, had argued that Jacobs' resemblance to the stuntman Karl Hennigan was proof that *Bachelor* was intended to expose Hennigan's murder by Leonard Blake. Yet as Clara told it, Jacob's casting was purely a chance affair. It only confirmed what Blondeau had determined from his own analysis: Woodford's theory was off the mark.

Except it seemed that no one had told Blake's daughter-in-law Valentina. He thought back to how she had assailed him at the party in Venice. How Victor Roache had nearly throttled him afterwards for even mentioning her name. Once again, Blondeau felt like he was straddling two different realities.

"I'm surprised I've never heard that story," he thought out loud.

"Who have you been listening to?"

"Anthony Hudgens, mostly."

Clara scoffed. "That hack. He had his silly little book ready to go before *Bachelor* even started filming." She stood up and excused herself to use the bathroom.

Fearing that remaining seated would only further advertise his suitability as a perch, Blondeau wandered over to the mantelpiece. He picked up the photograph of Paul Chekhov and brought it close. The legendary director looked about in his forties when it had been taken. It was a serious face, with hollow cheeks and sunken eyes, a bulbous nose, an odd clump of hair on top that wouldn't last much longer, a thick goatee that would. A serious face, even when smiling. A face that held secrets... almost certainly. But what?

He thought that if he could recognise the mansion in the background, he would be able to pinpoint when the photo had been taken. He sensed it was American – palatial and imposing, but not all that old. Perhaps something from the Gilded Age. That meant the pre-hiatus Chekhov, before he left his home country forever, but Blondeau still couldn't place it.

Then it came to him, like a cold knife drawn up the length of his back. He hadn't recognised the mansion from one of Chekhov's films. He had recognised it from a series of photographs, given to him by Barbara Zaniolo. The masked party. The giant stone statue out in the woods, half-human, half-bull. The pleading eyes of the girl in the white robe. His hands gripped the frame tight as he drew it closer.

Clara had silently re-entered the room. "Would you like a coffee, Mr. Blondeau?"

"Where was this taken?" he stammered, waving the photo at her.

"I think it was at the estate of one of his friends," she said, peering over, her wrinkled neck craned. "He and Diana would take the occasional weekend break there, to get away from the bright lights." She seemed to notice his expression for the first time. "Are you alright? You look like you've seen a ghost."

"I'm fine. Just thought I recognised it, that's all. Who was this friend of his?"

She paused to consider it. "I think it was Charles Chevalier's place. You know, of the Chevalier banking family? Yes, that's right. That was before Paul moved to your country, of course."

Blondeau nodded. Chevalier. It was a name even he knew. “Did Chekhov ever tell you what he did on those weekend breaks?”

She narrowed her eyes in confusion. “You do ask some strange questions, Mr. Blondeau. I assume he did what any other person does in such circumstances. A little relaxation, perhaps a bit of hunting on the grounds. He fell out of touch with most of those type of people when he left America.”

Blondeau dragged his eyes away from the photo to look straight at her. “Why *did* he leave America, Clara? And never return, for that matter. It almost feels like he was... hiding from someone?”

It was a long time before she responded. “Not someone. Everyone.” She sighed. “What you need to understand is that the Paul Chekhov that came out of the jungle after filming *Heart’s Desire* was a very different man to the one that went in. He came face to face with his own mortality, and he didn’t like it one bit.

“I’m not sure he ever meant the move to England to be permanent,” she continued. “At first he simply needed a break, not much different from his stays at the Chevalier estate that seem to interest you so much. But the weeks became months, then years. His world shrunk. Initially it was a fear of flying that kept him there. He had been reading up on air crashes and had gotten spooked. Then the crime rates in London led to him moving out of the city, to Ravenwood.

“Do you see how it works? Fear compounds fear. The only way he could guarantee his safety to continue his work was to hide away, to only film close to home, regardless of what an ordeal it was for people like myself to find suitable locations.”

She took the photo frame from Blondeau’s hands and placed it back on the mantel. “It’s a terrible thing – to become so afraid of death, that you stop living. But that was the way of it."

The room fell silent, for once even the birds. Blondeau turned it over in his head. Clara's pain was obvious, uncomfortably so. She looked older than when she had opened the door to him; the brightness that had been in her eyes back then had dimmed.

But there was still something about it that didn't add up...

He said, slowly, carefully: "It just seems hard to believe that we're talking about a man who ended up killing himself. So scared of flying that he refuses to travel, so scared of people that he hides away in the English countryside. And then... suicide? It doesn't make any sense."

Clara Davis walked over to the nearest cage and stroked one of the birds gently on the head.

"In a sense, you could say he lived as he died," the old woman said distantly. "Paul never liked to give his audience easy answers."

Nine
The Last Chekhov

Questions.

Far too many. And with every person he spoke to, the list only grew. Blondeau felt certain that the key to unravelling the *Bachelor* mystery lay somewhere in Paul Chekhov's past. The problem was that everyone seemed to tell a different version of it.

He poured out his bottle of Asahi into the glass and drank. The beer had a light, refreshing taste, perfect against the California heat. He was sitting in a sushi restaurant in Beverly Hills, recommended in his guide book. It was an airy, modern place, with two floors and large plate-glass windows that looked out onto a busy intersection. The other diners were smartly dressed, sunglasses pulled up to their perfect hair as they peered into mobile phones.

As he waited for his lunch, he had on the table his new weapon of choice: *Paul Chekhov: A Biography*, by an American writer called Carter Starling. He had bought it at a bookshop on Sunset Boulevard, shortly after leaving Clara Davis's house. Because even if Anthony Hudgens wasn't a hack, it couldn't hurt to get a fresh perspective.

Blondeau had previously been of the view that it all went back to the 1970s, the decade in which Chekhov had disappeared from public life. But it was another period that seemed to keep circling into view – Chekhov's last few years in America.

"He came face to face with his own mortality," Clara Davis had said, "and he didn't like it one bit."

It was a reference to Chekhov's experiences filming *Heart's Desire* in the late sixties. The film, his first project following the genre-defining sci-fi epic *Journey Beyond*, told the story of a doomed, early-twentieth century expedition in search of Paititi, the legendary lost city of the Incas. In his quest for authenticity, Chekhov had ignored the advice of all around him and chosen to film on location in south-eastern Peru, home to some of the densest jungle on the planet.

It was, as Carter Starling explained, a disastrous choice:

> When some of their equipment was held up by customs authorities at Cusco airport, it was an ominous sign of things to come. Camping in dismal conditions and constantly harried by biting sand flies known as the *Pumahuacachi* (literally translated from Quechua as "he who make the puma cry"), the morale of the camp soon plummeted. Within weeks a scorpion had stung a cameraman, Chekhov only meters away when it happened, and the supporting actor Peter Franklin was struck down with amoebic dysentery, forcing his role to be recast with Jason Robards and his scenes reshot. A local workman was later killed during the construction of a set.

The crew's troubles would only continue:

> The initial aim was that filming would wrap by the end of the Peruvian dry season in September. By August that seemed a hopeless proposition. It wasn't just the recasting of Franklin's part that caused delays. Chekhov was constantly rewriting the script, now barely recognisable from the original. He shot hour after hour of footage of the actors simply hacking through rainforest, climbing up hillsides and sailing down rivers, to the bafflement of the cast.
>
> Almost inevitably, filming overran into the wet season. Chekhov and the crew were left with no choice but to push on. Soon after, a storm caused the Vilcanota River to flood, drowning much of the nearby camp and set. It took weeks to rebuild. Chekhov filled up the time by shooting more footage of the cast hacking through rainforest, climbing up hillsides and sailing down rivers. Some of the actors began to joke (mostly) that he was intent on making a silent film.

> Worse still was the crew's relations with the local indigenous tribes, who were long suspicious of any encroachment into their territory. Though Chekhov tried to assuage the Indians with jobs as labourers and assurances that he was not moving in permanently, the

film became mixed up in the complex web of tribal politics, and rumours about the crew's true purpose began to spread: that they were smuggling arms, that they would destroy the Indian's food supplies, that they were going to rape their women.

On November 13, 1968, things came to a head. A group of armed Indians surrounded the film camp and ordered everyone present to leave. When the camp was empty, the Indians burned it to the ground, as Chekhov and crew fled downriver on rafts built for filming.

Chekhov would later write to his friend, the war photographer Bill Argyle, about the incident:

> "I watched the smoke come up from the jungle as we were heading downstream. I think any hopes I had that things were going to work out went up with them.
>
> What happened that day wasn't unique – it was the fear of the outsider, fear against all rationality or logic. There is a darkness inside of man that is universal."

Chekhov and crew returned to the United States a few weeks later. The studio baulked at a rough assembly of the footage, feeling the film lacked genuine drama and a satisfactory ending. Chekhov spent the Christmas of 1968 at his home in Los Angeles, trying to come up with a finale that would satisfy his financial backers. He eventually settled on the capture of the remaining explorers by the tribe, not dissimilar to the ending of the original screenplay.

And so, in early 1969, Chekhov, sixty pounds lighter, and with a gauntness in his face that remained to the end of his days, returned to Peru and resumed filming. Many of the original crew refused to join him.

Carter Starling's account of the rest of the story lined up with Blondeau's own understanding. When *Heart's Desire* wrapped for the second time, Chekhov had spent over two hundred days filming in total, far beyond initial expectations. The project had ballooned to more than double its original budget.

The director spent the next six months editing the film into shape. But by the time it finally released, he had left America, never to return. What rare promotion he did for the film was conducted from his home in London.

Another quote from the man himself seemed to sum it all up:

In one of his final interviews, given over the phone from his Chelsea home in 1970, Chekhov said:

> "We went into it thinking what a great adventure it would all be. That's the kind of naivety that Hollywood gives you, I guess, that it's all a great game, a spectacle. It was probably the first time in my life I'd faced real danger. I hope the film captured some of that, [he laughs], because it's certainly not something I intend to repeat."

Blondeau took the book off the table as the waitress brought over his king crab roll. He thought about what he'd read as he ate. It was a story that was well known in the industry – that Paul Chekhov had never fully recovered from his time in the jungle, that his retreat into the English countryside was his own way of dealing with that trauma.

But what if a story was all it was? An excuse, publicised to hide Chekhov's true motives for leaving the country.

Blondeau noted how Carter Starling had described the Chekhov who had returned from the jungle: "sixty pounds lighter, and with a gauntness in his face that remained to the end of his days". The Chekhov in the photograph on Clara Davis's mantelpiece certainly fit that description. He had the hollow cheeks and thousand-yard stare of a man who had known true suffering.

Did that mean the picture had been taken in the short period of time between the filming of *Heart's Desire* and Chekhov's departure from the United States? It would mean that Chekhov had found time, in the middle of post-production work, to take a trip to see his old friend Charles Chevalier. And then... an argument between the pair about the activities taking place on Chevalier's estate? Had Chekhov threatened to expose the whole depraved business; with Chevalier making threats in return? Were they enough to spook Chekhov into leaving the country forever?

Blondeau slumped back in his seat and rubbed his eyes. His mind was running away with him. He had heard all that Barbara Zaniolo had to say about the matter, had scoured *Bachelor* for any trace of it, and had been left unconvinced. So why did it seem to keep coming back around?

Too many damn questions.

There was one person who might be able to answer them. She was the reason that Blondeau was in Los Angeles in the first place.

That night on the beach in Venice, under the moonlight, as the waves churned and the party rumbled in the background, there was something that Victor Roache had said that planted a seed in Blondeau's mind. And in the days following, as he returned to London and fell back into his day job, the seed began to grow.

It all had to do with the journey of Chekhov's version of *Death of a Bachelor* on the night of his death. That Clara Davis had flown it out to New York for the actors and studio executives to view had never been in doubt. But Blondeau had initially believed that the film had remained there, providing a window of opportunity for Roache and his people to make changes following Chekhov's death.

Roache had denied that, and now Clara had confirmed his story. She had travelled back with the film to England, and had taken it to Chekhov's estate the following day, only to discover the director's body. The next day Constance Chekhov arrived at the estate and took ownership of the film. Roache had not seen it again until weeks later, and, as he had complained, Constance had barely allowed him access to it until its release.

Which all meant that Victor Roache could not possibly have edited Paul Chekhov's cut of *Death of a Bachelor*. Someone else could have, though.

And Blondeau was about to go meet her.

He left the sushi restaurant with a heavy gut and the usual post-lunch inertia. He clambered back into the Corvette and checked the map. Constance Chekhov lived in Benedict Canyon, a wealthy enclave a short drive north of Beverly Hills.

As he pulled out of the car park he considered all he knew about the last surviving Chekhov. Paul and his wife Diana had never had children. As such it had been Constance, his brother's only child, who had inherited the Chekhov estate. Not that Paul would have minded. It was well known that he doted on her as if she were his own daughter.

Constance had the window of opportunity. She probably had the means as well. She had been known to hang around her uncle's sets as a youth, sponging up any advice the director deigned to offer. As she blossomed to adulthood it even seemed she might follow in his footsteps. She had directed a few music videos for local rock bands in Los Angeles, nothing too big, but surely enough to demonstrate some semblance of the basics.

Could she have edited *Bachelor* herself? Possibly. But even if not, it wouldn't have been a challenge for her to find someone in her hometown, skilled – and discrete – enough to help her out and keep their mouth shut.

As Blondeau left Beverly Hills, crossing Santa Monica Boulevard and beginning the steady climb up the canyon itself, the landscape began to change. The city's signature palms gave way to oaks, sycamores and cypresses, which covered the gently winding road in shade. Where at first there were modern mega-mansions with pristine lawns and imposing gates, soon the houses were smaller and older – 1920s Spanish and English-style country homes, even a few little bungalows. The area felt rural. The hillsides above had groves, shrubs and wild grasses. The traffic had thinned out. It was hard to believe he was only a few minutes' drive from the heart of the city.

So Constance Chekhov had the opportunity, and she likely had the means. As for the motive... well, for the last few years she had run her own charitable foundation, sponsoring conservation projects in Central America. Blondeau had looked it up. The foundation held a few, very exclusive-looking fundraising events every year in L.A. He got the impression that they were dependent on the turnout of Hollywood's finest to loosen up the purse strings.

It stood to reason that if Paul Chekhov did have some dark secret buried in his past, it would be in Constance's interest to keep it that way, to keep the family name clean. The rich and famous abandoned their friends in a scandal faster than a Tony Scott camera cut.

Further up the canyon, Blondeau turned off onto the side road that Constance had given him. The road was too narrow for cars to cross, and was hemmed in by tall walls of ivy. It felt almost suffocating. The road coiled around until a wrought-iron gate appeared at its end. Blondeau gave his name through the intercom and the gate opened.

He drove slowly through onto a gravel path. It opened up to the left and a building came into view. It was a French-style country house, single floored with a steep roof, paned windows and dark brown bricks and tiles. At first it seemed small, but as Blondeau drove along the front of the house, he saw that it was a sprawling affair. There looked to be an additional building behind the main, perhaps a guest house. There was a small lawn, and the entire area was surrounded by thick pine trees, spreading down the hillside. It would have been hard to find a more secluded spot in the whole of Los Angeles.

A porch ran along the front of the house, held up with wooden pillars. There, the last Chekhov stood, waiting for him.

The damn dog kept trying to hump his leg. It stared up at him with a glint in its eye, panting and wagging its tail.

It still wasn't Blondeau's worst animal encounter that day.

"I'm really sorry," Constance said, actually seeming to mean it. "He was my uncle's, you know. I couldn't bear for him to be given over to some other family, so he's lived with me ever since. He's just a bit too friendly, that's all." She picked up a battered-looking toy and flung it down the hallway. The dog, a yellow Labrador, gave chase and began to savage it.

Blondeau hadn't known what to expect from Constance Chekhov. On a physical level, the only thing she shared with her uncle were the slightly sunken, darkened eyes. Past that, she had perfect porcelain skin, a heart-shaped face and straight, shoulder-length chestnut hair. Blondeau had calculated her in her late forties, which looked about right. She wore a sleeveless blouse that showed off surprisingly sculpted arms. Her manner thus far had been cordial but firm; she was not one to pause or equivocate. Blondeau had the sense it would be a mistake to get on the wrong side of her. He also had the sense he might end up there before the day was done.

He emptied his glass and set it down on the low wooden coffee table. They sat opposite each other on a pair of worn-in, blanket-covered sofas in Constance's living room. It was a cluttered, cosy space with a stone fireplace and wooden-beam ceiling. The exposed brick walls were peppered with photos of Constance with the brightest lights of the celebrity world – actors, musicians, politicians. Her uncle was there too, mainly in photographs taken on various film sets over the years. Blondeau looked over at one, a black and white of Paul Chekhov's face in side profile, as he peered down the lens of a camera. A magician and his wand.

He looked down at his notepad. The page was covered in his scrawl, all of which completely useless. That was all part of the plan, though, and, for once, it was going off without a hitch.

He had decided to approach Constance Chekhov in a different manner to his previous encounters. Instead of trotting out the usual line about an article on the final films of the great directors, he would appeal to her ego. He was writing about the children of famous directors, he had written to her saying, and though she wasn't Paul Chekhov's child per se, it was clear their closeness merited her inclusion. He would very much like to hear all about her conservation work and her memories of her uncle. The last bit, at least, was the truth.

Now, nearly an hour after he had walked through the front door, with the turgid talk of deforestation and the plight of the pygmy three-toed sloth done and dusted, he felt safe to move on to the real business without raising her suspicions.

"Did you have much contact with your uncle in the 1970s?" he asked casually, stifling a yawn. "People always talk about that period as the start of his reclusiveness."

"They act like my uncle spent the whole decade hiding under his bed," Constance scoffed. "He had projects, it was just that nothing came to fruition. Not for want of trying, either. He spent years working on a biopic of Alexander the Great. It would have been one of the great epics. He had planned to shoot entirely on location, across Greece, the Middle East and India. The problem was no studios were willing to put up the kind of money needed after *Heart's Desire*."

"That's strange," Blondeau said. "I'd heard the opposite. That he had become scared to film away from home?"

"All of that came later," she replied. "And even then I wouldn't say he was scared, it was just convenient for him." She drew a breath. "By the late seventies he'd finally realised what everyone else had a long time ago – the age of the epic was done. Those big projects were just too hard to get off the ground anymore. For the first time in his life, my uncle thought smaller. That was what *The Fox and the Henhouse* was to him: a reminder that you could make a great film on a limited budget, filming entirely at a studio, not traipsing halfway across the world. Once he'd done that, once he'd proved it, why bother with anything else?"

She gave him a stern look. "But he wasn't 'scared', do you understand me? This notion that he was hiding away from the world is untrue. He had simply found an approach that worked better for him."

Blondeau found he wasn't entirely convinced by her explanation. From what he'd heard, the requirement to film close to Chekhov's estate had been a major challenge for production.

He asked, "Did you talk to him much during that time?"

"Of course," she said. "Over the phone, or I'd travel out to see them – him and Diana – maybe once or twice a year. He'd transformed that old country house into a base of operations. He had an editing room installed, an office, storage for all his notes and records. Heaven knows what the next owner will do with it all, if I ever get around to selling the place. Who wouldn't work from home like that, had they the chance?"

She finished off her glass, hurried out of the room and brought back the bottle, a 1946 Pommard. She poured herself another glass and offered one to Blondeau. He declined. So she poured the rest of the bottle out into her own.

Blondeau wondered if he'd have been better off bringing James Raikes along to this one.

"Speaking of editing," he began, although in truth it was a stretch, "am I correct in thinking that it was you who took ownership of the final cut of *Death of a Bachelor* after your uncle's death?"

Constance shrugged. "What of it?"

It was a strange reaction, Blondeau thought. Needlessly defensive.

"We went over it with the lawyers early on," she explained, as if sensing his thoughts. "I had legal right to creative control of the film as the sole inheritor of my uncle's estate. But it was more than that – I had a moral duty. Living in this city, I know exactly what type of person Victor Roache is. He'd have butchered that film had he got his way. Can you imagine a ninety-minute version of *Bachelor*, all so Roache could cram in an extra screening each night?"

Blondeau's first thought was that it might have made for a better film, although admittedly a less enigmatic one. He decided to keep that pearl of wisdom to himself.

"Someone needed to protect my uncle's legacy from the wolves," Constance continued. "It was one of the reasons I flew out so quickly to my uncle's estate after it happened. I wanted to take control of the physical film before Roache could get to it."

"You were fortunate then, that Clara Davis brought it back so promptly."

Constance nodded. Chekhov's dog had wandered back over, she stroked its head absentmindedly, swilling her glass with her other hand. "I have fond memories of Ms. Davis growing up. I must have been annoying as hell the way I buzzed around my uncle's sets all day, but she always found time to introduce me to all the actors and keep me entertained."

She smiled. "I remember one time, during the filming of *Fortune's Kiss*, we played hide and seek. I crawled into a wardrobe at the back of the set while the crew were taking a break. I waited patiently there in that stuffy old box for what felt like hours, not saying a word, keeping perfectly still. At last my uncle and the crew came back and the scene started filming, that's when I decided I'd finally had enough, and I burst out, shouting, 'I win!' You should have seen his face." She laughed warmly at the memory.

"Of course, the irony is," she continued, "it never even crossed my mind that Ms. Davis had brought the film back to England that night. I'd talked to my uncle a few days beforehand – the last time I ever talked to him, for that matter. I knew he had asked Ms. Davis to travel with the film to New York, but I suppose I must have assumed it had remained there, and that Vic Roache already had it in his possession."

Blondeau paused. He wondered if he had misheard her. "I'm not sure I quite understand," he said. "If you thought the film was still in New York, why did you say that you flew straight to

England to get it?"

"I went for the neg."

"The neg?"

She looked at him as if it needed no further explanation. "Like I told you, my uncle edited at his home, at Ravenwood Manor. The original negative of the film should have still been there. I'd thought that taking control of it was the only way I could hold Roache's feet to the fire, in regard to the creative control stipulated in the contract."

She looked at him uncertainly. "We can go off the record, right? You won't use this if I tell you?"

"Sure."

"Well, that's what I meant, when I said it was ironic. I flew to England to pick up the negative, but when I arrived, Ms. Davis was already there, sat with the print she'd taken to New York like a faithful guard dog. In the end, we never even found the negative."

"You never found it?" Blondeau repeated incredulously.

Constance nodded. "We searched everywhere, without luck. On a practical level, it didn't make a huge amount of difference, we had Ms. Davis's positive print from New York to work with. It sure was strange, though."

That's putting it bloody lightly. "But..." Blondeau struggled for words. "How can I have possibly not heard about this?"

She sighed. "I agreed with Roache to keep it hushed up. He thought not having the original negative would make the studio look like a bunch of amateurs. It wasn't that I owed that asshole anything, but I was worried if the truth came out it would only add to the speculation. I thought people might claim that my uncle had destroyed it himself, that he had never wanted the film released."

"You don't think that was the case?"

She shook her head firmly. "That would have been the last thing my uncle would have wanted. He had worked for years on that film, why would he choose to destroy it?"

Not for the first time, Blondeau had no answer. That *Death of a Bachelor* was missing its original negative was a potential scandal all of itself. It was standard practice for negatives to be archived away in state-of-the-art, climate-controlled vaults, accessed only rarely for purposes such as restoration work.

It was a shame he was off the record about the whole subject. Not that it made what she had told him entirely useless. If Constance and Clara hadn't found it, and Paul Chekhov hadn't destroyed it... what *had* happened to *Bachelor*'s original negative?

"What did your uncle sound like?" he asked. "The last time you spoke over the phone. I mean, if you don't mind me asking."

"Tired," Constance replied. "But that was nothing new, he always worked so hard. He was editing that film right up until he sent Ms. Davis away with it. I think if he had his way, he would have never released any of his films, he'd have just spent his days endlessly tinkering with them."

"And he gave no indication that he was... going to–"

"Of course not. If he had then I would have sent someone out there for his welfare." She frowned. "And if your next question is whether I know why my uncle did what he did, then, once again, the answer is no. And no one else does, as far as I'm aware. Don't let the hacks with books to sell fool you on that front."

Blondeau had caught Constance stealing a glance at her watch as she spoke. They had already gone longer than agreed.

He decided he had nothing to lose: "I take it you're aware of the rumours that *Bachelor* was altered after your uncle's death?"

For the first time she hesitated, not much, but enough. "Of course."

"I just think it's funny," Blondeau said. "All those stories, they all talk like it would be Victor Roache's doing. The big bad studio man trying to cover up some scandal from years ago. But from the timeline as I know it now, it couldn't have been Roache. The only one who could have changed that film was... *you*."

Constance smiled stiffly. Somehow, without moving an inch, her whole demeanour had changed. "It's a good job that they are only rumours then."

Blondeau noted how she clutched her glass tightly, the bones visible in the back of her hand. Though her expression was stony, he had the feeling her mind was racing away behind it. Was she regretting her previous candour?

"I didn't ask for any of it," she said, staring at the dark red nectar in her glass. "To be the one responsible for the film's release. And I didn't much enjoy that pressure, either. I kept everything exactly as it was, exactly as my uncle intended, yet even then I knew that if the critics didn't like it, people would blame me. People like you, the 'experts.' Like I told you, the only thing I ever wanted from any of this was to protect my uncle's legacy."

Blondeau smiled. "I never thought otherwise, please don't be offended." He stroked his chin. "Though, I suppose, when you talk about protecting a legacy, there's more than one way that could be–"

Constance rose to her feet, a little unsteady. "I think we've gone far beyond our subject matter here, Mr. Blondeau. If you don't mind, I have social plans this evening that I should prepare for."

"Of course," Blondeau said. "I understand."

Constance Chekhov looked at him with a coldness in her eyes. Her lip was pulled up into the hint of a snarl.

"I will look forward to reading your article," she said, without the slightest sense she meant it.

Blondeau switched on the light on the bedside table. It had just gone midnight. His flight back to London was in the morning. He'd been trying to get an early night, but his mind wouldn't let him.

The strange thing was, it wasn't anything that Clara Davis or Constance Chekhov had told him earlier in the day that was keeping him up. It was something else, something that had been gnawing away at him for a while now.

In the week following his trip to Venice, a friend had helped him out with access to the BBC archives, probably the biggest single store of historical media content in the country. They resided in a series of drab, nondescript buildings in Brentford. Amongst the towering shelves of film, videotape, vinyl and cassette, Blondeau had tracked down the news footage from the days following Paul Chekhov's death.

It was largely as he'd expected: career retrospectives, public statements from his peers and the current cream of Hollywood's crop, speculation on the imminent release of *Death of a Bachelor*. There was one clip in particular that had caught his eye. The presenter referred to it as Chekhov's final public appearance (a detail confirmed in Starling's biography), made only a few months before his death.

Chekhov was presenting a lifetime achievement award at the

Evening Standard British Film Awards in London, to his friend and frequent collaborator, the cinematographer Francis Gould. It was a surprise appearance by Chekhov, and had caused quite a stir at the time. Blondeau couldn't recall why he hadn't attended the event himself. Probably, thinking it was going to be no more than a bog-standard awards show, he had chosen to go to the pub with James Raikes instead. That was usually the way of those things.

Watching the brief clip back, there was something about Chekhov's demeanour – the way he walked across the stage to the podium, the way he looked around the room, the way he greeted Gould – that seemed decidedly off. Perhaps it was being away from such events for so long that explained it, but Blondeau had the sense there was something more going on. He just couldn't put his finger on it.

The memory of that scene had burned away in the back of his mind ever since, and now, at midnight in Los Angeles, for reasons he couldn't quite explain, its flame was brighter than ever.

He felt he almost had it, that he finally understood its significance, but it was as if he was reaching for a cloud; his fingers brushed the edge and passed right through. Then the moment was gone, the cloud drifted away, out of his grasp. It wasn't coming back tonight.

He took a bottle of Budweiser from the minibar and turned on the TV, just to give his mind something else to do. Conan O'Brien was on the late-night circuit, interviewing Adam Sandler about his latest abomination.

Blondeau sat back on the bed and happily let the drivel wash over him. It felt good to hear about something other than Paul Chekhov for once. It felt like the time before, before he'd headed off on the bus to interview Chase Ashley, before it had all begun. What had the biggest worry in his life been back then? He couldn't even remember.

His thoughts were scattered as something struck against the window.

He flinched in his bed, nearly spilling his beer. He looked over – the glass was undamaged, no sign of any impact. A bird perhaps? He considered going over to look, but decided he couldn't be bothered.

Back on screen, Adam Sandler was prattling on about something or other as Conan cackled along. Blondeau slunk down in his bed and pulled the duvet up past his shoulders. He yawned.

Bang! The window, again.

Either he was dealing with a particularly stubborn bird, or something else entirely...

No good can from me looking out that window, he thought. But his curiosity got the best of him. He slipped out of bed, made his way over and peered out.

His window looked out onto the rear of the hotel. There was a patio area with a swimming pool, shaped like a teardrop. It glowed in the night like neon.

A lone figure stood in front of the pool. He wore a light brown trench coat, a fedora obscured his face.

Blondeau stared down at him from his second floor window. He was surprised how calm he felt. It was different to that night in Venice; the distance offered the sense of safety. The man in the trench coat couldn't get to him from down there, so what was he doing?

They watched each other in silence, neither making a move.

Then the man in the trench coat took off his hat.

Blondeau's mouth fell.

The man's face looked as if it had been severely burned; it was unnaturally smooth and taut. There was only the slightest sense of a nose and the mouth was a jagged slit, like it had been hacked out with a knife. Worst of all, though, were the eyes: small, pitiless black holes, from which dark tear stains ran halfway to his mouth.

It took Blondeau longer than he would care to admit to realise he was looking at a mask. *And not just any...*

The man slowly drew gloved fingers across his throat, never taking his eyes off Blondeau, stood at the window above him. Then he put his hat back on, low over his face, turned and walked away, out of sight.

Blondeau realised he'd been clutching the curtain tight to his chest the entire time. Very macho. He rushed over to make sure his door was locked. He didn't really think it mattered, though – that wasn't what tonight was about.

It was a warning: "I know what you're doing, and I know where to find you. So back off."

Blondeau wasn't sure that he could anymore, even if he wanted to.

He went to his bedside table and picked up Carter Starling's Chekhov biography. He flipped through to the final set of images, and brought one photograph in particular close to his face.

He already knew what he would see.

Ten
The Talk at The Dyer's Eye

The village of Ravenwood didn't have much to it. It mostly comprised a single, curved road, along which were a pub, a shop and a small church with an overgrown graveyard. There were perhaps fifty houses in total, most were semi-detached, not so old, with low picket fences, cut lawns and garden gnomes. Bikes leant on walls without locks, on the lamp posts were faded posters for that summer's arts and crafts fair. There was a small war memorial, a stone obelisk on a plinth.

It was no more than ten minutes' drive from Maidenhead – flat English countryside, surrounded by a pastoral patchwork of farmland, copses and open meadows. The trees wore the brown and orange dress of autumn.

The estate itself was a little further on. They'd driven to the front gate, then turned back. *Not yet.*

Other than the church, the pub was the oldest building in the village. It was an old hall house, black-and-white, half-timbered, with a thatched roof. It was called The Dyer's Eye. The public area had two main rooms, the bar extending across both, with dark stone floors and worn wooden tables. It could probably have housed the village's entire population. The only visible source of entertainment was a dartboard. The middle-aged woman at the bar had gawked at them as they'd entered as if their very existence was a prank being played on her.

Blondeau and Raikes sat at a table by an unlit fireplace. It was the middle of the afternoon. There were a few others inside, mainly old men, sat with airs of comfort as if being in their own living rooms.

"And you're sure that was it?" Raikes asked Blondeau, pointing at the photo in the book.

"Positive," Blondeau said. "You don't recognise it?"

Raikes screwed his face up then shook his head.

"Unbelievable," Blondeau muttered. "You're seriously telling me that you haven't seen *The Night Sessions*?"

Raikes repeated his previous gesture. "Give us a hint."

"It was the second film he made after his hiatus. It's set in a psychiatric hospital in New York. The main doctor at the hospital, Krauss, is a serial killer. He terrorises the inmates at night while wearing *that* mask. It's supposed to embody their fears or something. I can't remember exactly. The plot got a little lost towards the end."

Raikes had an utterly blank look on his face. "Any good, then?"

Blondeau could only grind his teeth in reply.

"So what's he trying to say?" Raikes asked him. "Your masked man, I mean. That you're an inmate in his world? That he's in control?"

Blondeau groaned. "I guess? He could have spelt it out a bit clearer. That mask though – it wasn't some cheap plastic crap brought from a shop for Halloween. It looked the real deal. It was either from the film itself, or a damn good replica. Expensive stuff, either way."

The hint of a smile appeared at the edge of Raikes's lips. He took a swig of his beer. "You know who it is, right?"

"Obviously not." Blondeau grew impatient. "Who?"

"It's your man."

"Who?!"

"Chekhov."

"Chekhov?"

"You know – the director? The guy who made the film featuring that exact mask? The guy you've been on about nonstop for the last two months?"

Blondeau couldn't help but laugh. "You're not serious?"

"I am. Think about it. You told me he shot himself in the head, with a shotgun, no less. His face would have been completely unrecognisable from the blast." Raikes smirked. "How convenient. *It wasn't him*. The body was switched with some other poor bastard, and the real Chekhov has been hiding out the entire time. He'd spent half his life trying to hide away, that's what you said. This was just taking it one step further. That's why he has the mask, and that's why he's trying to scare you off. Whatever it is that was in that film, he wants to keep it hidden." Raikes dusted his hands off with satisfaction.

Blondeau scrutinised him. "Then why did he put it in the film in the first place?"

Raikes shrugged. "I don't know. It's your story, I can't solve it all for you." He finished off his drink and yawned.

Blondeau chuckled to himself. Of all the ridiculous things he'd heard in recent weeks, that had to take the biscuit. James Raikes would have fitted in perfectly with the Chekhov obsessives, if he could only sustain an interest.

It couldn't be true. It couldn't be Chekhov. It was utterly impossible.

It was, wasn't it?

"It's not Chekhov," Blondeau said. It suddenly felt important to state it out loud. "Definitely not."

The barmaid had come over to take their empty glasses. Blondeau finished his off and ordered a couple more pints of the Old Speckled Hen.

"So that's why you're here," she said to them in a friendly enough tone. "I should have known – it's the only reason anyone comes around here, tell the truth. *Chekhov*. Are you fans or professionals?"

"Just fans," Blondeau answered quickly. He paused, wondering whether to broach the subject. "We were actually thinking about heading up to the house itself, to see if someone could give us a quick tour of the place."

An old man sat alone at the table behind them turned in their direction. He had a coarse, weathered face, mutton chops and constantly squinting eyes. "You'll be needing a ladder then, boys," he rasped, "cos ain't no one up there."

"No one?" Raikes repeated. "There surely must be a security guard or a caretaker–"

"Ain't no one up there!" the old man exclaimed with unnecessary anger. "The girl – his daughter, I think – comes by maybe once a year, but that's it. The place is deserted."

"Interesting..."

"You'd best be heading back to London," the old man warned them, as if he thought Londoners couldn't possibly survive more than a couple of hours outside of the capital. It was likely not an uncommon view in places like Ravenwood.

"I'd rather you didn't send all my customers away so quickly, Albert," the barmaid said wearily. She turned to Blondeau and Raikes. "He's right, though. The whole place has been left alone for a while now. Strange, really. You'd think they'd try to sell it or at least do something with it."

"Do you know much about the days around the time of his death?" Blondeau asked them both. "There's all sorts of rumours."

A man with a long face who was sat in the corner of the room lowered his newspaper and spoke up: "You should ask Peter about that."

"Peter?"

The man nodded. "Peter Doyle. He's a policeman, he was first on the scene." He looked at the barmaid. "Give him a call, Julie, I'm sure he's in."

"It's really no bother," Blondeau said. "If he's not here–"

"Not to worry, boy," old Albert waved his hand dismissively. "He only lives down the road. He'd never give up the chance to tell his story."

"It's about the only interesting thing that's ever happened to him," Julie agreed.

The spring in Peter Doyle's step when he entered the pub three minutes later seemed to confirm it. He had friendly brown eyes, a straight moustache and a round bald head. His stomach was pretty round, too. Blondeau put him not more than a few years from retirement. For a policeman in the movies, that was the most dangerous time. For a policemen in Ravenwood, it was hard to imagine there was one.

Blondeau, now feeling a little embarrassed by the whole commotion, bought the policeman a drink.

"When I got there," Doyle recalled, having taken a seat at their table, "it was his assistant who had discovered him. An old American lady. Awful sight for her, poor love."

"Did you recognise him?" Raikes asked. "Chekhov, I mean."

"Couldn't much recognise anyone in that state," Doyle winced. "A shotgun at close range, hell of a way to go. I suppose they didn't want to leave anything to chance."

Raikes gave Blondeau a smug look. "How could you be sure it was him, then?" he asked the policeman.

"That was the old lady's doing," Doyle replied. "He had a birthmark on his shin, she pointed it out right away."

"Why did you say 'they'?" Blondeau asked Doyle suddenly.

"Come again?"

"You said, 'they didn't want to leave anything to chance.' Not 'he'. Strange choice of pronouns."

Doyle slowly shifted in his seat. "Well, I don't know much about pronouns, but I suppose what I was getting at was that I was never truly certain the old boy did the business himself."

"You don't think it was a suicide?"

For the first time Peter Doyle showed signs of unease. He tried his answer out in his mouth before releasing it: "I can't honestly say I do, no. I mean, they took him away for the autopsy and the inquest and so forth, and the folks who are a lot smarter than me determined that to be the case. But I always thought that it seemed a bloody big coincidence, what with everything that had been going on the previous few months."

"What do you mean?"

"He'd called us out three times," Doyle said, counting them off with his fingers. "Kept claiming he'd seen an intruder, was all worked up." He chuckled. "He'd lived up there for near three decades, and that was the first time any of us had seen hide or hair of him. Funny how that works, isn't it?"

Blondeau thought it over. It tallied with what Cain Xavier had told him, back at The Zebra, what now felt a long time ago. It appeared Xavier was not a total bullshit merchant. He wondered how much else of what the UFO man had told him had something to it.

"I don't suppose any of you were around in the 1970s?" he asked the room. "When Paul Chekhov first moved to these parts."

"Only me, I think," the man in the corner with the newspaper said. The others agreed, surrendering the stage.

Blondeau asked him, "Someone told me about seeing vehicles with tinted windows at his estate around that time. Does that ring a bell?"

The man was nodding his head before Blondeau had finished speaking. "Quite regular at one point they were. Four by fours, always in black. Quite a sight in these parts. Then it all stopped, just like that."

Blondeau pressed the man for further details but that was the lot of it. He considered it. At the least, it was another thing Cain Xavier seemed to have been telling the truth about. It was strange. Ever since the weekend he'd spent studying the *Bachelor* film, little things kept coming up, suggesting that the stories the Chekhov obsessives had relayed to him had some element of truth to them. It had him doubting himself, questioning his own skills of analysis. Perhaps time had made him rusty, and he had ruled out their theories too soon. The Leonard Blake murder story from Adam Woodford, Barbara Zaniolo's sex ring – those he could tolerate. But the possibility that Cain Xavier's tale of UFOs and secret government projects could turn out to be true, now that was too much...

As he sat there mulling it over, Peter Doyle turned to Julie and laughed. "It's funny we're talking about this," he said. "I finally got around to watching that film the other day. *The Bachelor*, or whatever it's called. Not my type of thing, I must admit. I didn't have a clue what was going on. Made me wonder what he was so worked up about."

“What do you mean?” Raikes asked.

“Well, that was all he kept on about,” Doyle said, “when he called us out thinking he had intruders. He just kept repeating it, again and again: ‘They’re after my film. They’ve come to take it from me.’”

The room fell to silence. Raikes had placed a cigarette in his mouth, his thumb hovered over the lighter without engaging. A man at the bar called to Julie but she swatted him away.

“I don’t suppose he told you who ‘they’ were?” Blondeau asked Doyle eventually.

The policeman shook his head. “Can’t say he did. I tell you one thing, though: that man, so rich, so well known – he looked scared out of his wits.”

Eleven
Before Sunrise

Back to the gates. They were wrought iron, about ten feet high and ended in spikes that were more than just a warning. A brick wall of the same height ran around the rest of the sprawling estate. Beyond the gate, buildings were visible as no more than dark outlines in the moonless night.

"So... we're really going to do this, then?" Raikes asked.

"We're really going to do this," Blondeau answered, as much to convince himself as his friend. He pulled down his homemade balaclava and motioned for Raikes to do the same.

They had left Blondeau's car – a silver Audi A4 sedan – in amongst some trees at the edge of a small, possibly eponymous wood half a kilometre away. Only the darkness kept it fully hidden. They would need to be back and gone before sunrise to avoid risking its discovery, and all the drama that would bring.

Behind them, further down the drive, was the road that ran through Ravenwood village and back to Maidenhead. They'd passed no other cars at that time of night. The air was cool, the grass glossed with dew.

Raikes clasped his hands together. "Give us a boost, then." He walked from the gate to the wall, slung the loop of rope over his shoulder and gestured at Blondeau expectantly.

Blondeau obliged, helping him to scale the wall. Even that

wouldn't have been enough, had his friend not been such a beanpole. He'd finally proven good for something.

Raikes dropped down to the other side silently. Seconds later the coil of rope came sailing back over. Blondeau took it with gloved hands, then, with the rope taut, climbed up and over in an ugly and graceless manner. He dangled down and then dropped onto wet grass, steadying himself. In all truth, he'd expected that part to be harder.

He looked around. Anthony Hudgen's biography had included an aerial photograph of the estate, so he had a vague idea of his bearings. The foremost building had to be the main house. Chekhov had purchased the estate from a famous horse breeder, who had built a stable block to the rear of the house. It was this that Chekhov had used as his work area, his "base of operations," as Constance had called it. If the original negative of *Death of a Bachelor* remained somewhere on the estate, it seemed the best place to start.

They walked up alongside a wide gravel path. There were patches of grass growing through the stones. Blondeau directed Raikes round the side of the main house to the rear. There was no sign of another person. He hadn't spotted any security cameras either, though it was too dark to be sure.

"I've been thinking about it," Raikes whispered to him ominously as they crept along. "I'm standing by my theory – that your man in the mask is Chekhov himself."

"So that birthmark on his leg," Blondeau replied, "he just transferred it to some other poor sod, did he?"

"We only have the old woman's word for that, remember. She must have been in on it. You can't trust old people, Stevie. They've had longer to learn how to lie."

"Whatever you say."

Raikes continued to mutter to himself, "Or maybe she was the one who killed him?"

They reached the rear of the house. There was a patio area and a garden. Shadows of shrubs and small trees rose from the darkness, leaves whispered in the gentle breeze. The rest of the estate was partitioned by a tall hedge.

"The stable block should be just past this," Blondeau said.

That wasn't quite right, though. First came the tennis court and what looked like a covered-up swimming pool. There was a Victorian-style gazebo and in the distance large areas of open land, likely where Paul Chekhov had practised with his guns. The nearest neighbours wouldn't have heard a thing.

An archway in a brick wall led to the stable yard. The traditional half-doors had been replaced with standard types, or in some cases bricked up entirely. There was a statue in the centre of the yard, a life-size bronze of a stallion rearing up beside its handler.

It was an eerie feeling, standing there in the perfect quiet, in an area that was built to be anything but. It was like walking through an abandoned hospital or an empty school, it just didn't feel right. Blondeau felt a chill from the night air and pulled his coat close. Somewhere nearby an owl hooted.

"Where do we start then?" Raikes asked him.

Blondeau counted six doors in total. "Clockwise, I guess."

As they approached the first door, they saw it was shut with a bulky padlock. Blondeau signalled to Raikes. "Now's your moment to shine."

Raikes took his rucksack from his shoulder and pulled out a small leather case and a flashlight. He switched the light on and inspected the padlock. "This is good," he said. "Laminated padlock – should be four pins, five tops. Doesn't look too old either."

"I dread to ask how you know about this kind of stuff."

"It's nothing sinister," Raikes replied nonchalantly. He opened the case and ran his fingers across an assortment of small metallic tools. "The manner in which I choose to live my life has left me liable to having need of such services. It might be a lady friend, shutting me out of my house in a fit of pique. Or perhaps I simply misplace my belongings in a drunken stupor. Either way, at the point I'd become on first name basis with every locksmith in London, I decided I should take matters into my own hands."

He picked out an L-shaped tool, about the length of his index finger, and another one which looked like a miniature screwdriver. "It's not all that complicated with a bit of practice," he continued, "and a life of leisure has given me plenty of time for that. I have acquired other skills in the same manner, if this little adventure of yours has need of them. I can juggle, for instance. And I can tell you what you've been eating purely from inspecting your vomit..."

"I'll bear it in mind."

Raikes pulled up his balaclava, passed Blondeau the flashlight and inserted the L-shaped tool into the lock, turning it slightly. Then he did the same with the other tool and began to gently rock it back and forth, his ear to the lock. After a couple of minutes he replaced the second tool with a similar one and went back to work.

Blondeau soon grew bored and peered around the yard. Moments of pause like this were the last thing he wanted – the opportunity to reflect on exactly what it was they were embarking upon. It was a definite step up from telling a few fibs and sneaking into a party off another man's name. He was almost certain it was illegal, for one thing. A part of him hoped that Raikes would fail to pick the lock, and they could pack up and go home. Give up on the whole business. As he considered the possibility, he heard a loud *click*.

Raikes looked up at him with a smug expression. "Ladies first," he said, raising the padlock in triumph.

The door opened with the lethargy of one that had not been tried in some time. Blondeau fumbled for, found and then pressed a switch on the wall. The room became bathed in an ominous red light. It was long and narrow. Along one side were shelves, cabinets and counters with trays on top. On the other, at the far end, was a metallic sink, with big glass bottles beside it. There was a wire, like a clothesline, running along the middle of the room.

It was a photography darkroom. Or at least it had been – there wasn't much sign of recent activity. The clothesline was bare, save for a few pegs.

Blondeau walked towards the shelves. Most were empty. He picked up a folder and took out the photographs within. There were various shots of a city that he was probably London – streets, apartment blocks, warehouses, parks. There was one in particular that Blondeau recognised from *Death of a Bachelor*; it was the exterior of the school that the son of Chase Ashley's character, Sam, attended.

The photos must have served as part of the location scouting for *Bachelor*. The work of Clara Davis or another of Chekhov's assistants, trying to capture the bright lights of New York in the murk of London, two cities similar in population but entirely different in character. Blondeau knew their efforts had been largely in vain – Chekhov had given up in the end, choosing instead to recreate the streets of New York in purpose-built sets at Pinewood Studios. It was one of the things that gave *Bachelor* its unnatural, dreamlike quality.

There were more folders. Again, some looked to be for *Bachelor*, shots of islands and large houses that must have been considered for the performance of *Hamlet* in the film's second half. There were others that Blondeau couldn't place, either in *Bachelor* or any other part of the director's oeuvre. Shots of barren land, crumbling churches, grimy tunnels. These ones were dated from the year of Chekhov's death, the locations spanning the counties surrounding London. *Interesting*.

"What exactly are we looking for?" Raikes asked.

Blondeau blew out his cheeks. "Reels of film, I suppose, though I imagine they'll be in cans or a box or something."

There was no sign of such in the room they stood in. There were a few folders they hadn't yet touched, a treasure haul in itself for Chekhov aficionados, but there was no time for any of that.

Raikes picked the lock of the darkroom shut, then moved to the next door. He was getting the hang of it – the second padlock was open less than a minute later.

Blondeau was an unashamed fan of horror films, from the classics, the likes of *The Exorcist* and *Psycho* that even the snootiest critics could no longer turn their noses up at, right through to trashy slasher flicks like *The Last House on the Left*. It was well known in the industry that no amount of blood, guts or pure psychological dread could put him off.

But as he switched on the light in the next room, the sight of a dozen or so people standing there, perfectly still, gave him a fright unlike anything he had ever experienced before.

Only for a moment, though.

Mannequins. Half-clad in odd garments, the room must have

been used for costume design. He recognised some of the clothes from *Death of a Bachelor* – dresses and doublets and headwear worn by the House of the Damned theatre group.

And again, there were others that didn't fit. What he could only think of as *Mad Max* garb: battered leather coats and jackets, cargo pants, knee-high boots. Scavenger chic. Some wore necklaces or earrings of bone. There was nothing that came close in any of Chekhov's films.

He thought back to the photos from the darkroom. Barren land, crumbling buildings. Was Chekhov planning some sort of post-apocalyptic sci-fi film? He recalled the director having been a fan of the genre from his biographies, he had praised works such as *A Canticle for Leibowitz* and *La Jetée*. It was a genre he'd never before touched, there was a certain logic to it. And having a darkroom on his estate, a place for costume design, all presumably to maximise secrecy. No wonder it had never reached the press.

Most importantly, if Blondeau had it right, these were hardly the actions of a man planning to kill himself anytime soon.

There were more clothes of similar designs on racks and in boxes at the back of the room. Behind the boxes they found a stack of those cardboard cutout displays used at cinemas, timeworn, depicting characters from Chekhov's films over the years – heroes and villains, damsels and dames.

Of the *Bachelor* negative, there was no sign.

"I wonder if they have little parties in there?" Raikes asked, grinning as he locked the mannequins back in their tomb. "I always used to think about that when going through clothes stores as a kid."

"And yet you've matured so much."

The next two rooms seemed to serve no purpose beyond

miscellaneous storage. There were tools for decorating and repair, chemicals that might have been used in the darkroom, old bits of furniture.

Blondeau and Raikes picked through the junk with a sense of boredom. Even Paul Chekhov's couldn't escape the day-to-day mundanity of existence. Blondeau had no real expectation they would find the negative of *Bachelor* there, the great director's prized possession tossed in with such clutter. They didn't.

After that they reached the editing rooms. There were two, the final two rooms of the repurposed stables. They were set up identically. At the end of each there was a table upon which sat a monitor and speaker, a desktop lamp, six plate-sized disks and a central deck of rollers and switches. In reality, the tables and all that sat on top of them were part of the same machines – they were a pair of Steenbeck flatbed editors. Above the machines and around the rest of the two rooms were a series of shelves that were mostly empty.

As Blondeau explored the first room, he couldn't resist taking a seat in the chair by the editing machine. He placed his hands on the table and imagined scenes from *The Night Sessions* or *High Upon the Hill* unfolding before his eyes. He pictured Chekhov leaning in to the monitor, waiting for the perfect frame, marking it out and then literally cutting the film and splicing it to the next shot. Good editing was both an art and a science, but it was more than that still – it was a feeling. Every shot has a natural rhythm, a great editor can sense it, can tell the exact moment at which the shot itself *wants* to be cut. It went without saying that Chekhov was one of the best.

There were a couple of empty boxes on the shelves above. Elsewhere there was the odd reel of film, mainly referencing Chekhov's pre-*Bachelor* work. There were none related to any works that Blondeau was unfamiliar with. Chekhov might have been planning a new film, but there was nothing to suggest he had gone beyond that.

The second editing room was the same. Blondeau pulled out Carter Starling's biography and flipped to the final set of photos. There was one of Chekhov sat in front of the same type of machine, his back to the camera, his head resting on his chin as he worked. It could well have been taken in the exact room Blondeau now stood in, though he couldn't be sure – all the editing rooms he had ever seen were much the same. Regardless, the shelves in the photo were crammed with film cans and boxes, not the sparsity Blondeau now saw. He could only think of one explanation: Constance Chekhov had cleared these rooms out.

Not entirely, though. As with the darkroom, there were scraps left behind, or perhaps found elsewhere and hastily put back in the most suitable place. Plus there were larger items like the editing tables, which didn't exactly come cheap. It was as if Chekhov's niece had lost interest in the entire affair, the removal of her uncle's possessions a job half-done and forgotten.

Blondeau and Raikes found no reels of film referring to *Death of a Bachelor*. In a way it made sense. If Constance and Clara Davis had searched for the *Bachelor* negative like the former had claimed, the editing rooms would likely have been the first place they'd have looked. It was still a disappointment, though. Blondeau and Raikes had trawled the entire stable block, with nothing to show for their efforts except more damn questions.

"What now?" Raikes asked as he finished locking up.

Blondeau had already thought it through. "There's an office here," he said. "I read about it in one of the books. There's an extra house nearby. The previous owner had it built for the stable manager and his family; Chekhov turned it into offices. It's where Clara Davis and the other assistants must have worked when this place was more than just a ghost town."

Raikes pulled a hip flask from his rucksack and took a swig. "I guess it's going to be a long night."

The building in question was a short walk away. It was an unremarkable two-floor cottage. Pretty enough. The front door was painted turquoise. The sign read: "Summerset Lodge", with a bouquet of roses between the words.

Raikes picked his way in the front door. As Blondeau walked down the hallway, he soon realised his night was not about to get any easier.

The first room he looked into was normal enough. There were two desks, upon one was an old typewriter, the other was clear. There was a photocopier, an empty coat rack and a set of filing cabinets.

The rest of the house was an ocean of boxes. Some on rows of shelves that spanned the length and height of rooms, others piled between the aisles. There were boxes in the kitchen and the bathroom upstairs, boxes tucked in an empty fireplace in what must have once been the family's living room. The amount of boxes in that cottage could have filled the warehouse at the end of *Raiders of the Lost Ark*.

Every box was identical in shape and size. It would have been a challenge to carry more than one. Most were labelled with a code that must have made sense to someone: "PCA-23-11" and so forth.

Blondeau opened one at random. Inside were about fifty lime-green folders, ordered by date. He picked one and examined the contents. The first page was a memo. It read:

To: Susan
From: Paul
July 15, 1974

Please check with the weather bureau and find out what the pollen count in Oxfordshire was last Friday, July 12 between 9am and 6pm. Also, find out what the average pollen count is by month of year, what is considered extremely high and what is extremely low and any other information on how they would describe the pollen count on Friday, July 12 during the times I mentioned.

Thanks,
Paul

The following pages proceeded in a similarly fastidious vein. There was an instruction to keep the house stocked with a minimum of three pineapples at all times. Then came a request for one of the family's cats to be moved to a weaker painkiller for an unspecified injury. The current dosage had the creature "buzzing around all day like a hummingbird," Chekhov claimed. After this he had asked for information on the dismantling of the Californian public trolley lines in the 1930s and '40s. Because of course he had.

What had Chekhov been up to in the 1970s? Blondeau wasn't yet any the wiser. It seemed impossible to sort the wheat from the chaff – the man was an obsessive, about everything. There was seemingly no knowledge he did not consider useful.

Other boxes were labelled more intelligibly. There were

multiple boxes of résumés, stretching back decades. They found an entire shelving area dedicated to fan letters. These were divided into three groups: positives, negatives and, "cranks". Blondeau, naturally, went straight to the last group. Each folder inside the box he selected had the name of a town or city typed on the front – Hamilton, Ontario; Hartford, Connecticut; Hayward, California; and so on. He opened one. The letter inside was very neatly handwritten:

> Dear Mr. Chekhov,
>
> I was recently unfortunate enough to attend a screening of your latest "work". It bothers me greatly that a man of your obvious talents has chosen to dedicate his life to purveying such filth. The violence in your films is both a cause and a product of our sick society. Rather than seeking to alleviate our ills, you seem to revel in it. I can no longer resist the urge to contact you about these matters. Would your parents be proud to see what you have given the world, Mr. Chekhov? Mine would be rolling in their graves to see what we have become of ourselves.

It carried on in this fashion for another three sides. It wasn't even the only one from that city, either. Blondeau had received the odd crazed letter of his own over the years, but nothing to this scale. It put Chekhov's retreat from the world in a different light. And if the director had been murdered, he'd at least been helpful enough to leave behind a ready-made list of suspects.

James Raikes was wincing beside him, as if scared to broach

the subject: "We're not going to have to look through all of these boxes, are we?"

Blondeau chewed his lower lip. *How to put this nicely*? "It might be in here, somewhere. We can't yet rule it out. We just need to, you know, open a box, check that it's all just papers inside, no film cans, no reels, then move on to the next one. It can't take that long."

Raikes took another swig from his flask and raised his head to the heavens. It was the most work he'd been asked to do since the days his parents had unwisely attempted to bring him into the family business proper, and he was starting to realise it. Eventually he let out a deep breath and said: "Let's get it over with, then."

An hour later it was over with. It wasn't so bad once they'd got a routine going; it soon became mechanical. And, of course, they hadn't found the *Bachelor* negative. The boxes were nothing but paperwork. Blondeau hadn't been able to resist the occasional read. He found many more memos to a litany of assistants, fragments of long-term correspondences, financial records of a mostly mundane variety, decades of plans, both realised and abandoned: location photos, scripts, plot summaries to obscure novels.

Blondeau felt certain there were clues somewhere in those boxes to the *Bachelor* mystery. He also felt certain that he wouldn't find them. He needed a lifetime and he only had a night.

They sat on the carpet in the old living room, backs propped against boxes, passing the flask of whiskey back and forth.

"Are we going to search the main house now, then?" Raikes asked in a quiet voice.

Blondeau didn't answer. He really hadn't wanted it to come

to that. The stables and the office he could rationalise, but breaking into Chekhov's house felt like a step too far. It was an invasion of privacy, an intrusion into the inner sanctum of a man whose work he had long admired. Everyone deserved to keep a certain part of themselves away from the world.

But deep down, he had always suspected it would end that way. Chekhov wouldn't have left his most valued treasure where he worked on it. Amongst the boxes in the office would have been a decent enough hiding place, but that didn't fit right either. As the policeman Peter Doyle told it, Chekhov was wracked with paranoia that people were after his film. He would want it close to him at all times, the only way he could guarantee its safety. If they wanted it, they would have to go through him first. *And perhaps they had?*

Blondeau and Raikes retraced their steps. The main house loomed over them. It was rectangular, with a flat roof, three rows of large paned windows and imposing chimney stacks on each corner. When Blondeau glanced his flashlight at the walls he saw they were smooth and cream coloured. The front door sat under a regal portico, held high by four stone columns. Raikes knelt and set to work on the lock.

Blondeau stood idly by once more. He pulled up his balaclava and rubbed his eyes. The cool night air buzzed at his face. The search of the stables and the office had cost them a few hours, but they still had time on their side. As long as they were smart with it.

Then Raikes remarked: "Shit."

"Hmm?"

"Don't get too angry," Raikes cringed, "but I may have broken off a pick inside the lock."

Blondeau couldn't claim to be an expert in the field, but he had the feeling that wasn't a good thing. "Can you get it out?"

"I can try." Raikes opened his case and took out another tool. It looked like a tiny barbed spear, like a harpoon. He inserted it in the lock and jigged it around, a bit more aggressively than with the others. His face was riven with the effort.

"I don't think it's going to work," he said to Blondeau eventually. "The lock's completely jammed up now." He scrunched up his nose. "To be honest, I'm surprised we got this far."

Blondeau nodded and helped him to his feet. Without his friend's help he'd have got nowhere, or at least would have been forced to resort to more drastic measures. He couldn't be too mad at him. "Let's look round the back," he said. "I think I saw a door there, must be worth a try."

The back door was rather less ostentatious than the front. The paint was cracked and peeling; the area around the handle looked damaged. Raikes rediscovered his form with the lock but there was another problem. Even unlocked, the door wouldn't budge. It must have been bolted from the inside.

Blondeau cursed his luck. If they couldn't find a way in, their search was over. There was one side of the building they hadn't yet visited; they traipsed over in the hope they would find an additional entrance. They found something else instead.

They looked up at the open window on the top floor, then back at each other.

"Seems like fate," Raikes offered.

There was no light coming from the window. The caretaker or Constance or whoever else must have left it ajar.

"Seems like fate," Blondeau agreed, his voice faint. He remembered seeing an extension ladder in one of the rooms at the stables. They retrieved it and lined it up against the wall.

Even at its fullest, the ladder only just reached the sill of the window in question. To Blondeau's coddled, middle-class eyes, it looked a hell of a climb.

Raikes gestured to him in a manner that suggested he was happy for Blondeau to take the lead on this one.

Blondeau climbed the ladder. He took steady breaths and careful steps, passing the first window, then the second, making sure more than anything to not look down. The ladder, dug into the flowerbed, held steady. The window sill came into view above him, just past the top rung. As he reached the summit, he clambered into the darkness and landed on a carpeted floor. His foot struck something that felt like an empty bottle, it rolled softly away. He spotted the outline of a bed and sat on the edge, allowing the relief to flood over him.

Something in the bed moved.

One of the shouts that followed belonged to Blondeau, the other came from a figure that rose from under the bed covers and seized him by the shoulders. They struggled together for a moment, but the other person was stronger, they pushed Blondeau back and pinned him down on the mattress.

Blondeau heard a switch and suddenly the room was alight. The face in front of him was unfamiliar. He had bleary eyes and straggly shoulder-length hair. His breath reeked of cigarettes and alcohol.

The two man stared at each other in confusion, then pulled away so they stood on either side of the bed.

"Who the bloody hell are you?" Blondeau panted.

"Who are *you*?" the man responded in a gruff voice.

"I asked first."

His opponent seemed to accept the logic of it. "Well… I'm him aren't I? The big movie man."

"Chekhov?"

The man nodded. "That's it."

"You most certainly are not."

"I'm in his house, aren't I? That should be enough."

Blondeau couldn't contain his outrage. "You're just a damn squatter, aren't you? You have no right to be here."

"What right do you have?"

"Well, I er... I..."

Suddenly James Raikes came tumbling through the window. He held out the little lock-picking harpoon like a weapon. "Hands up, buster!"

Blondeau groaned, massaging his shoulder where the man had grabbed him. "Relax. He's just a- a..."

The man let out a bitter laugh. "Go on, say it then – 'just a homeless guy.' That was what you were going to say, wasn't it?"

"Well... you are, aren't you?"

The man shrugged. "S'pose so."

Blondeau looked around the room. It was small and fusty and plain. The only furniture was a single frame bed, chest of drawers and bedside table. The wallpaper was a damask pattern in white and grey. There was a duffel bag by the door; the carpet was dotted with empty beer bottles. It was hardly the most luxurious bedroom Blondeau had ever seen. Perhaps Chekhov's uninvited guest had found the others a touch overwhelming.

"Let's all just calm down, OK?" Blondeau said, motioning to Raikes to lower his weapon. "None of us should be here, so the best thing is if we all forget this ever happened. Agreed?"

The man on the other side of the bed offered a grudging nod of the head.

"How long have you been living here?" Raikes asked him.

"About two months," he said. "I didn't break in, neither. The back door was unlocked. If you can't take the care to properly lock up, then really you're just asking for someone like me to take advantage of it."

"I suppose the front gate was unlocked as well, was it?"

The man responded with a scowl. "What are you two doing here anyway?"

Bloody good question, Blondeau thought. "We're... looking for something. Something that's ours, we're not stealing it. And while we're on the subject, I hope you haven't been putting anything from here on the back of a lorry, if you know what I mean."

"Oh, typical," the man sneered. "Every homeless person has to be a criminal to you posh bastards, doesn't he? Can't simply be a well-adjusted member of society on a run of bad luck." He grimaced as he looked around at the empty bottles on the floor. "Anyway, I wouldn't know what to flog from this place if I tried. The house is full of old crap, damned if I know what's valuable and what ain't." There was a sudden glint in his eyes. "Though if you're looking for something, I could always help you find it? Dare say I know this place better than either of you."

Blondeau and Raikes glanced at each other. He had a point. From the outside, the house could have half a hundred rooms or more, there was no way they'd get through them all before morning. If they could be directed to the ones that mattered, it might make all the difference.

"Alright," Blondeau said.

"Fifty quid," the man immediately replied.

Blondeau swore under his breath.

"Plus another twenty to keep my mouth shut about this," he added. "Because whatever you say about none of us supposed to be here, I reckon from the way you two talk you've got a lot more to lose than I have." He grinned, unveiling a row of yellowy-brown teeth.

Blondeau walked over and slammed the notes into his palm. Their newly acquired guide immediately became amicable, as if this was something he did often. He told them his name was Jon. Neither Blondeau nor Raikes offered theirs in return.

"We're looking for a film," Raikes explained. "It might be in metal cans or something similar. Have you seen anything like that?"

Jon mulled it over. "There's a home cinema on the ground floor. Never managed to get it running myself, but it might be your best shot."

Raikes gave him a pat on the back. "Show us the way."

They exited the bedroom and emerged halfway down a hallway. Jon directed them leftwards. The carpet displayed geometric patterns in shades of red, the walls were porcelain white and lined with frames containing photos of the Chekhov family with friends, colleagues and luminaries, movie posters in a dozen different languages and dour abstract art canvases that probably each cost more than Blondeau's house.

One of the first rooms they passed had tall bookshelves on all sides, and all of them full. A single armchair sat in the middle of the room, a small coffee table beside it.

"Is that the library?" Blondeau asked.

Jon smirked. "Sort of. I call it the Alexander Room. Every single book in there is about Alexander the Great."

Blondeau's mouth fell. The room must have comprised everything ever written about the man. All for a film that Chekhov had never got beyond planning. It was incredible. It was tragic.

"Read one myself the other day," Jon grinned. "Did you know he named a city after his horse? Takes all sorts."

As they continued through the upper floor of the house something became clear: there were very few bedrooms left in Ravenwood Manor. Like the cottage, the main house had been taken over by boxes. What Blondeau and Raikes had trawled through earlier apparently only represented a fraction of the total. Chekhov's mind had been consuming the estate like a virus. The idea that they could search through them all was for the dogs.

Jon took them down a stairway and then another, wider one, which brought into view at its end a large entrance hall. The stone floor had a black-and-white spiral design that somewhat hypnotised as they approached. There were Chinese vases on either side of the front door, a pair of bronze fawns at the foot of the stairs and the chandeliers were of an Art Deco fashion. It typified what Blondeau had seen of the house so far – a strange hodgepodge of styles and eras. Chekhov's films were so meticulously crafted; yet in his own house, nothing seemed to quite fit together.

Blondeau's first thought upon seeing Chekhov's cinema room was that it put his own to shame. There were five rows of red felt folding seats that could have been torn from an actual cinema. The floor had been set on an incline, the walls on either side were covered in acoustic foam panels and there were recessed lights in the ceiling. It was clear that Chekhov had gone to great expense to replicate the full cinematic experience. Blondeau might have expected to see a popcorn machine had he not remembered the director's vocal loathing of such "desecrations".

They walked through to the projection room. Blondeau

briefly admired Chekhov's projector – a Cinemeccanica Victoria 5 – before turning his attention to the row of metal cabinets at the back. Most were empty. None of Chekhov's films were present, which Blondeau had to assume was Constance's doing once more. The labels on the film cans that remained reflected Chekhov's own influences: titles from Max Ophüls, Sergei Eisenstein and Orson Welles; as well as his peers – Andrei Tarkovsky, Federico Fellini and Sam Peckinpah; and more recent fare from Quentin Tarantino, the Coen Brothers and Terry Gilliam. There was only one box that was unlabelled. Blondeau opened one of the cans inside and inspected the film with his flashlight. Whatever it was, it wasn't *Bachelor*.

He closed the final cabinet, leant back against the metal door and sighed. "Where else?"

Jon scratched his chin. "His study is up on the top floor?" he suggested. "And I'm pretty sure it's his bedroom that's next door to it. It's the biggest one in the house, at least."

"Let's try the study," Blondeau replied. He left the word "first" unsaid.

They trudged back upstairs, their footsteps echoing off the stone steps. Blondeau could tell from Raikes's slumped shoulders that his friend's spirit was about to break. He wouldn't be able to count on him much longer. As for their other companion... he was an unknown quantity, to put it lightly. Blondeau didn't trust him one bit. He felt desperation choking his pores and coursing through his body. He was running out of time and he was running out of ideas and he was running out of hope.

Chekhov's study was on the opposite side of the house from the room Jon had claimed as his own. It contained the largest desk Blondeau had seen outside of pictures of the Oval Office. It dominated the room. A buttoned office chair was behind it, a few shelves and filing cabinets nearby. There was a large map of the world pinned to the wall facing the desk, which seemed a strange choice for a recluse.

Blondeau and Raikes began a perfunctory search of the room. Jon must have concluded that such activities were outside the terms of his contract; he leant back in the chair, his feet propped on the desk. The toes of his trainers were worn right through. He yawned loudly. "More trouble than it's worth," he muttered.

"What's that?"

"I said, it's more trouble than it's worth. This house. Thought I'd get some peace and quiet out here, but instead there's people coming and going like it's Oxford Circus." He scratched his stubbly cheek and began picking his nose. "Least I made some money out of you two."

Blondeau stopped rooting through a drawer and turned to look at him. "Are you saying that someone else has been here recently?"

Jon began to answer then stopped. "Might be," he said with caution. "It'll cost you, though."

Blondeau swore out loud. He slammed another twenty into his palm. "Talk."

Jon unfolded his hands and smiled wide. "About a week ago, it was. I woke up in the middle of the night and went to take a piss. I step outside my bedroom and take the route, just like I showed you earlier, when, as I turn the corner, I see a man at the top of the stairs. He sees me at the same time. We stare at each other for a few seconds, then he scarpers, back down the stairs and out the back. I realised the next morning he must have forced the door open with a crowbar or something – that's why I started bolting it shut. Not that even that was enough to put off you two resourceful chaps."

Blondeau recalled the damage to the back door. He had seen similar not long ago, in his own home. "Was he wearing a mask?" he asked without thinking.

Jon's confusion seemed genuine.

"Forget it," Blondeau said quickly. "What did he look like?"

He shrugged. "Looked like a man, I suppose. Nothing too out of the ordinary."

Blondeau snatched the biography of Chekhov from his rucksack and shoved it in Jon's face. He pointed to the front cover. "Was it this man?" He could feel Raikes watching him with a smug satisfaction; but at this point, the question had to be asked.

"You mean the one who's in every photo in this house?" Jon smirked. "No, wasn't him. This guy was younger, not all that young, but younger." He squinted. "Dark hair, that's about all I can say. I thought for a flash that I knew him, but I can't have, I suppose. It was the middle of the night, remember? You know what it's like when you get up, you're barely aware of your own feet."

With an increasing sense of desperation, Blondeau showed him the rest of the photographs in the book, but none contained the man that Jon had seen.

"Hardly worth the twenty quid," Blondeau scowled.

"Yeah, well, no refunds, OK?"

Blondeau perched on the edge of the desk and closed his eyes. He hardly had the energy to think about what he'd just heard. If the man Jon had seen was the same that had broken into his house and taken his papers, the same that had stalked him in Venice and Los Angeles... what on earth was he doing at Ravenwood? Was he attempting to remove the crucial evidence before Blondeau got to it? Alternatively… was he chasing the same answers? Things seemed to only become ever more twisted up and tangled.

As for Chekhov's study, it was a bust. It was the same story as all the other rooms, nothing but paperwork. Which only left…

"Show me the bedroom," he said to Jon.

Jon showed him.

They stood, hushed, at the entrance to the dead man's bedroom. Paul Chekhov's bedroom. The inner sanctum of the inner sanctum. It didn't come more personal than this.

Blondeau took a deep breath, setting aside any feelings of guilt, and entered.

The room was large but sparsely furnished. The bed was king-sized. Much of the wooden floor was covered in an enormous Persian rug. There was a walk-in wardrobe that was empty and an en-suite bathroom the same. Behind silk curtains, paned windows looked onto the front lawn and the gravel path that Blondeau and Raikes had walked up at the beginning of the night. It felt like a year ago.

The only thing that was strange was the amount of lights in the room. In addition to a crystal chandelier, there were lamps on both the bedside tables and another pair by the windows, as well as golden wall lights that Blondeau had the sense were a recent addition. It seemed excessive, though now he thought about it, he realised much of the house was the same way. Chekhov's electricity bill must have been through the roof.

An unwelcome thought came to him – was this where it had happened? Chekhov's suicide, or whatever it had been. The exact details of the location had never been disclosed, but he supposed the bedroom was as good a place as any. He searched the floor for leftover bloodstains, squinting. He saw nothing.

Perhaps under that enormous Persian rug, he thought. He left it there.

He poked through a chest of drawers, dressing and bedside tables. All empty. And just that, their search was done. Talk about ending with a whimper.

"I guess that's that, then?" Raikes offered gingerly.

Blondeau ignored him, turning instead to their guide. "Where else is there?"

Jon gave him a disconcerted look. "There's more rooms, loads of them. But... I don't know, you know? I've been here a couple of months, and there's still parts of the place that seem new to me. I don't fancy your chances."

"Time to give up, mate," Raikes said. He offered a sympathetic smile. "We're never going to find it, the house is too big. It probably isn't even here anyway."

"I'm not giving up," Blondeau said through gritted teeth. "I just need to think. I just need to- I just need to..." his words drifted away into nothingness. He knew by then that they were right. He wasn't going to find the film. And without it, his investigation was over. There were no more paths to tread. Chekhov's Cut would remain nothing more than a legend. He pictured returning to his normal life, with nothing to show for his efforts. Then, looking back in his old age, telling his grandchildren about the one time something interesting had happened to him. They'd just have to take his word for it, of course. *Sure you did, Grandpa*.

He sat on the side of the bed and sank his face into his hands. He felt grimy and worn out. "Give us a drink," he said to Raikes wearily.

Raikes chucked the hip flask across the room at him. Badly. It skidded across the floor and disappeared under the bed.

At first Blondeau couldn't make sense of it, couldn't see the beacon in the mist of his mind. He rose to his feet and looked at the bed with curiosity. There was a frilly valance that ran from the mattress to the floor. He'd assumed that the bed was solid wood behind it, but perhaps not.

He lifted the valance. There was a hollow area stretching the width of the bed. The hip flask was not far away, but there was something else down there as well, something bigger, further back.

He reached deep under the bed and, with effort, dragged it out. It was a wooden storage trunk, just shallow enough to fit under. He opened the lid. Inside the trunk were nine film cans.

He knelt over the trunk, perfectly still. His skin suddenly felt very hot, he could feel the sweat on his forehead. Raikes was saying something but it barely reached him. He sounded muffled, as if he was talking through a pillow.

He let his fingers brush lightly over the cans. Maybe he was imagining it, but it felt like they tingled to his touch, like a low buzz of static electricity.

None of the cans were labelled. It didn't matter.

Outside the window, the first glimmer of sunlight peeked over the horizon.

Time for some answers.

Twelve
Chekhov's Cut

Katherine enters the living room from the kitchen, a large glass of wine held loose in one hand.

"Was this"–she gestures around–"the way you thought things would be for us?"

Sam closes his eyes and pinches his forehead. "What are you doing this for?"

Katherine shrugs. "I'm not doing anything."

"Yes, you are. You know you are. You're making this all bigger than what it needs to be. I don't- I'm not saying this isn't a big deal, but it's not more than that. We don't need to talk like this. I just need to... fix it."

She studies him, swilling her glass. "And then what?"

"Then... whatever's normal."

She places the glass on the coffee table and slumps on the sofa beside him. "Sometimes when it's normal... I don't feel anything. Like I'm in a fog." She sighs. "Perhaps this is good for us."

He eventually responds: "This is good for

no one. You shouldn't think like that."

"At least I'll remember it."

Sam stands. He walks over to the window, opens it and leans out. The New York night is heard below, distantly.

"If that's really the way you think," he says, "then perhaps I shouldn't even bother. I should let this continue, let this chaos go on."

"Is that what you want?" she asks him. Her tone is professional.

He turns back to her with a scowl. He shakes his head and walks out of the room.

Blondeau watched as the scene changed to one that was more familiar, just the way Paul Chekhov had intended. *Chekhov's Cut*. So it existed after all. What's more – it was *his*. If he could somehow explain how he came to own it, he might well become a rich man. He'd need a story, one that didn't involve breaking into the Chekhov estate with the heir to a chocolate biscuit empire and a homeless guy.

At least the staff where he'd had the positive print made from the negative hadn't asked too many questions, hadn't known its true significance. Which brought him to another problem. He would now need to find somewhere to hide *both* copies. He had already suffered one break-in and things hadn't exactly calmed down since.

But all of that could wait for a more pressing matter. After all, wasn't that the point?

Blondeau yawned. So that was that, then. Chekhov's Cut. Three extra scenes, each about three minutes in length. All three took place in the first half of the film; all three were set in Sam and Katherine's spacious Upper East Side apartment. No other characters appeared. There was no obvious plot development, the dialogue was uninspired. The scenes were... forgettable, inessential. Disposable.

It was a twist Blondeau hadn't seen coming: whoever it was that removed those three scenes from the released version, Blondeau probably would have done the same.

Except that couldn't be it. There had to be something else going on. Something below the surface.

He thought about the three scenes in their totality. Each explored Sam and Katherine's relationship. They were depicted as the stereotypical well-heeled, somewhat bored, married couple. Part of the modern academic elite. There was the sense, made explicit in the third scene, that Katherine somehow enjoyed the drama of Lindsay's intrusion into their lives. It was similar to that old film *The Night Porter*, the sense that it is only trauma, or the memory of such, that allows one to truly feel alive. Normal life is "a fog."

Katherine was played by Miranda Hamilton, an Oscar-winning actress who deserved more than what she got from the version that made it into cinemas. There, she is an afterthought, a clichéd nagging wife who exists solely to make the plot function. In the version that now resided in Blondeau's attic, she at least approximates a three-dimensional character, with her own thoughts, needs and motivations.

Blondeau wondered whether the additional emphasis on Sam and Katherine's relationship offered some kind of link to Chekhov's own marriage. He considered what he knew about Diana Chekhov. It wasn't much.

Paul and Diana had met through mutual friends in the late 1950s. She had worked for a time beforehand as a costume designer. In more than thirty years there was not the slightest hint of marital troubles. There was not much hint of anything for that matter; Diana was barely mentioned in anything he had read about Paul Chekhov's life. She was by his side throughout, but quietly, unassumingly. It was never revealed why the Chekhov's had not had children, though neither was it presented as something with any deeper significance. Diana had died of pancreatic cancer in 1991. Unsurprisingly, the funeral was a private affair.

Was there some kind of reference to the Chekhovs' marriage hidden away in those scenes; something Paul felt suitably guilty about; something Constance would want to keep hidden? But how bad could it possibly be? If it was along the lines of Paul Chekhov having had an affair, it would hardly be cause for great scandal. You weren't a filmmaker worth your salt in Hollywood if young women didn't throw themselves at you, either for a career break or just to say they had. It would have been unusual if Chekhov *hadn't* strayed once in a while.

Perhaps their marriage had been a violent one. That would have soured Paul Chekhov's reputation. But was there the slightest sign of such in those three scenes? If there was, Blondeau couldn't see it. There was tension, distrust, passive-aggressiveness for sure, but neither Sam nor Katherine ever even raised their voices. The overall tone was no different to that of any other scene of theirs in the film.

Blondeau groaned and sank back on the sofa. He listened for a while to the rain patter on the attic window. He'd spent much of the past four evenings watching the film, over and over again. Watching the new scenes in isolation, watching them as part of the whole. Jotting down in a notepad the exact time of each scene change to make sure nothing else was different. It wasn't.

Just those three scenes. Three little, inconsequential scenes. He'd studied the dialogue, the editing, the shot composition and framing. The lighting and use of colour. He'd ramped the sound up to see if something was buried in the audio mix.

He'd found nothing. It didn't make sense.

And now... the only thing he could think to do was to try again. It would come to him eventually. It had to.

He rose from the sofa and stretched his limbs until the joints cracked. Then he walked over to the projection room and brought the film back around to the first of the extra scenes:

> Sam stares out the window, saying nothing.
>
> Katherine watches him from the sofa. "You need to tell me if you're not going to be able to make these things. At least then I'll have time to make up an excuse."
>
> He turns around quickly to face her. "It won't happen again. I'm sorry. I lost track of time."
>
> "It's fine," she says with forced casualness. "I don't think we both need to attend every single time."
>
> Sam shakes his head. "It's important we're both there. We have to understand what's going in our kids' lives. Like I said, it won't

"Can you seriously not hear me calling you?" The voice – exasperated – was Andrea's.

Blondeau turned to her as if waking from a trance. "Huh?"

"The takeaway's here. I've been shouting up here for five minutes."

He blinked rapidly. “Right.”

She walked forward a few steps, looked at the projection screen and frowned. “Perhaps an hour off will do you some good. Perhaps a week off for that matter. I’m trying my best to be patient and understanding with this whole enterprise, but you don’t make it easy.”

Blondeau screwed his eyes shut. “I’m sorry,” he said. “You’re right. I lose track of time up here.”

“I’d noticed.” Eyes still on the screen, Andrea tutted and said: “That’s stupid.”

“What?”

“It’s a stupid pun,” she replied. “I hate when they do things like that.”

Blondeau was now totally lost. Perhaps he really had been in a trance, and hadn’t yet come clear of it. “What are you talking about?”

She turned to him as if suddenly realising who she was talking to. “The painting there – do you see it? Behind your best friend Chase.”

Blondeau looked back at the screen. The painting in question was mounted in Sam and Katherine’s living room. It depicted a medieval scene in portrait: a knight slumped in front of a tree, eyes closed, his shield resting in his arms. The arrow sticking out of his side told that he wasn’t sleeping.

Blondeau pursed his lips, still none the wiser. The painting was a little incongruous amongst the modern décor of the apartment, but other than that, there didn’t seem anything all that strange about it. Either it wasn’t shown clearly in the released version, or he’d never before made note of it.

“It’s a pun,” Andrea explained disapprovingly. “The film is called *Death of a Bachelor*, yes? Well, there’s your bachelor.” She saw his blank expression and rolled her eyes. “It’s the original meaning of the word. Haven’t you ever heard of a Knight Bachelor? It’s like a junior knight, one not belonging to any particular order.”

Blondeau didn’t respond. His eyes were glued to the screen. Glued to the painting of the dead man by the tree.

Andrea shook her head with mild disdain. “I thought a highbrow guy like Chekhov would be above such things. Anyway, if you’re not coming down, I’m going to start. Don’t get mad at me when there’s no spring rolls left.”

She went back downstairs muttering. Blondeau barely noticed.

There were two things said to him in recent months racing through his mind.

The first was from Anthony Hudgens. A trivial example of Chekhov’s maddening perfectionism, the tale of how the director had commissioned a painting specifically as part of the set design for *Bachelor*, a painting that never even appeared in the released version of the film.

The second came from Cain Xavier, that night in The Zebra.

This time Blondeau remembered the exact words: “Don’t worry about the plot. Chekhov always hid the interesting stuff in the background.”

Thirteen
Death of a Bachelor

The studio looked out across the Thames. There was a clear view of the Millennium Dome, the soon-to-be great white elephant of the age. It was a hell of a view.

It was part of the loft of an old warehouse in the Docklands. Blondeau had needed to take a freight elevator up to reach it. Enormous steel frame windows flooded the room with light. The floorboards were covered with sheets then littered with scraps of paper, tins, jars, pots and tubes. Industrial shelves were stacked with books and newspapers. In the centre of the room was an easel, the first layers of a pastoral landscape laid out on a canvas.

The owner of the studio was a thin man of about fifty. His hair receded into a widow's peak above a wiry face with gentle brown eyes. He wore an apron that looked as if it was his only one.

The man squinted at the photo for a while then, finally, shook his head. "Not one of mine, I'm afraid."

Blondeau watched him. "Are you sure about that? It was painted in London, a few years ago."

The man shrugged. "Quite a lot of artists in London, you know."

Blondeau smiled. *He had him.* He was starting to get the

hang of this. "There's not many that do historical painting, though. Chuck a tin at a canvas and call it art, sure, there's hundreds of those types. Want someone to stick their dirty bed in the Tate, no problem. But historical painting? It's a pretty niche genre these days. Only five such artists in the entire city by my count."

The man turned away from him back to the easel, hands on hips. "You've got four more chances then. You can probably get round them all today if you're quick."

"I've already have," Blondeau said at once. "All four said the same as you – it wasn't theirs. But two of them were at least able to point me in the direction of a certain Andrew Jestin."

At first there was no obvious reaction. Then Jestin turned back around and let out a snort of laughter. "You could have said that straight away instead of letting me make a prat of myself, you know."

Blondeau made to reply but Jestin cut him off, "And don't think I don't realise I could make a lot more money chucking a tin at a canvas, as you so eloquently put it. But this"–he gestured at the easel–"is what I like, so this is what I paint." He winced. "Good job I was a banker for twenty years first."

That explains the view. Blondeau gave him an apologetic look. "I just have a few questions. I hope it won't be too much trouble."

Jestin waved his hand dismissively. "I should have told you the truth from the start," he sighed. "It was him that said to keep quiet about it."

"Chekhov?"

Jestin nodded. He picked up a rag and began to wipe his hands with it. "I wasn't exactly pleased when he said it. It was the biggest commission of my life and I wasn't allowed to tell anyone! I couldn't resist bragging to a few of my colleagues – I guess that's what led you to me in the end."

He makes three days of grinding through phone directories and traipsing across the city sound easy, Blondeau thought as he smiled politely. "Did Chekhov say why he didn't want you to talk about it?"

"He just said that it would be better for me if I didn't. Wouldn't say anything more. Proper cryptic, but then, creatives are like that sometimes. I was never completely serious about honouring it in the long term, but then he died..." Jestin grimaced. "It felt wrong to break a pledge to a dead man."

Blondeau wasn't sure he'd have had Jestin's sense of honour in such circumstances. Surely the dead have bigger concerns? "Can you tell me how it all happened?"

Jestin tossed the rag on the floor and walked over to the window, staring out at grey sky and murky waters. "He came in, unannounced, one day, much like yourself. I had a place in Richmond at the time, near the theatre. Strange fellow, I thought. Odd mannerisms. He didn't give his name but, of course, I knew who he was. Everyone did, not just for his films, but all the rumours and crazy stories you used to hear. He asked if I'd paint something for him as a matter of urgency. Didn't even ask about the price."

"What did he ask for?"

Jestin worked it over in his mind. "He wanted the knight, I remember that for sure. I'd done a few previous, though never dead, as he requested, normally something a little more... heroic. I think it was me that had the idea for the placement – in front of the tree."

He scratched his cheek with a paint-stained finger. "The only other thing he wanted was the symbol on the shield." He pointed to the shield's bottom-right quarter. "That one. The other quarters I added, all standard heraldry, but that one he was specific about. He'd sketched it out on a piece of paper so he could be precise. I suppose it was a reference to something or other."

Blondeau peered at the symbol in the photo. He could just about make it out. The outline of two eyes, overlapping vertically; an iris and pupil at the join. He didn't recognise it. He'd try to get a clearer image back home later.

"Did he explain what it meant?"

"He didn't and I didn't ask. I was a bit starstruck, to be honest. Anyway, a week or so later, he comes to pick it up, and I never saw him again."

Blondeau puffed out his cheeks. He'd hardly expected Chekhov to reveal his innermost secrets to the man, but a little more candour wouldn't have gone amiss. "Did he seem happy with it?"

"As I recall," Jestin frowned, "he barely looked at it."

Blondeau decided he'd got about all he could from the man. Happy for an interview for once to end without acrimony, he thanked him for his time, and made to leave.

"Are you going to buy it, then?" Jestin called out as he neared the door.

"Excuse me?"

"The painting," Jestin said. "I assume that's why you wanted to know about it. It must have re-emerged onto the market somewhere?" His eyebrows rose optimistically.

Blondeau's words caught in his mouth. It didn't seem the kindest time to start telling the truth. "Right. Yes, I think I might do, actually."

"It would be great to see it in a gallery or somewhere else

public. I remember being quite proud of the final effort."

"Don't worry," Blondeau grinned. "People will know all about it soon."

That evening, Blondeau sat in his study with a glass of shiraz, staring at a sketch he'd made of Chekhov's symbol:

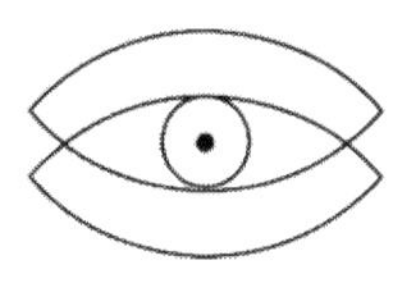

It was a curious design. It felt at once familiar and alien, modern and ancient, sinister and benign. It could have been anything. An old rune or glyph, the logo of a business or organisation, something from a religion, astronomy, the occult... anything.

How in God's name was he going to be able to identify it? Even Andrea hadn't been able to help him this time. Perhaps one of her colleagues could. A professor of symbology, if such a thing even existed. But what if Chekhov had just made it up, its importance known only to himself and a few others?

The one thing he was sure about was that the symbol was the key to the whole mystery. He'd rewatched *Bachelor* one more time after Andrea had unwittingly enlightened him. Jestin's painting appeared in the background in all three of the additional scenes, but never in the released version of the film. What's more, Chekhov appeared to have gone out of his way to make sure the image – including the symbol – was visible. Certain shots were in "deep focus," a rather convoluted filming technique requiring the precise use of lighting, composition and camera lenses to keep foreground and background in focus at the same time.

It had to be the reason those scenes had been removed – someone had seen it, understood its importance and had taken one hell of a risk to make sure it didn't reach a wider audience. Someone out there knew what it meant.

He kept thinking back to the hours he'd spent up in his attic, poring over every frame of the released film, searching for the truth of it. It would have been time better spent sat in traffic for all the use it had been. He'd been right all along, of course. The various theories of the Chekhov obsessives as to what was in those missing nine minutes were all wide of the mark. There was no murder, no plot twist, no little green men. There was only the painting. The death of a Bachelor in its most literal, original sense. And from the painting, the symbol. And from there...?

He ground his teeth in frustration. His investigation felt like scaling a sheer cliff wall, continually latching on to the next hold or niche or nook of information, painfully aware that he could slip away at any minute, or that without the next hold or niche or nook he'd become stuck, with nowhere to go. He'd always managed to find it so far, somehow, but how long could it possibly last?

Perhaps there was another who could help him. He wasn't an academic, Blondeau wasn't sure he even knew him by his real name. A man with an ability to pull together obscure information. A man whose claims about the strange goings-on at Chekhov's estate seemed to have at least some basis in fact.

Blondeau put the page with the symbol to one side and took a fresh sheet of paper. He opened a drawer in the desk, brought out a pack of felt tip pens and began sketching a crude scene – a house, a smiling family beside it, a cat and a dog that could have been a dog and a cat.

Then he went downstairs and taped the picture up in his dining room window for the whole world to see.

Fourteen
A Sunday Drive

"This is *not* a shortcut," Andrea concluded with irritation. "We should turn around and get back on the main road."

Blondeau smiled and drummed his fingers on the steering wheel. "I know what I'm doing." It was almost the truth.

His stomach felt fit to burst. He loosened his belt with his spare hand. The roast at The White Hart had been exquisite; well worth the drive to Fyfield and back. Killing two birds with one stone had never felt so enjoyable.

The narrow country lane went on seemingly without end. It had been minutes since they'd seen another vehicle. Tall hedgerows on either side closed down their view. Thick gnarled branches leant over the road, almost forming a tunnel. At every turn Blondeau craned his neck, looking for a sign they had arrived. If it was here, it was hidden away well.

One of the photos had shown a sign by the entrance. He'd thought it impossible to miss, but they'd been travelling down that road for a long time now...

"I think we should get the map out," Andrea said gently.

"We must be nearly there," Blondeau replied without thinking.

She turned on him with suspicion. "Nearly *where*? I thought we were going home?"

Thankfully for Blondeau, a sight appeared that made her questions redundant. The hedges on the right of the road became a touch more manicured. Then a gap appeared. A gravel path running out of view. A sign close to the ground, white text on a black background. It read: "THE SHEPHERD INSTITUTE". Beside it was a symbol that was no longer unfamiliar.

Blondeau slowed the car to a halt on the opposite side of the road and let out a deep breath. He placed his shaking hands in his lap.

Of course, Andrea had recognised it too. "You've got to be kidding me. Please don't tell me *this* is why we drove out here?"

Blondeau winced. She seemed angrier than he'd thought she'd be. "I had to see it," he explained. "I found it – aren't you at least impressed?"

If she was, she wasn't showing it. "And what are you going to do now? Have you even thought that far?"

"I- I don't know," he admitted.

"What is it, anyway?" she asked, conceding her interest only grudgingly.

"I'm not sure. I looked up their website." He chose to ignore her obvious surprise that he'd managed such a feat. "It talks about 'spiritual healing' and so forth, but I think that's just a cover. I've heard other stuff. This is it though, I'm sure of it. Chekhov had some kind of involvement with them."

She shrugged. "Why are you still sitting here, then?"

It was a fair question. Blondeau's entire journey had led him to this place; but now he'd reached it, it felt like his legs were frozen. Had stage fright finally hit? Perhaps it was the sense of the unknown that did it. All times previously – in Venice, L.A., even at Ravenwood – he'd at least had some sense of what lay ahead. But beyond that hedge, up that path, it could be *anything*.

"I don't know," he said at last.

Andrea grumbled under her breath. She seemed to be losing respect for him by the minute. "If it means we get home quicker," she said plainly, unbuckling her seat beat, "I'll go see what they're up to." Without further comment, she exited the car, crossed the road and headed off down the path.

Blondeau watched his wife disappear from view. He didn't know why.

It had only taken a few days after leaving the drawing in the window for Cain Xavier to make contact. A typed letter, no stamp, instructing him to meet the following midday at Trafalgar Square, under Nelson's Column. Once again, Blondeau had the feeling Xavier was trying to impress him with his sheer commitment to clandestinity. Regardless, he had skipped out on a press screening of Disney's animated version of *Tarzan* to show up on time. At half past the hour on a cold grey day, with Blondeau on the verge of giving up, Xavier had appeared beside him in a baseball cap, sunglasses and three-day stubble.

"I think I'm onto something," Blondeau told him straight away. He pulled out the sketch of Chekhov's symbol from his bag and passed it to Xavier.

The American examined it. Eventually he answered: "Leave it to me. Be back here – same time, next week." Then, just like that, he was gone.

The next week, Xavier hadn't showed. At least not then. Blondeau had wandered forlornly around the square for an hour before deciding that enough was enough. Later that day, trying to put the whole business out of his mind for at least a few hours, he and Andrea had gone for a drink in The Holly Bush, a cosy little pub hidden away in the picturesque back alleys of Hampstead. As Andrea went to the bathroom, Xavier dropped into her seat, seemingly out of nowhere.

Blondeau was stunned. "What the hell are you doing here?! And where were you earlier, for that matter?"

Xavier had dark circles under his eyes. He had buzzed his hair down till there wasn't much left. "You had a tail," he said. "Didn't you see him?"

"A tail? You mean, someone was following me?"

Xavier nodded. His eyes were constantly darting around the room. "An elderly Chinese man. He was with you from Leicester Square."

"How do you know?"

"I followed you as well," he said matter-of-factly. "It wasn't safe for us to meet."

Blondeau looked in the direction of the pub toilets. "Yes, well, now's not exactly the best time either."

"We have time," Xavier said without concern. "Women take on average six minutes to use the bathroom. Plus there's a queue – one of the stalls is out of order."

Xavier really did think of everything; Blondeau didn't know whether to be impressed or disturbed. "What have you got to tell me?" he asked him. "Have you identified the symbol?"

Xavier let the tension build up, then showed his hand: "You were right. You *are* onto something." He took a folded brown envelope out from his coat pocket and handed it over.

Blondeau opened it. Inside was a single sheet of paper. It was a printout of a webpage. So much for Xavier's investigative skills; he must have just posted the symbol on one of those internet forums and let his fellow cranks from around the world do the hard work for him.

The page showed photographs of the exterior of a large Georgian country house. Underneath it were the words "The Shepherd Institute". There was an address below that, somewhere in Oxfordshire.

"What is it?" Blondeau asked.

"My sources differ on the Institute's exact purpose. They talk varyingly of experiments in telekinesis, mind-control, precognition–"

Blondeau rolled his eyes. "No little green men?"

Xavier looked pained. "Not that has thus far been established. All are in agreement, however, that the Institute is a front. A way for the British and possibly American governments to conduct research of a 'questionable nature' off the books, without scrutiny."

"But what's Chekhov got to do with any of this?" Blondeau wondered out loud.

Xavier held his hands up. "I was hoping that you would tell me."

Blondeau hesitated. He wasn't yet willing to tell Xavier quite how far he'd gone, especially in regard to his discovery of Chekhov's cut of *Bachelor*. It was still his story, and only his, to share with the world, when the time was right. "I found it in a book," he offered flimsily.

Xavier looked like he could smell it. He'd no doubt already had the same thought as Blondeau: the Shepherd Institute was within comfortable driving distance of Chekhov's estate. It put the stories he had heard about seeing strange vehicles there in a different light.

He stared at Blondeau for longer than was comfortable. "Look," he began, "normally I'd help you bring down these bastards, but I have to leave the country tonight. It's no longer safe for me here. It's best you don't know the full details."

Blondeau was happy not to. "Oh."

Xavier leant in close. "I'm afraid you're on your own."

Then he was gone, just as before. Blondeau had managed to stuff the envelope into his pocket only moments before Andrea returned to their table.

And now here she came again, walking back up the gravel path towards him. Alive, at least. Unharmed, from the look of it. Her expression was inscrutable. She got back in the car and put her seatbelt on, saying nothing.

Blondeau eventually couldn't let the silence drag out any longer: "Well?"

She looked surprised he had spoken. "I talked to them," she said. "Very interesting."

Blondeau struggled to hold his frustration. "And?"

"I'll tell you what I know," she said coolly. "But first you need to talk to me. Properly."

Blondeau shrugged. "Sure."

"What's going on?"

"I told you. I think this place is the–"

"No. What's *really* going on?"

He narrowed his eyes. "What do you mean?"

She sighed. "Is this a midlife crisis? Because if that's what it is, then that's what it is, but you need to be open about it."

Blondeau could hardly believe his ears. Was she really going to do this, now of all times? "A midlife crisis?" he scoffed. "Come on. This is a real mystery we're talking about. I'm hardly making this stuff up, am I?"

But Andrea was ready for him: "You drove around Los Angeles in a top-down Corvette. You snuck into a party full of celebrities with a fake ID. You're putting even less effort into your job than usual – don't think I don't know you've been getting Damian Scott to summarise films for you so you can skip out on screenings to go... wherever the hell it is you go."

"I've been doing that for years!" Blondeau protested. "Everyone does it."

"You've been doing it more than normal. A lot more. People are talking. I'd almost think that you're having an affair, except you don't seem to be making any more effort with your appearance than usual. Less, to tell the truth."

"I'm not having an affair," he said, happy to latch onto the one thing he could be honest about.

"I know you're not," she replied. "I'm starting to think I might prefer it, though. At least that's what normal couples do. You seem to positively relish the idea that there's some grand conspiracy behind all this stuff."

"It's true!"

"And if it *is* true, did you ever stop to think you might be putting yourself- putting *us* in danger?" Her bottom lip began to quiver.

Blondeau thought he understood at last. He unbuckled his seat belt so he could look at her straight. It somehow felt like the first time he had done so in months. Her auburn hair, straight to the shoulder; her languid hazel eyes. Faint freckles on her cheeks, the slightest dimple in her chin. It was a face he knew as well as his own, and like his own, he rarely had cause to really think about it.

Twenty years of marriage it had been. Twenty-five altogether. Happy years. They had been together in the struggle, when he was out of work, desperately trying to find someone foolish enough to pay him to watch movies all day while she toiled over her doctorate, when they'd lived on beans and rice and suspiciously cheap wine from the off-licence down the road, the one that ended up being raided by the police and then turned into a TV repair shop, though strangely it still had the same guy behind the counter. They had raised two children that had come out better than most seemed to these days. They had settled down, enjoyed the years that were supposed to be enjoyed. Two foreign holidays a year and the occasional city break. Private school for the kids. A stupidly expensive dog. They had done it all, together.

He felt a sudden sense of guilt, of shame. She deserved better than what she had got from him the past few months.

He took her hand in his, squeezed it gently. "You have my word," he said. "We are *not* in danger."

"You can't know that for sure."

"Yes, I can. This is all just a quirky little tale. Something that will make a fun documentary. Talk of danger is ridiculous. And if it ever does get to that point – which it won't – I'll turn back."

"Promise?"

"Promise."

She nodded. There was the hint of a smile at the edges of her lips.

That was that dealt with. "Now then," he began with forced cheer, "what have you got to tell me?"

She smiled fully now. "You're booked in for next weekend."

Fifteen
"Spiritual Healing"

He was halfway down the stairs when he heard her voice. He froze. It could only mean that it was still going on. *How was it still going on?* Yesterday's session was done by half past the hour. He thought about turning round, heading back upstairs, back under the bed covers, skipping breakfast altogether; but they must have heard him by now, the door was directly opposite the bottom of the stairs. They would all know the truth. He would have to face them down instead.

"*And now,*" the voice – composed, melodious, tranquil – drifted up towards him, "*start to roll out the neck, left ear to left shoulder, chin to chest, right ear to right shoulder, then lifting the chin, round and round and round...*"

He reached the ground floor and looked into the room opposite. There were seven altogether, including the instructor. All with their own mats, sat cross-legged, hands on knees, eyes closed, heads lolling around their necks. James Raikes was among them, right at the back. Even sitting, he loomed over the rest.

"*Then gently bring your head to a neutral position, let us take one cleansing breath to end our practice. Take a big breath in through your nose–*"

Breathing, Blondeau thought. She's teaching them how to

breathe. Why didn't they know this already? Even babies can do it.

"*–open your mouth and exhale it out.*"

They did.

"*Finally, let us bow our heads together.*"

They did.

The instructor concluded, as always: "*Namaste.*"

They all opened their eyes and made dreamy smiles at each other. Then they looked to the door and saw him. Judged him. *What did they want from him?* It wasn't his fault he wasn't a morning person. It wasn't his fault he had the flexibility of a piece of old wood. Why couldn't they understand that?

Truly, the Shepherd Institute was hell on earth.

He had to give it to them, though – if the Institute *was* a front, it was certainly a committed one.

He and Raikes had arrived – a few pints down – late Friday afternoon, finally making it up the gravel path to the large Georgian country house from Cain Xavier's photographs.

They had been welcomed by the beaming staff, who promptly forced them to fill in questionnaires detailing their lifestyle habits. In defiance, Blondeau decided to leave nothing out. The poor girl who took his form looked suitably horrified.

After that they were shown to their rooms. They were small but, like the rest of the house, had a certain rustic charm, with creaking floorboards, open beams and crisp white bedding. A bag of dried lavender had been left on Blondeau's pillow. He still didn't know what he was supposed to do with it.

In the two days that followed there had not been the slightest sense that the Institute was anything other than a health retreat for well-off Londoners. The other guests included a BBC executive, a political editor from *The Guardian* and several academics whose work would have likely led the *Daily Herald* to label them as "lefty." Blondeau's line about needing a break from the stress of his career was met with sympathetic looks from all. He could only imagine what Andrea would have said to *that*.

As well as yoga, there were guided meditations, exercise classes, massages and plenty of time for the guests to log their every inane thought in notepads. No electronics were allowed, of course. There were talks on nutrition and healthy living. The house included a sauna, a steam room and a cold water plunge pool for the true masochists.

The wider estate had extensive gardens and a wood where the guests were encouraged to forage – blackberries, elderflowers and honeysuckles in the summer months; sweet chestnuts and sloe berries in the winter. All hidden away in the sleepy Oxfordshire countryside.

The meals, prepared by a soft-spoken Finnish lady, usually involved berries, too; alongside a plenitude of pulses, nuts and grains. The evenings were spent together in the communal kitchen and lounge, complete with open fireplace, or alone in quiet contemplation. Blondeau soon came to prefer the latter. He quietly contemplated becoming a grumpy old man before his time.

The person who seemed to be in charge of the whole affair was a middle-aged woman called Parvati, a name she claimed to have adopted after joining an ashram in Los Angeles at an earlier, particularly trying point in her life. Her manner was about what would be expected from such a tale.

Blondeau had attempted to get the details of the Institute's history from her over a cup of herbal tea. It had been established in the late 1960s by a British psychiatrist named Henry Shepherd, its goal to "explore human potential." When Blondeau pressed Parvati on what exactly that meant, she became vague, though it was difficult to tell whether she was hiding something or simply didn't know the details. She claimed that at some point in the 1980s the Institute had started to struggle for funding, at which point the transition to its current state had begun.

Parvati was the oldest member of staff, none of the others looked much over thirty-five. Did any of them know anything of the origins of their employer? Blondeau doubted it. They seemed completely oblivious to the possibility of anything sinister lurking amongst them. He once dropped Paul Chekhov's name loudly into a conversation, just to see if it elicited any sort of reaction. It elicited sod all.

"We're running out of time," he moaned to Raikes as they traipsed around the gardens together for the umpteenth time. "We're out of here tomorrow morning and still none the wiser."

"I'm not sure there's anything to be wise about," Raikes responded. "I think these are just good, honest people. Especially that yoga teacher, Penelope. I sense a connection between us."

"Maybe *she* knows something," Blondeau wondered aloud.

"I think I should be able to drill her for information," Raikes said with a wink. He paused. "And when I say, 'drill,' I mean–"

"I got it, thanks." Blondeau looked back at the house. Some of the other guests and staff were on the terrace doing *tai chi* moves. Who'd have thought it would come to this?

"We need to try the basement," he said at last.

It was the only place left for answers. The only part of the house not being used for accommodation or stuffed with yoga mats, massage tables or miscellaneous exercise gear. A locked door down a flight of stairs just past the reception area. A member of staff had disinterestedly told him it was for "storage." Blondeau hadn't pressed the matter.

Raikes looked pained at the prospect. "I don't know, Stevie. Realistically, what could possibly be going on down there?"

"Who knows? It must be locked for a reason, though. Devil worship, alien autopsies, a portal to another dimension – there's only one way to find out."

Raikes knelt down and pulled out a few weeds from the staff vegetable patch. "Maybe you should listen to what these guys have been saying," he said gently. "It can't be healthy to obsess like this. Instead of thinking about Chekhov, you should think about your thoughts, like, observe them as if they are hovering around you. I think that's what they keep going on about anyway." He stood up, weeds clutched in one hand. "That reminds me – have they given you your life plan yet?"

Blondeau had noted one of the staff heading in his direction with a plastic folder several times earlier in the day. Each time he had sped off out of sight. "I've managed to avoid it so far."

"Mine was way off," Raikes chuckled. "But you can't fault them for the effort."

"To hell with the bloody life plan. We're here to find out the truth. And there's only one place left to look. So I guess the question is, are you – and your lockpicks – going to help, or am I going to need to kick that door down and get us in a whole new world of trouble?"

Raikes stared at him, hands on hips. Eventually he let out a deep breath and bowed his head. "Fine."

***

That night – at precisely midnight – Blondeau knocked lightly on Raikes's door. Several minutes later his friend answered in a silk dressing grown, rubbing his eyes, his usually slicked-back hair flopping over his face. It seemed longer that way. Blondeau wondered whether he grew it out to cover a bald patch.

"I told you to be ready!" he hissed.

Raikes yawned. "Yeah, yeah, yeah."

As Raikes closed his door behind him, Blondeau sensed movement in his friend's bed. A yoga teacher-shaped mass reconfiguring under the covers, perhaps. He decided he must have imagined it. Things were simpler that way.

They crept down the stairs together, their attempts to minimise their impact on the floorboards failing, as was always the way with such attempts. The lights were out. There was no sign of another person.

Eventually they reached the stairs to the basement. Raikes went down to try and unlock the door with his usual set of tools while Blondeau kept watch, crouching in the dark next to a potted plant. His fingers dug into the soil from nervous tension.

The clicking of the lockpicks sounded enormous amongst the silence of the rest of the house. As Blondeau waited a series of absurd possibilities flickered through his mind as to what they would find down there. Someone had altered Paul Chekhov's final film to obscure his connection to this place. Perhaps even gone as far as to kill the man. And now, it all came down to one locked door. On previous occasions, this would be the moment where he'd have second thoughts about what they were about to do. Whatever happened to that guy?

He heard footsteps coming up from behind him. Raikes appeared at the top of the stairs. He mouthed: "We're in."

Blondeau led the way back down to the basement. He slowly,

gently pushed the door open.

He looked into darkness. There was no sense of movement. No chained-up monster – not awake, at least.

He felt for a switch. He found it, he pressed it. The lights came on.

Blondeau groaned.

Shelves full of cardboard boxes. That old story again. The room was long, with a corridor running along the right-hand side. There must have been about ten rows of shelving units in all. The square recessed ceiling lights gave off a low hum. It could have been the basement of any office in the city.

Blondeau strode past the shelves. The corridor led through to another, smaller room. Here there were yoga mats, massage tables, miscellaneous exercise gear. "Storage," in other words. He couldn't say they hadn't tried to tell him. Tucked away at the back was a Buddha statue with a chipped nose.

There was nowhere to go beyond that. No more doorways, entrances or exits. *Fin*.

Raikes clasped his hands together. "Well, we gave it a try," he said, unable to hide his relief. "We should probably get back upstairs now."

Blondeau ignored him. He walked back to the shelving area. He picked a box at random and opened it. He took out some of the papers within. They were the questionnaires that the staff made the guests fill out when enrolling. He was surprised they even bothered to keep them. Another box had copies of the life plans he had tried so hard to avoid. Another held employment contracts. He grit his teeth.

"Let's look through these," he said, gesturing to the rest of the shelves. "We need to find stuff from the 1970s."

"1970s?"

Blondeau nodded. It had to be. It was the only way the puzzle fit together. Chekhov's absence from filmmaking at the time; the vehicles at his estate, the ones with the tinted windows, transporting him somewhere on a regular basis. And then, the Institute's struggles for funding the following decade, its gradual repurposing into a health spa, corresponding to Chekhov's return to filmmaking. The director had been involved with them in some way. But how? Blondeau could put the pieces together, but he still couldn't see the whole picture.

They took positions at opposite ends of the room and began to rifle through the boxes. Just like old times.

It was Raikes who struck first. He called out: "I've got something!"

Blondeau rushed over. Raikes waved a handful of tabbed folders. "1975," he announced proudly, handing them over.

Suddenly they heard footsteps, clear and unmistakable. It sounded like they were coming closer. Blondeau and Raikes froze. Then, so did the footsteps.

The door to the upstairs of the house opened.

"Hello?" a man's voice called out. "Is anyone in there?"

Blondeau and Raikes silently moved behind the end of the shelving units on the far side of the room. Hidden, for now. Blondeau could feel his heart thumping. No one's in here, he silently urged. Go away.

But the man was not so easily assuaged. He began to walk down the corridor on the right of the room. Blondeau caught a glimpse of him from his hiding place. It was one of the masseuses. A muscle-bound clod with blond hair who had something of the air of a Bond henchman. The bastard had given Blondeau a proper thrashing the previous day. His thighs still felt sore from it.

The masseuse slowly walked past them towards the second room, his footsteps echoing off the hard floor. Raikes made a gesture that could have meant anything. He slid the cardboard box back on the shelf and began to creep along the aisle. Blondeau numbly followed.

With the masseuse out of sight, they dashed to the door, opened it and fled upstairs.

It was only when he reached his room and dove under the bed covers that Blondeau realised he still clutched the folders in one sweaty hand.

Blondeau and Raikes didn't wait around for breakfast the next morning. They sped off in Raikes's Range Rover with barely a goodbye to the staff. The blond masseuse gave them a funny look, but nothing more. And, as they reasoned, who's to say he wasn't doing the same to everyone?

Blondeau hadn't even dared look inside the folders they'd taken from the basement. He'd laid with them the previous night under his pillow, eyes open. At one point he heard footsteps in the hallway outside, but they came no closer than that.

They crawled through the Monday morning traffic, not saying much, until they reached Raikes's townhouse in Fitzrovia. It had been a while since Blondeau had visited; the cleaners had left it as spotless as usual. Raikes set to scrambling some eggs for them both.

It was then, finally, that Blondeau allowed himself a proper look at what they had taken. He opened the first folder and pulled out a single water-stained typewritten page:

Patient Name: Alushi, Daniel
Patient Number: 10000217
Date: 18th June 1975
Dr Graham Renwick

Mr Alushi seems to have had an inadequate response to treatment so far. He continues to speak of violent thoughts. His anxiety and paranoia continue. He harbours a great anger towards his father. He is frustrated with treatment and speaks of wanting to stop, regardless of the consequences. He is sleeping well. There is no incontinence, there is no mutism, there is no retrograde amnesia.

Current treatment:
Four-hour sessions every two days
Repetition of Eden #2 Fortitude #3 Worth 5
with LSD-25 100micrograms, mescaline
300mg, scopolamine 600micrograms

If no improvement in one week, increase
dosage in line with standard procedures.

Blondeau didn't know what scopolamine was, but judging by the other "medicines" Daniel Alushi had apparently been subjected to, it wasn't hard to muster a guess. It was the other terms that puzzled him – Eden, Fortitude, Worth; plus the numbers beside them. That didn't fit right at all. It might have been some kind of code, but his mind was drawing a blank. Why couldn't things ever be straightforward?

He skimmed through the rest of the folders. Mr. Alushi must either have carried through on his threat to quit the "treatment", or something else had happened to him, but there were others – James Beale, Carl Burgess, Agnes Cairns. Different conditions, too: manic depression, schizophrenia, a severe case of anorexia. The Shepherd Institute didn't seem picky. Still more names: Jamal Daniels, Irene Dawson, Reginald DeLarge.

Reginald DeLarge...

"Hey," Blondeau called out from the kitchen table, "come and take a look at this."

Raikes walked over with a spatula in hand. "Hmm?"

Blondeau handed him the last paper and pointed to the patient's name. "Is that... is that the same name as the guy who..."

Raikes's eyes got just a little bigger as he took it in. "Yeah," he said. "I think so."

"Do you think it's... the same one?"

Raikes was reading on. "Might be. Yeah."

The only sound came from the hiss of the eggs on the pan as they thickened.

Blondeau could feel his heart pumping. His throat felt tight and his mouth dry. He said at last: "Holy fuck."

Raikes stared straight ahead, as if dazed.

"Fucking hell."

"Fuck me."

Fuck.

"What the hell did Chekhov get himself into?" Blondeau murmured.

Raikes handed him back the paper. No, it was more like he was pushing it away. "It's not Chekhov I'm worried about, to be honest."

Blondeau looked at him. He saw something in his friend then that, in all their years together, he had never before seen. A distant look in the eyes, a slight trembling of the jaw. *Fear*.

"Look," Raikes began, trying to hide it, "I think we've gone as far as we should with all this. It can't make sense to dig something like *that* up again."

Blondeau started to respond but Raikes cut him off, "And actually, I reckon I might get out of here for a while." He nodded his head, as if convincing himself of it. "I was thinking about heading down to Cancun anyway, you know, a little winter sun. You're welcome to join me, of course, you and Andrea both."

Blondeau said nothing. Raikes was slowly backing away from him, perhaps without even realising it.

"Don't get me wrong, Stevie – I love you like a brother. But if you really want to keep going with this, you're on your own."

Sixteen
Lost Men

Not for the first time in recent months, Blondeau had the uncanny feeling he was starring in his own movie. It was the great, hulking microfilm machine in front of him that did it this time. After all, where were such contraptions seen other than as lazy expository tools in thrillers and horror films? Sharon Stone in *Sliver*, Virginia Madsen in *Candyman*, Jodie Foster in *The Silence of the Lambs* – all diligently uncovering some ghastly secret, shrunken onto a roll of 35mm film.

Presumably the men of such pieces preferred to blunder through without the requisite research. Well, not Stephen Blondeau. One of the advantages of being a film critic was you had plenty of chances to learn from the mistakes of the myriad teens, drunks and wide-eyed fools who so frequently came to a gruesome end.

Besides, it offered him a rare opportunity to make use of his membership to the British Library. The machines were situated in a narrow dark room that smelled faintly of vinegar. It was late Tuesday afternoon; he'd been there for several hours already. The evenings were drawing in. There were few others about.

The rule had held true so far – whether in real life or celluloid, microfilm never bore good news. An example stared back at him from the screen. It was the front page of the 25th

September 1978 edition of *The Times*. Blondeau zoomed in to save the strain on his eyes:

LAKEWELL SUSPECT CLAIMS BRAINWASHING, HYPNOSIS
By Ian Harrison and Jacob Morefield

A lawyer working for Reginald DeLarge, the suspect in the murder of MP Philip Lakewell, has sensationally claimed Mr DeLarge was brainwashed into committing the act.

Jeremy McClair told media that his client remembered everything about Friday except for the moment of the shooting. Referencing the 1962 Hollywood film "The Manchurian Candidate", the lawyer alleged that Mr DeLarge, 36, had undergone extensive hypnosis and related therapies in recent years, though failed to provide further details.

The claims were dismissed as "ludicrous" by police sources close to the case. The current belief is that Mr DeLarge, who has known links to the left-wing group the Revolutionary People's Liberation Force (RPLF), carried out the assassination of Mr Lakewell, 53, in retaliation for his support of the Israeli government.

It has now been confirmed that police at the scene found a newspaper article in Mr DeLarge's pocket which discussed Mr Lakewell's likely inclusion in a potential

Conversative government led by Mrs Thatcher, including a reference to Mr Lakewell's long-term, strident support for the state of Israel.

Turn to Page 2, Col. 1

Most of the page was taken over with a photograph of Reginald DeLarge being "escorted" to a van by a group of police. It captured the exact moment that DeLarge, a short dark-skinned man with an afro and a ragged beard, looked into the camera. He had a blank, glassed-over look on his face, his mouth was ajar. More succinctly – he looked zonked out of his mind.

Blondeau pressed forward on the machine to reach the inside pages:

EYEWITNESS SPEAKS OF 'CHAOS' AT SCENE

By Robert Fisher

An eyewitness to the murder of Philip Lakewell has spoken exclusively to "The Times". Mr Lakewell was shot three times at a constituency surgery in Abingdon on Friday. Joseph Fairclough, a 51-year-old local restaurant owner, had spoken to Mr Lakewell only minutes before the attack.

He recalled: "The first shot dropped him to the floor. The other two were fired from close range into his head. It was only after that that people seemed to realise what had happened. The place erupted into chaos and confusion, it was pandemonium. There was blood everywhere."

Mr Fairclough identified Reginald DeLarge, currently in police custody, as the attacker. "He had walked in without anyone noticing him." He added: "He never said a word. After the third bullet, he dropped the gun and just stood there, next to him. A few people tried to drag him away, but they struggled to move him, even when the police turned up. He was only a small man but he was much stronger than he looked."

Blondeau had never been one to pay much attention to politics, but even he remembered the furore at the time. Some of his friends who ran in left-wing circles had been terrified the police were going to burst through the door with raised truncheons at any minute, others murmured sympathy for DeLarge behind cupped fists. Blondeau remembered being more interested in *Midnight Express*, *The Driver* and François Truffaut's *The Man Who Loved Women* at the time. Who could blame him?

He had spent the afternoon putting together the story. At the time of the attack, Reginald DeLarge was a small-time criminal who had been in and out of prison most of his adult life. As for Philip Lakewell, he was a Tory, that was about all Blondeau understood. A close ally of Margaret Thatcher apparently, who had offered a rare display of emotion in a television interview hours after Lakewell's death.

DeLarge's lawyers had soon dropped the hypnosis claim, instead pleading diminished responsibility at the trial. An unconvinced judge and a furious public, whipped up by the press (not least among them Blondeau's current employer), showed little mercy on DeLarge, sentencing him to life imprisonment. And there he had languished ever since.

There was an additional mystery, the matter of who had supplied DeLarge with the gun he had used, that remained unsolved to this day.

And then there was the piece of paper lying on the base of the microfilm machine. A page from the basement of the Shepherd Institute. Blondeau picked it up and read it again:

> Patient Name: DeLarge, Reginald
> Patient Number: 10000241
> Date: 21st January 1976
> Dr Henry Shepherd
>
> Current treatment:
> Two-hour sessions every third day
> Hive # 4
> Nourish #3
> Worth #5
>
> LSD-25 75micrograms
> scopolamine 500micrograms
>
> Reginald is showing an excellent response to treatment. He has spoken of regret of his previous life and a desire to change. He displays a strong aversion to violence and criminal behaviour. There is no evidence of adverse effects.
> Reginald is a model example of the potential of

> our work and a prime candidate for release back into the community. We will check progress in one week's time, maintaining current programming and dosage.

Blondeau placed the page back – face down – rubbed his eyes and sank low in his chair. So Reginald DeLarge had been a patient at the Shepherd Institute two years before murdering Philip Lakewell. Apparently a rare success story, too – of the patient files Blondeau had taken, DeLarge was the only one they seemed to have made any progress with. It was hardly surprising the Institute had lost its funding.

None of the articles Blondeau had read mentioned DeLarge's involvement with the Shepherd Institute. It seemed an important detail – and a suspicious omission, especially given his lawyer's claims. Had the Institute not divulged DeLarge's history, or were the press deliberately ignoring anything that detracted from the "official" narrative, clearly already being constructed in the days following the attack?

Blondeau ran his fingers through his hair. No doubt the murder of Philip Lakewell was a mysterious affair, but it wasn't Blondeau's mystery, and he didn't much want it either. The key point still evaded him – what had any of this got to do with Paul Chekhov?

Was Chekhov another patient at the Institute? There was certainly no lack of issues the man could have used some help with. He was an obsessive, without doubt; a control freak, too. Depending on who you spoke to, a sociopath, a sadist, perhaps worse. His efforts to maintain secrecy on his productions spoke of a deep paranoia. And then there was the breakdown he had apparently suffered in the Peruvian jungle while filming *Heart's*

Desire. In short, Paul Chekhov was a psychiatrist's wet dream.

But Blondeau didn't get the impression that Chekhov was the type to ask for that kind of help. There was a quote, buried in his memory, about the director's long-held interest in the extremes of the human mind. That the only other career he imagined for himself would have been as a psychologist.

An alternate explanation: Chekhov was helping *them*. Blondeau considered it. Those strange terms that kept coming up in the patient notes – Eden, Hive, Nourish. They could have been experimental drugs or similar. But Blondeau had another idea, just from the way they were written. It was just possible...

They could have been films.

The following afternoon, Blondeau drove out to an L-shaped brown-brick building just outside of Southwold on the East Coast. He parked up in a car park that was largely empty. Stepping out of the car, he could smell the sea salt in the air, could faintly hear waves churn and for just a fraction of a second felt a sense of nostalgia for childhood holidays past.

He walked into the central reception area and released the words that had been on his tongue the last few miles: "I'm here to visit Graham Renwick."

Henry Shepherd had, rather inconsiderately, died of a heart attack two years earlier. Of the three other doctors listed on the Shepherd Institute's patient files, one more was dead, another untraceable. The final doctor lived here, at the Beech Hill care home.

The middle-aged woman behind the desk looked him over. "Who can I say is visiting?" she asked with a hint of suspicion.

"I'm his nephew," Blondeau answered. To be safe he added, "Twice removed."

"I've not seen you around here before."

"I just moved to the area. To be honest, I've been trying to trace that side of my family. I've an interest in genealogy."

The woman mulled it over, then rose from her chair and walked stiffly off down a hallway to one side of the front desk.

In fairness, Blondeau had never expected his story to fully convince. His hope was that the likely forgetfulness of the old man, combined with a desire to provide *any* kind of visitor on a rainy midweek afternoon would be enough for the staff to decide, "What the hell?" and allow him in, setting any misgivings to one side.

Moments later when the woman returned, Blondeau could almost read that exact calculation on her face. "You can try to talk to him," she offered after a moment, "but you must prepare yourself – his mind is not what it once was."

She led him down the same hallway and into a large communal room with a grass-green carpet and bright lighting. Some of the residents were playing cards or checkers around circular tables, others knitted or sewed from high-backed armchairs. Others still simply stared off into space. There was a piano in one corner, a television on the opposite side. A row of large plate-glass windows offered a stunning view of the nearby roundabout and petrol station.

The woman from reception led Blondeau towards the windows, to an old man in a wheelchair. He sat watching the cars circle in the rain.

"Graham," she said sweetly. "Your nephew Stephen is here to visit you."

The old man turned in Blondeau's direction and squinted through thick black-framed glasses. He had a bald head, closely shorn, and a large round nose. He wore a thick woollen cardigan that couldn't disguise his frailty.

"Stephen?" Graham Renwick repeated.

The nurse gestured to Blondeau as if to say, "I tried to warn you," then wandered off.

As Blondeau looked down at the old man, he felt a stab of pity, and of guilt at what he was about to do. Then he remembered the patient notes of Daniel Alushi: "There is no incontinence, there is no mutism, there is no retrograde amnesia."

On second thought, Blondeau decided, *fuck this guy.*

Talking to the eighty-something Dr. Graham Renwick felt like trying to work under a flickering light bulb. He came and went, there were occasional moments of sustained illumination and you hoped against hope that he would stay that way. He never did though. At Renwick's age, things only went one direction in the long run.

Blondeau had just about convinced him of their relation, and had broached the old man's career, which he seemed to remember as well as anything. He couldn't get anywhere without prompting though. He finally bit the bullet: "I hear you used to work for the Shepherd Institute?"

Renwick smiled. "That I did. A great man that Henry Shepherd, never let anyone tell you otherwise." His tone was wistful, though Blondeau had the sense it would have been the same had he been speaking about that morning's round of toast and jam.

"What kind of work did you do there?"

"All sorts, son. We dealt with some real troubled characters, I tell you."

"Of course," Blondeau said, "but what, *specifically*, did you do to them?"

Renwick gave a nod of understanding. He looked about to answer when suddenly his face fell. "Who did you say you were again?"

Patience... "I'm your nephew, Stephen, remember? I was asking you, what exactly you did there?"

The old man paused, narrowing his eyes. "Where?"

Blondeau grit his teeth. How the staff had the will to deal with this all day was beyond him. The next time he saw his boys he'd make sure to tell them to press a pillow over his face at the first sign of trouble.

He tried a different tack, "Do you remember Paul Chekhov?"

"Who?"

"The film director. You knew him in the 1970s."

"Ah!" Renwick wagged a finger and laughed. "Of course. Such wonderful things he came up with."

Now we're getting somewhere. "Can you tell me more about them?"

"Oh, it's hard to describe, son. All colours and words and sounds. Wonderful, they were."

While they were talking an old woman had staggered over to the piano nearby. She began to play a faltering version of "The Entertainer" at about quarter speed.

"There she goes again," Renwick chuckled. He swung his hands in the air as if conducting an orchestra. "Wonderful."

"What did Chekhov come up with?"

Renwick turned back to him. It was clear from his face that he was gone again. "*Who?*"

The old woman finished her recital to scattered applause, Renwick included. Blondeau could have throttled her.

The room fell quiet again. The beat of the *Countdown* clock could be heard from the television set on the other side of the room.

Blondeau asked: "What can you tell me about Reginald DeLarge?"

Renwick's eyes flashed with recognition in a way that hadn't happened previously. "We're not supposed to talk about that," he said coyly. He put his hand over his mouth and smiled like a naughty schoolboy.

"Why not?" Blondeau asked, feigning innocence.

"Because of"–Renwick looked around the room, then leant in closer–"what happened afterwards."

"You mean the shooting?"

Renwick gave a near imperceptible nod of the head.

"What happened to DeLarge at the Shepherd Institute?"

Renwick looked pained. "They told us never to talk about it," he said, almost pleading.

"Who did?"

The old man didn't answer.

Blondeau's voice grew louder: "Who told you not to talk about it? And why?"

Renwick was breathing heavily. His hands shook on the arms of his wheelchair. He looked at Blondeau through the thick lenses of his glasses, a look of desperation, slowly sinking to defeat.

Then...

"Who did you say you were again?"

Blondeau groaned and sank his head into his hands. "I'm your nephew, Stephen," he said with an air of resignation.

"No," Renwick shook his head sternly. "I don't know you. I don't know you at all." He rotated his wheelchair around and started calling out across the room for help.

Blondeau sensed his visit was almost up. "Tell me what happened to DeLarge. What did you do to him there?"

Renwick called out again. A member of staff came over. "What's going on here?" she said, eyes darting between them.

"I was just asking him some–"

"I don't know who *he* is."

The woman turned on Blondeau. "I think you should leave. Now."

He didn't bother to argue.

The rain was still falling as he was practically bundled out the front door. A long line of residents stared at him from the window, Renwick included. The whole, not-quite-a-scene scene was probably the most interesting thing that had happened there in months.

It was a starless, moonless night. The clocks had only gone back a few days ago and Blondeau still hadn't got used to it. The last summer of the twentieth century was officially done.

As he started the long drive back to London, he wondered whether it felt worse for a psychiatrist, if they would somehow be more conscious of their own deterioration. Like a barber finding hair on their pillow, or himself suddenly starting to enjoy Steven Seagal films.

If James Raikes had still been involved, he'd have probably claimed Renwick was faking it to avoid having to tell the truth. Blondeau didn't believe it for a minute – Renwick's current condition was no act. The most frustrating thing was that he'd come agonisingly close to parting the fog at times, but there was still nothing he could be certain of.

Were Paul Chekhov's "wonderful things" the likes of *Journey Beyond*, *Eternal Fire* and *Zenobia*; or something else, something only for the eyes of the Shepherd Institute and the poor bastards who got sent there? Who was it that had ordered Renwick and his colleagues to silence about Reginald DeLarge; was it their boss, Henry Shepherd, or someone higher up the food chain?

Perhaps he'd never now know for sure. The memories of that time were fading away, almost gone. *That damn woman and her piano.*

In the absence of evidence, Blondeau decided to let his speculation run away with him, just for a minute. Say Chekhov had been working with the Institute. Creating pieces of film to somehow help brainwash patients like DeLarge. How would it have even worked in practice?

It was telling that DeLarge's lawyer had referenced that old Sinatra thriller, *The Manchurian Candidate.* The film, and talk of brainwashing in general, were products of Cold War-era paranoia, rather than anything substantive. Techniques such as subliminal messaging had been debunked in more recent years, at least as far Blondeau knew. But had Chekhov somehow managed to make it work – well enough even to drive a man to murder? Ignoring the ethics, it would surely have been the director's greatest achievement of all.

He knew he was basing a hell of a lot on a few out-of-place words on some old documents. But that didn't make it any easier to get the idea out of his head. That's speculation for you.

He was driving down a quiet two-lane road, fiddling with the radio, awaiting the turn onto the A12, when he first noticed the car come up behind him. It was a black four by four and it was too close for comfort.

They continued in this way for a while, Blondeau growing increasingly annoyed, until the car moved over into the other lane and began to draw alongside him. Blondeau saw the outline of the driver reach up and turn on the interior lights, and that's when everything changed.

The man stared down at him from the four by four. The fedora was gone but the mask wasn't. Even having seen it before, it was such a grotesque sight that Blondeau only narrowly avoided skidding off the road in recoil.

The four by four pulled ahead then moved back across, then maintained its speed. Blondeau couldn't work out what the driver was intending. Whatever it was, it couldn't be good.

At the last second, Blondeau took the next turn on his left, a muddy track leading into darkness. He hoped to find a place to turn around and head back in the opposite direction.

The track soon opened out. There was a building in Blondeau's headlights. It looked like an old stone barn. He glimpsed a hand-painted sign – something about a farm shop. There were no other cars in sight, no people.

He turned the car in a wide circle, hoping to complete the U-turn in one clean manoeuvre. Then he saw headlights that weren't his own. The four by four approached from the same entrance, Blondeau's Audi was now facing it. The other car had him trapped.

Without thinking, Blondeau shut off the engine, clambered out of the car and ran around and behind the barn. He immediately regretted it, realising he had shorn himself of his last layer of safety.

He waited behind the barn, leaning against the wet stone wall. His heart was thumping, his fingers tingled. He heard the other engine stop, a door open, a door close. Trudged, deliberate footsteps. He saw a beam of light flash past the edge of the left-hand wall.

He ran through his options. He could try the same trick as in the Shepherd Institute basement – wait until the man came round, then run back the other way to his car. But even if he made it, if the four by four was blocking the only exit, it wouldn't make a difference.

Beyond the barn he could see only darkness. He could run off into it, but if there was a flashlight in play he'd soon be spotted. Besides, where the hell would he go?

Absurdly, at that moment he thought again of James Raikes. Raikes would have known what to do. He was used to such situations, angry husbands and barroom brawls and the like. Raikes had been right about all of it. He should have stopped this madness when he had the chance.

There was one more option available – to face his pursuer down. It was time to stop running, things had gone far enough.

Blondeau crept over to the left-hand corner of the building. He leant back, waiting, controlling his breath, flexing his fingers. He heard footsteps approaching, saw the beam of the flashlight press into the darkness.

His opponent had been complacent. Had he taken the corner from a wide angle he'd have had Blondeau caught in the beam of the flashlight, exposed and helpless. Instead he took it close on, and was met with Blondeau's fist crashing into his face. The man staggered back, a grunt of pain coming from behind his mask. Blondeau had timed it perfectly; he could hardly believe how well his gamble had paid off.

Blondeau then ran at him, crashed into him, tackled him to the ground. They landed in grim dark mud, Blondeau on top. He attempted to bring down another punch but the man blocked it, then raised a knee up into Blondeau's groin. He screwed his eyes shut and swore.

The man in the mask used the opportunity to muscle

Blondeau off him, then struggled to his feet. With Blondeau still on his knees, the man aimed a kick straight at his chest, but Blondeau caught his leg and twisted it at the knee, taking him back down to the mud.

It had all happened in a matter of seconds but Blondeau was breathless. His hand brushed against something solid on the ground. It was the flashlight. He picked it up and, with his last ounce of effort, crashed it into the head of the man in the mask.

They both lay there then, still, as the rain hammered down from the black night sky. If there had been stars, they'd probably be spinning.

Blondeau could hear his breaths through the rain. A voice came to him from the darkness, staggered and pained: "You goddamned bastard."

Blondeau had the strangest sense that he recognised it. But from where? The question brought him back to life. He tried the flashlight – miraculously it still worked. He crawled over and kneeled on top of the other man.

He reached his hand up, roughly pulled off the mask and shone the flashlight in the man's face.

He didn't know what he had expected, but it certainly wasn't *that*.

He was staring at Hollywood royalty. Noah Blake. Son of the great Leonard Blake, and a star in his own right.

"What are you doing?!" Blondeau spluttered stupidly.

Blake grimaced, squirming under his weight. "Just get off me and I'll tell you, OK?"

Blondeau allowed him up. Something about unmasking Blake had immediately nullified him a threat. He was no longer sinister, no longer dangerous – *he was Noah Blake*. And frankly, he looked a little chagrined.

"Why have you been following me around?" Blondeau demanded.

Blake spat and gave a sullen look. There was a trickle of blood running down the side of his face from his hair. He was soaked through and muddy. He wiped his hands on his sides. "Can't we do this somewhere else?" He scowled. "I'll tell you everything, but I've got to get out of this damned rain."

Blondeau scrutinised him. "Fine," he said at last. "There's a pub half a mile back, we'll talk there. And don't think about driving off the second I let you go. If you don't tell me what the hell you've been playing at, I'll give the press their biggest field day since Hugh Grant went for a spin down the Sunset Strip."

The pub was called The Lamplighter. It stood opposite a garden centre in the middle of a small row of detached houses on the main road into Southwold. It had a large car park and two decent-sized rooms which were busier than Blondeau had expected. The bar was wood-panelled and the lighting low. Too low, he would normally have thought. Tonight, it was probably for the best.

He ordered two pints of Adnams Broadside from a dour barman. He carried them over to a small table in the corner of the room and took a seat. Noah Blake sat opposite, staring down at an unemptied ashtray.

When it came to looks, Blake was no Chase Ashley, but he wasn't far off either. He had jet-black hair, piercing green eyes and a rugged square jaw he'd inherited from his father. Not that anyone in the pub could tell. Blake had pulled down a baseball cap to cover his face. Even so, he kept taking nervous glances around the room. His head had stopped bleeding and he'd managed to clean himself up with some wet wipes from

Blondeau's glove compartment – he refused to use the pub toilet – but there was still dirt under his fingernails and mud stains on his familiar light brown trench coat.

So it was Blake who had been stalking him, all this time. Blondeau could still hardly believe it. *Noah Blake.* The leading man of terrible romantic comedies and, in fairness, a few good dramas earlier in his career. Maybe not an Oscar winner but he probably had a Golden Globe or two. Not that Blondeau needed a performance right now. The truth would do just fine.

"I can't believe you took me down," Blake grumbled out of the side of his mouth. "Do you even go to the gym?"

"I've got a membership," Blondeau replied concisely.

"Yeah, well, I don't know how I'm going to explain *this*"–Blake pointed to his head–"to the makeup department tomorrow morning."

"Oh, what are you working on at the"–Blondeau stopped himself, holding up his hands–"Forget it," he said. "I want answers. *Now.* I'm assuming this isn't the first time you've followed me?"

Blake had a drink of his beer and gave it a funny look. Clearly not a bitter man. "That's right," he said eventually.

Blondeau asked, "Venice?" and then, "L.A.?" and both times Blake nodded. "And you broke into my house as well?"

By this point Noah Blake might as well have been a bobblehead.

"What the hell?" Blondeau exclaimed, allowing his outrage to come to the fore. "*Why?!*"

Blake scowled. "You know why. I couldn't let you put that story out to the world and destroy my family."

"You mean, about your dad and the stuntman?"

"You know that's what I mean." Blake's face sank into his

hands and he let out a long sigh of defeat. Then he sat back up, meeting Blondeau's eyes. "It was Victor Roache who first contacted me, saying that a British journalist was sniffing around the story of Chekhov's version of *Bachelor*. This was way before you braced him in Venice, by the way – he knew all about you within minutes of your little interview with that junkie Ashley.

"I couldn't believe it when he told me. I thought we'd dealt with the whole thing when the film came out. We used every trick in the book to keep the speculation to a minimum, especially on the *Zenobia* link. It mostly worked. The only people we ever saw linking *Bachelor* to my family were cranks on internet boards, and who the hell cares what they think, right? And then, three years later, you come along acting like you'd never heard a thing of it. Some expert you are, by the way.

"I was between projects at the time," Blake continued, "and my wife was driving me crazy back home, so I decided to take matters into my own hands and check you out. I saw you meet up with the little hack who wrote that biography of Chekhov. That was the confirmation I needed that you were a threat. Then..." he trailed off.

"...you broke into my house?"

Blake looked away. "I'm not proud of any of this, OK? Even at the time I knew it was madness. I just needed to see what you had. Only, as soon as I got inside, this great dreadlocked beast came out of nowhere and started attacking me. He must have been sired by Cerberus himself from the way he went on. I had to get out of there. There were some papers on the kitchen table, I picked them up without looking at them, then ran out the front door."

Blake peered at the ruby-red liquid in his glass. "In a way, your dog saved my ass. I passed you in the street only a minute later, as I imagine you soon realised. I don't know what would have happened if you'd have arrived home with me still there. It wouldn't have been good for either of us."

Worse for you, Blondeau thought smugly, judging from tonight's encounter at least. He decided it wouldn't exactly help things to say it out loud, though.

"I returned to my hotel that night," Blake continued, "and finally looked at what I'd taken. Sure enough, there was all the old *Zenobia* crap. Newspaper clippings, that damned Tatlock book. There was some other stuff as well, things that didn't seem so relevant, so maybe you weren't certain yet, but I knew you'd at least connected the dots."

Blondeau noted Blake's head shift an inch. He turned and saw a short, somewhat rough-looking bald man in a muddy high-vis jacket approaching their table. *Now this could get interesting...*

"Evening, chaps," the man smiled. "Will you be partaking in our quiz this evening?" He waved a bundle of papers at them.

Blondeau smiled back. "Sorry, not this time."

The man walked away, grumbling something about tourists. He didn't seem to have noticed Blake, which was strange, as by now the actor's efforts to be inconspicuous had to be accomplishing the opposite. If he pulled down his baseball cap any further the bill would be brushing his chin.

"I understand the break-in," Blondeau said once the other man was out of earshot, "but what about Venice and Los Angeles? What about the mask? What were you even hoping to achieve?"

"I just wanted to scare you off," Blake muttered. "I was never going to hurt you. I followed you all the way from the party in Venice. When that didn't seem to deter you, I decided to get a little cinematic. Hey, it's in my blood, OK? I got the mask made up from a prosthetics guy I know, told him it was for a Halloween party. It wasn't cheap, believe me."

"I'm sure you could afford it."

"I didn't say I couldn't. I just want to put you in my shoes, to try and understand my desperation. If the truth ever came out about that Chekhov film, about what happened back then, it wouldn't just be my career down the pan, it would be my entire family's. No one would ever think of the name Blake again without thinking..." he faltered. "Murderer."

Blondeau started to laugh. He wasn't trying to be cruel, he just couldn't help it.

Blake frowned. "What the hell's so funny?"

"Not that I owe you an answer," he said, "but Chekhov's cut of *Bachelor* has absolutely nothing to do with what your father may or may not have done in a Jordanian hotel forty years ago."

"What do you mean?" Blake asked, eyes narrowed. "Of course it does. The kid he cast looks exactly like the guy who... well, you know."

"Just plain old nepotism I'm afraid. I'd have thought *you'd* have recognised it when you saw it."

Blake ignored the dig. "There was an additional nine minutes from the screening in New York that never made it into the final picture."

Blondeau shrugged. "Completely unrelated."

"Huh." Blake slumped back in his seat. The conversation he had never expected to have was clearly not going the way he had expected. He picked at his picture-perfect, shiny-white teeth, working it over in his mind. "How do you know this?" he said finally.

"I have my ways." Blondeau smiled. Wide. His knees were

rocking. He was thoroughly enjoying the shift in the power dynamic between them. Should he go further? He had learned by now to not reveal more information than was absolutely necessary; but sometimes, he simply couldn't resist.

He said, "It's too bad you were interrupted on your little visit to Ravenwood."

Blake's mouth fell for just long enough to confirm Blondeau's suspicions, then he recomposed himself like a true professional. "I guess we both know more about each other than we realised, huh?"

"Guess so."

"I'd been reading up on Chekhov's last days," Blake explained. "I got it in my head that his cut of *Bachelor* might still be somewhere at his estate." He shrugged. "My attempts to scare you off were evidently getting me nowhere, but I figured I could still cut your supply lines. If I could find the film and destroy it, you'd never be able to prove anything beyond what had already been said."

Blake had been right about that, Blondeau considered, though it had led him down a different path to what the actor had feared. He reckoned he owed Jon, Chekhov's enterprising squatter, another twenty quid for interrupting Blake in the act and scaring him off.

"Maybe if you'd been a little quieter that night," Blondeau said, "you'd have ended up in Paul Chekhov's bedroom and taken a peek under the bed." He didn't feel it necessary to add that his own reason for doing so was entirely accidental.

Blake could no longer keep composed. He said incredulously: "*You've* got Chekhov's Cut?"

"*I've* got Chekhov's Cut. And those extra nine minutes have nothing to do with your dear old daddy."

Blake was shell-shocked. He pushed his cap back up his face, forgetting his earlier caution, and slowly ran his fingernails down his cheeks. "You're not just saying this, right?"

Blondeau scoffed. "You think I'm trying to spare the feelings of the guy who's spent the last two months terrorising me?"

"Fair point."

"I don't know if your father killed that guy or not, and I'm getting the sense that you don't either"–Blake gave an unhappy nod–"but the truth about whatever went on all those years ago is probably going to stay hidden. At least from me." He could sense Blake's relief, mired among other emotions – a churn of regret, shame and barely contained rage at the injustice of it all.

At a table nearby, the pub quiz man was counting out change drawn from a deep coat pocket. The room was beginning to fill up.

"Look, man," Blake began, "I'm sorry for everything, I really am. This whole story just drives me crazy, you know? I finally mustered up the courage to ask my old man about it a few years ago, but... he's gone. His memories just aren't there anymore. And now I don't know what to do. A little part of me wishes Chekhov *had* revealed the truth about it, at least then I'd know for sure. Every time I drive my kids out to see their grandpa, I have it in the back of my mind that I'm taking them to a killer."

Blondeau had a long drink of his beer to cover for the fact that he really didn't know what to say. He had never been good at this kind of stuff. He forced a smile. "I think on balance, I preferred your wife's approach to this whole business. At least she was out in the open."

Blake cringed. "I'm sorry about that as well. It's the only way Valentina knows how to do things – fire, threats and fury. I guess that's the Latin temperament for you." He raised his eyebrows and puffed his cheeks. "I can't say I wasn't warned."

"Does she know about your... extracurricular activities?"

Blake shook his head. "No one does, for that matter." He added, grudgingly: "Except you. When she confronted you at the party in Venice, I knew I had to get her away from you as quickly as possible. I was certain that you'd put it together, that you'd recognise me as the man you passed outside your house that night."

"You're making me feel a little slow-witted."

"Or maybe I'm just not as instantly recognisable as I thought." His smile turned to a look of remorse. "My family have really done a number on you recently."

"I can't deny it's made the last few months more interesting. Stalked by a movie star, what a story!"

Blake seemed to suddenly remember his predicament. "Please don't tell anyone," he pleaded. "I'll make it up to you. Interviews, set reports – you name it."

"I've heard that before," Blondeau replied. But, in truth, he'd made his mind up about the whole matter minutes ago. "Fine. It's not like anyone would believe me, anyway."

At the bar the pub quiz man started testing his microphone. A family of four rushed in through the front door and headed straight to a table that must have been their usual. The kids were about the same age as Blondeau's. A simpler life, he thought with a sudden longing. He turned to Blake and sensed the actor was feeling the same thing. Blake wasn't a bad guy, he thought, just another flailing in the dark, trying to pick up the pieces from decades ago and finding only dust. Blondeau kept anticipating a great reveal, a moment when the true villain of the piece became clear and undeniable. Like Blofeld turning in his chair or Kevin Spacey losing his limp. Jason Voorhees' mom or Norma Bates's son.

All he found instead were lost men.

They sat together a while without saying anything, their thoughts each their own.

It was Blake who broke the silence: “Hey, if that film isn’t about my dad, what is it about?”

Blondeau looked at him and said nothing.

Seventeen
On the Run

Blondeau decided that *The Sixth Sense* was such a good film, he really didn't need to see anything else that week. He chose to skip his next appointment, a low-budget British thriller from a rookie director which none of his esteemed readers would likely have any interest in, and take the afternoon off. Unwind after a trying few days. Andrea had taken Marley to the groomers, a process that could never be described as quick, so he wouldn't even have to explain himself.

As he walked from Hampstead Underground Station to his home, he worked his way through the entirety of the Chekhov business, drilling his thoughts to a rhythm, repeating them until they became like a mantra. What he knew and what he didn't. What he'd discovered and what was left.

Paul Chekhov leaves America forever at the end of the 1960s – *attracted by the relative peace and privacy of England, burnt out after a gruelling stint filming in the Peruvian jungle; or fleeing, something, someone?* He becomes involved with the Shepherd Institute, a research centre not far from his country estate – *as a patient, attempting to treat one or many of his obvious issues; or working with the Institute, fulfilling his long-held interest in the extremes of the human mind?* A young man, Reginald DeLarge, is treated at the Institute. DeLarge goes on to assassinate a prominent politician – *did the Shepherd Institute somehow brainwash DeLarge into carrying out the attack? Nothing in his patient file suggests such an outcome, so why was Graham Renwick so scared to talk about it, all these years later?* Chekhov's involvement with the Shepherd Institute ends, he returns to the world of cinema – *a consequence of the Institute running out of funding, or a more acrimonious departure?* Decades later, Chekhov hides a reference to the Institute in his final film – *for whose eyes and what purpose?* Chekhov dies – *by his own hand or another's?* The scenes in question are removed before the film is released to the public – *but by who?*

There were still too many questions unanswered. He had still not been able to definitively prove Chekhov's connection to the Shepherd Institute in a way that couldn't be explained away as circumstantial. Worst of all, he was running out of people to ask. There was only one more he could think of and, given that he currently resided at Her Majesty's pleasure in Belmarsh Prison, it wasn't going to be easy.

Reginald DeLarge had been locked up now for twenty-odd years, almost forgotten by polite society. Imprisoned for a crime he surely did commit, but may not have had a choice in. Who could say what had happened to the man, physically and mentally, since.

Blondeau didn't know how he would gain access to him, nor how he would get him to talk even if he could. But he thought that if DeLarge could somehow confirm Chekhov's involvement with the Institute, perhaps recognising him from a photograph, it would be enough for Blondeau to finally take the story public and reap the benefits. There'd still be questions unanswered, sure, but by now it was likely as good as he was going to get. Someone else could iron out the remaining details while he was off shooting his TV show.

He arrived at his home and noted with relief that Andrea's car was nowhere to be seen. He was walking up the short path to his front door, fishing for his keys, when he caught a flash of movement through the living room window. Some intangible element of experience he'd gained over the past few months made him immediately duck down out of sight. He crept towards the door, then slowly along the wall. He peeked through the window.

Two men were standing in the middle of his living room. They wore grey suits in slightly different shades, their faces were pale, almost grey too. One looked about sixty, the other was younger. Blondeau had never seen them before in his life.

What the hell were they doing there? The answer, gained after a minute or so of observation, seemed to be looking around, in a fairly half-hearted manner. The younger one peered behind the sofa, the other was focused on a painting on the opposite wall, a watercolour of a fishing boat at sea that Andrea had picked up from somewhere years ago. He lifted the picture off the hook then quickly put it back.

Blondeau might not have known them, but he knew the type, somehow. It meant that the situation had changed. The past had charged out from the darkness and roared in his face, teeth bared.

Through the window, the two men exchanged a few words, then the younger one walked off out of sight. He came back a few moments later, clutching a box of teabags. The other man yawned and nodded.

Still low to the ground, Blondeau moved back along the path to his car, parked on the street a short distance down the road. He slipped his keys in the door, ignoring the curious look of a passing dog walker, and clambered inside.

He turned the engine on and drove away with as much calm as he could muster.

The pub was called The Green Man. It was in Hurley, a village on the south bank of the Thames, about a forty-minute drive from West London. Blondeau and Andrea had first visited it a few months ago, in the middle of summer. He had been surprised then to see the river run clear, swimmers in the shallows. A few small wooded islands were being used for picnicking. It was an idyllic scene. The roast had been alright, too.

Now he thought about it, sat in sight of the table they'd had that day, their previous visit had been just a few days before he had interviewed Chase Ashley, and all the trouble had begun. How simpler his life would be if only they had undercooked the chicken.

But the most important thing right now about The Green Man in Hurley? Accommodation.

Blondeau had driven straight from his home to the dog groomers, a small flat in Camden that seemed the only place in the city willing to take on such a task. The usual girl opened the door, a yapping Yorkshire Terrier beside her, and hastily informed him that Andrea had gone off somewhere while she toiled away. She invited him in to wait. He went and sat in the car instead.

Half an hour later he saw her walking up the street, coffee in hand. Then she saw him and her face fell. It was as if the moment she had been expecting for a long time had finally come to pass.

This time around Blondeau confessed everything. Even the

stuff he could have probably still got away with. He told her about the break-in at their house and the stolen documents. The barely believable tale of the man in the mask, their fight in the rain and all that came after. Finally, he told her about the grey men currently moping around their living room.

Andrea stayed calm throughout, listening without interruption, her only visible reaction a slow tightening of the jaw. Blondeau was disturbed by her lack of outrage. He had played the conversation in his head a dozen times as he'd waited, yet had never planned for *that*. It seemed that, with a level of cold pragmatism he had not before seen in her, she had decided to focus entirely on the problem at hand. Dealing with him would come later.

And so their life on the run began. Doing their amateurish best to make sure they weren't being followed, they dropped the dog off at Andrea's sister in Uxbridge, claiming they needed some time alone to deal with certain marital issues. Though Blondeau had remained outside in the car, he didn't think his wife would have to try too hard to make it sound convincing. Then they drove to The Green Man, simply the first place that came to mind, and booked a room for the night.

What came next – who knew? Blondeau was happy for tomorrow to wait until tomorrow.

Inside, the pub was all dark oak, stone floors, open fireplaces and shadowy nooks. The patrons looked different this time around, middle-class London day-trippers replaced with the kind of variety of locals only possible in a village with a single pub.

They sat at a table at the side of the main room, Blondeau facing out to the bar and the front entrance. His recent experiences had taught him to prefer it that way.

Every swing of the old wooden door cost his heart a beat.

This time it was a couple. Middle-aged, with faded clothes and fleshy faces. They seemed normal enough. Probably an accountant and a nurse, something like that. Happy for a night out, even just the local pub. Probably one of them would say as such soon. They shook the rainfall off their clothes. The woman looked around as the man headed to the bar.

Blondeau turned back to his table. Andrea hadn't taken her eyes off him. She drilled her cigarette into the ashtray and immediately lit another.

He smiled awkwardly. "I was thinking tomorrow we could try The Golden Eagle, up in Ashwell. Bob Starkey from *The Times* was raving about it the other day."

She said nothing, just kept staring at him. His forehead felt like it was burning.

A crack of thunder hushed the room. At the bar the accountant ordered a gin and tonic and a pint of Carling. Normal enough. A dog, sat with a lone drunk, gave a low growl. The students by the window huddled together conspiratorially.

Blondeau tried again: "Or there's The Clarendon Inn at Amersham? We've been talking about that one for a while, what better time to–"

"I am not," Andrea grit her teeth, "spending another single night in some pub in the middle of nowhere. While you... pretend everything's fine, all the while you're glancing over at the front door every ten seconds and thinking I won't notice."

He sighed. *So she'd noticed.* "I never said things were fine, OK? I'm just saying we should try and make the best of a bad situation."

She leant forward, her words barely more than a whisper, "And I'm just saying, that you need to go home and get those men out of our house." She scowled. "How many chances did you have to walk away from this? How many times did I tell you that some things were best left in the past? But you had to keep scratching away, didn't you?"

Blondeau held his hands up in protest. "How could I have possibly known things would end up like *this*?"

She moved closer to him still, he could smell the nicotine and red wine on her breath. "Tomorrow morning," she nodded as she said it. "Tomorrow morning, you are going to go home and get those men out of my house."

Blondeau grimaced but said nothing. In his periphery the door swung open again, but, for once, he held her gaze.

"Fine," he said at last. He finished off his IPA and slammed the glass down. "Fine."

The rain pattered on the windows. The thunder rumbled. The dog howled.

Eighteen
The Men in Blondeau's House

Up the path, keys in hand. No sign of life.

Key in the door. Open.

Breathe.

Enter.

The house was silent. The house was still. The lights were off, there was post on the floor. Blondeau crept forwards. The hum of the fridge slowly became audible. *Was it normally?*

He searched from room to room, downstairs to up, even the attic. And then back down, out and through the garden.

There was nothing.

The grey men were gone. Everything was as it had been. They could at least have washed up.

It shouldn't have come as a surprise, he supposed. It's not like they could stay there forever. It's not like they needed to.

He made a coffee, added a shot of whiskey to steady his nerves. He drank in before he should have, fire in his mouth and his belly.

With nothing better to do, he walked through to the living room and switched on the TV. It was the middle of the morning. *City Hospital* on BBC, Nick Knowles and Gaby Roslin. *Trisha* on ITV. Christ. Inane drivel. Didn't they realise the world might be ending in a few weeks' time? That *his* might be heading that way only minutes from now? He let the empty chatter wash over him, like a scalding shower numbing his senses.

It took half an hour for the knock on the door to come. Blondeau finished his coffee, turned off the TV and trudged to the front door. He opened it.

There they stood. The same men, the same grey suits and the same grey faces. The older one had a lined face with a short moustache, his hair was parted in the middle. He wore a silver tie clip that was somehow the most interesting thing about him. His younger partner was chubby, with short-cropped brown hair. He looked at Blondeau with hungry, wolfish eyes.

"Mr. Blondeau," Tie Clip smiled. "Perhaps we could come in?"

Blondeau smiled right back at him. "Of course."

He stood back from the door and allowed the men into the hallway. They looked around, admiring the pine console table and the paintwork as if they had not been there only a day prior.

"Can I get you chaps anything to drink?"

Tie Clip – apparently the senior of the duo not just in age – smiled again and shook his head. "No, thank you. We really can't stay for long." He spoke the Queen's English. Formative years at Eton or Harrow or similar, no doubt.

They went through to the living room, Blondeau gesturing them towards the sofa. They looked awkward sat there. Tie Clip leant forward, forearms on knees. Wolf Eyes reclined in the corner, spreading himself out. Blondeau sat in the armchair to the side of them.

Tie Clip cleared his throat. "We'll get straight to the point," he said. "I'm afraid it's about time for you to ease off on this business, old chap."

Blondeau went through the motions, "I don't know what you're talking about."

Wolf Eyes then spoke for the first time in a brusque tone: "Let's not waste any more time with this, eh?" His manner could not have been further from Tie Clip's. He had a coarse East End accent and made no attempt to hide it.

"We've tried to take a hands-off approach with you until this point," Tie Clip sighed. "We thought you might burn yourself out, but, in retrospect, that may well have been a miscalculation on our part. So now we are going to have to make an intervention." He motioned apologetically. "We don't like it any more than you."

Blondeau let out a short bitter laugh. "What I don't like," he snarled, "is an innocent man rotting away in jail."

Wolf Eyes scoffed. "'*Innocent*,' he says."

Tie Clip winced. "No one in their right mind could possibly like such a situation. But you surely realise you can't change anything about that? You don't have the evidence, old chap. All you can do is make an almighty mess."

"Perhaps that's good enough for me at this point," Blondeau replied, jaw clenched. "It's strange – I'd have thought people from your part of the world would have been very interested in what I'd uncovered. Sounds like you knew it all already, though. Which means, I suppose, that Philip Lakewell must have had more serious enemies than a bunch of lentil-eating crusties."

Blondeau thought he was pushing his luck, but Tie Clip only held up his hands in surrender. "You've got to understand, old chap, this is before our time as well. It was a terrible thing what happened, you won't hear any argument from us." He paused, lips slightly parted, as if considering whether to continue. "The impression I get is that Mr. Lakewell, while doubtless a man of great talent, was not exactly the sort our country needed in a position of power."

"Why not?"

Wolf Eyes grinned. "*He had big ideas.*"

Blondeau had the immediate sense it was about all he was going to get from them. "Fine. You've made your little intervention. Now what? Because I don't think the Shepherd Institute is quite equipped to send one of their zombies after me these days."

Tie Clip looked genuinely offended. "Come on, old chap. We don't do that sort of thing anymore." He shook his head. "This is the modern age. We're not here to scare you – we want to help you. We can do a lot to help our friends."

Blondeau shrugged. "I don't need any help."

"Are you sure about that?" Wolf Eyes smirked. "All happy at work, are you? No frustrations, no sense your life's slowly drifting away from you with nothing to show for it?"

Someone's talked, then. Though Blondeau would struggle to narrow the suspects down – he hadn't exactly been tight-lipped on such matters. Two pints were normally enough to open the floodgates.

Tie Clip leant across and patted Blondeau on the knee. "You've done some bloody good work with this, old chap. I admire you, truly. Dogged, determined, ingenious at times. We haven't had someone get so close to this whole business in a long time." He clasped his hands together. "We know you had in mind taking this all public and reaping the rewards. But there's no reason why you can't achieve the latter without all the bother of the former."

So that was it. They hadn't turned up to spray his brains over his luxurious deep-pile carpet – they wanted to cut a deal.

Blondeau didn't doubt they had the power to offer him all he wanted. At long last, the career boost he had chased was within touching distance.

He should have felt triumphant. He knew why he didn't. At the start, the whole Chekhov mystery had been a means to an end; but somewhere along the way, it had become much more than that. Could he really give it all up now? Could he live with himself, knowing he held the truth but could never reveal it to the world?

"What if I turn down your wonderful offer?" he asked tentatively. "What happens then?"

Wolf Eyes chuckled. "I find that no one ever asks that question without already knowing the answer."

Blondeau got his meaning. He tried not to let his imagination run away with him.

"It's not going to need to come to that though, is it, Stephen?" Tie Clip smiled like a man without the slightest doubt in the world. "You must see the logic in taking up our offer?"

What would Andrea say? Why even ask. She'd tell him to bite their hands off. To stop being such a bloody fool about the whole thing. Hell, even James Raikes would say the same by this point. These weren't men to mess with. Tie Clip might have been playing the friendly uncle, but Blondeau was certain the man would act without hesitation, just as easily as Wolf Eyes, if it came to it. They wouldn't have been in that business otherwise. They were offering him a way out, how could he refuse?

Wolf Eyes was showing signs of impatience. He rubbed the face of his watch with his thumb. "You must know that we were here yesterday, which means you also know that we have the papers from the Institute that you stole. All we need now is the film."

Blondeau thought he saw Tie Clip shoot his younger colleague a look of annoyance, and he thought he knew why, too. Wolf Eyes had slipped up, and changed the whole balance of things.

The film. His thoughts traversed from his current surroundings, across the city to a safety deposit box in Bromley that he had opened the day before his visit to the Shepherd Institute. It was funny how things worked. He'd been considering closing it and bringing the film home, thinking that his unmasking of Noah Blake meant it was no longer in threat. If these men had turned up just a few days later, the whole situation would have been very different.

So they didn't know where Chekhov's Cut was. Which meant he still had leverage. Whatever they hinted at, they surely wouldn't harm him, knowing the evidence was still out there. He still had a choice in all of this. He thought he might prefer it if he didn't.

"The film," Tie Clip gently prodded, "and your word."

And my soul.

Wolf Eyes bared his teeth.

Tie Clip smiled.

Blondeau gave his answer.

TEN MONTHS LATER…

Nineteen
The Premiere

> "A curse?" Blondeau smiled darkly. "Who among us can truly say? But whether simply a series of unfortunate events, or something *more*"–he raised an eyebrow–"one thing remains clear. More than twenty-five years since its release, the horror of *The Exorcist* lives on."

The camera cut to black and the credits rolled. Applause broke out in Blondeau's living room that seemed genuine enough. Someone patted him on the shoulder. Someone else called for an encore.

It wasn't a bad effort, Blondeau had decided. And the Bruce Lee episode next week was a hell of a follow up; he'd really hit his stride with that one. The lighting could use some work, though. He'd seen lines on his face he was certain weren't there in real life.

He stood up from the sofa and made his way across the living room, claiming to be bringing drinks, actually seeking to soak in the adulation.

James Raikes was leaning in the doorway to the kitchen, a bottle of Kronenbourg in one hand. A banner proclaiming

"Congratulations" hung above his head.

Raikes feigned a look of concern as Blondeau approached. "Promise me you won't forget about your old friends now that you're a big star, OK?"

Blondeau shrugged. "I suppose I might still be able to fit you in at some point."

"Hey, I'm the one who helped you with all of this, remember? The party in Venice, the mansion–"

"It's probably best if we don't talk about that anymore," Blondeau said through gritted teeth. "I thought we'd discussed this."

Raikes raised his bottle. "Whatever you say. After all, you're the man of the hour."

Blondeau couldn't argue with that. Channel 4 had said they'd inform him of the ratings as soon as they had them, but it would surely be in the millions. *Millions.* He'd have to get used to being recognised more frequently, and not just by oversensitive football thugs.

It surely couldn't hurt to start thinking about the second season either. There were plenty more tales from the dark side of Hollywood to tell. It was just a shame there was one in particular he'd never be able to...

In the corner of his eye he spotted movement near the front door. His parents were putting on their coats.

"Are you leaving already?" he asked them. "Why not stay for another drink?"

His father shook his head brusquely. "We must get going, son," he said, without explaining why.

"Did you like the programme?"

His parents glanced at each other, memories of Linda Blair's projectile pea soup clearly not far from their minds.

"Oh, yes," his mother said eventually. "We're er... we're very proud of you."

"That we are," his father added. He looked around, as if searching for the words. "You've got a very nice house here, son."

Blondeau thought it was about as good as he could reasonably expect from them. He watched as they wandered off down the path from his house, bickering about in which direction they had left the car, before closing the door.

He could hear the opening strings of *The Exorcist* itself coming from the living room. Max Von Sydow was about to spend ten minutes wandering around Iraq, while all those who had never before seen it were about to spend ten minutes wondering if someone had changed the channel.

It was genius scheduling. The film had been banned for years and yet now, suddenly, the censors had changed their minds about the whole matter. It would surely do wonders for his ratings. Funny how so many little things like that seemed to be going in his favour these days.

He walked through instead to the kitchen. The counters were covered with bottles, cans and glasses; the table with plates of cocktail sausages, crisps, scotch eggs, skewers with cheese and pineapple cubes and a nondescript quiche. What the hell were they going to do with it all?

Andrea stood by the sink. She was peering down at a glass of red wine, held loose in one hand.

Blondeau cleared his throat to announce his presence. "So that's that, then."

She looked across at him, studied him. Then she smiled. "That's that, then."

He walked over and stood beside her, just close enough to feel the hint of her arm on his. "You know, I really feel like this is the beginning of a new chapter in our lives."

He felt her tense up. She shifted away, just slightly. *What had he done now?*

"*I* was happy with the old one," she said, measuring her words. "But I guess... we are where we are."

She walked into the middle of the room, pressed her hands on the kitchen table, shoulders hunched. Then she turned back around. The coolness fell away and she came closer once more, rested her arms on his shoulders, leant her head against his.

"I did do the right thing, didn't I?" he asked her. He hadn't planned to, and he couldn't say why now, of all times, the thought had come to him. But for whatever reason, he suddenly had to know.

"You did the right thing," she said straight away, with no doubt in her voice. She arched an eyebrow. "Well, actually, you did the wrong thing, repeatedly, for months, and then finally the right thing, only at the last possible moment. It's almost depressing how well it seems to have worked out for you."

He grinned. "How else would anything interesting ever happen in life?"

She rolled her eyes. "Just remember you're a married man now that you're famous, OK? Any groupies will have to answer to me."

It was essentially the same joke Raikes had made but Blondeau didn't mind. He was about to recycle his response when suddenly there was a shout – and a bark – from down the hall. They rushed over.

Turnbull from down the road was being accosted by Marley just outside the downstairs toilet. The dog had him pinned against the door, his arms held up in a feeble defence. It was immediately clear that there was only going to be one winner.

"Down, boy!" Blondeau pulled the dog off his neighbour and dragged him out into the garden to cool off.

He came back over to the scene of the crime. Poor Turnbull looked near catatonic.

"I'm really sorry," Andrea was saying to him, her hand on his shoulder. "It's why we don't have too many gatherings like this around here. All these people, all the noise. He's just not the right kind of dog for such occasions."

She carried on talking but Blondeau no longer heard her. He no longer heard anything for that matter. Just that phrase, repeating in his head.

Not the right kind of dog.

Hmm. Interesting.

That surely couldn't be it. Could it?

He left them there, standing in the hallway. Made his way over to the stairs. Someone waved to him from the living room but he barely noticed it. He walked up the stairs.

Not the right kind of dog.

He continued all the way up to the attic, then switched on the lights. Entered the projection room, rummaged around.

He found it.

The videotape of Paul Chekhov's final public appearance, at the awards show in London. He'd discovered the footage at the BBC archives, just before his trip to Venice the previous year, and had requested his own copy made. Just in case.

He put the tape in the VCR. Fast-forwarded to the moment in question. Pressed play.

He walked back through to the main room and watched as Chekhov appeared from the side of the stage, award in hand.

Blondeau had thought the whole thing strange when he'd

first watched it. How Chekhov walked across to the podium, how he looked around the room as he spoke, how he greeted the recipient of the award. But he'd never been able to place it. Until now.

Not the right kind of dog.

Yes, he saw it now. It had been right there in front of him all along.

At last he knew the truth.

Twenty The Life and Death of Paul Chekhov

The front gates to the apartment block were open when he arrived. He walked through to the courtyard, centred on a large olive tree. There were koi fish and turtles swimming in a fountain, an outdoor fireplace, wooden benches tucked in the shade. And plants, all around.

There was not a person in sight. Blondeau walked down the narrow stone pathway to the rear of the building. He reached the door at the end and knocked.

He heard muffled sounds and a female voice coming from beyond the door. It opened. An elderly woman stood there, smiling. Her face was lined and thin, her hair a natural grey, but there was a brightness in her eyes that belied her years.

"Come in, Mr. Blondeau," Clara Davis said.

Blondeau followed her through to the living room. The racket had already begun, but at least he was prepared for it this time. He counted four birds, all in their cages. The last cage was gone.

"I'm afraid dear Conrad has passed on," Clara explained, following his eyes. "It happened only a few weeks ago."

"Oh," Blondeau said. "I'm sorry. Are you going to er... replace him?"

Clara gave a wistful look. "In time."

Blondeau didn't think that any of the other birds looked particularly upset. He didn't rule out foul play.

Clara gestured for him to take a seat on the sofa. "I must admit I was a little surprised when I received your call," she said. "I'd thought we'd covered all there was to cover last time. And I never did manage to track down that article you were writing. Not for want of trying, either."

There was more than a little suspicion in her words, but Blondeau ignored it. "There were a few details I think we missed."

"Such as?"

He fixed his eyes on hers, as if steadying his aim. *Here goes nothing...*

"That Paul Chekhov was blind, for one thing."

Clara's smile froze on her face like a mask. "Now where would you have got such an idea from?"

Blondeau raised his eyebrows. "He had the wrong kind of dog."

She looked at him with puzzlement. "I'm not sure I quite understand–"

"All those stories about intruders at Chekhov's estate in the weeks leading up to his death. He'd been so concerned that he'd bought a dog for protection, apparently. The strange thing is I met that dog, at Constance Chekhov's house. A nice boy, a bit over affectionate perhaps, but I've always liked Labradors, ever since my family had one when I was growing up."

He paused for dramatic effect. "Though I hardly think they'd make the best guard dogs," he added finally. "A little too friendly, a little too sleepy, a little too greedy. I'm no expert, but I imagine you'd probably want something like a German shepherd or a Dobermann for that kind of thing."

Clara had shown no reaction to any of it. She must have known by now where Blondeau was heading, yet seemed content to let him go.

He concluded: "Labradors do make pretty good guide dogs, though." He chewed his lip, bunched his hands, waiting for the response.

Clara smiled stiffly. "Very impressive, Mr. Blondeau."

"*Very impressive!*" one of the birds agreed. "*Very good!*"

Blondeau couldn't deny he felt much the same way. It *was* impressive, even if it had taken him a while. Watching Chekhov at the awards show had been the confirmation he needed. The director's mannerisms, the way he peered out at the audience – it all fit a man struggling with his sight and trying to hide it. Once you saw it, it was clear as day.

He'd realised soon after that there had been another clue, one he couldn't share. The bewildering array of artificial lights at Chekhov's Ravenwood estate. For a normal person it was excessive, almost absurdly so. But a man battling the loss of his sight needed every soldier he could muster.

"Why didn't you tell me?" he asked her.

"Why on earth would I?" she replied with what seemed like genuine confusion. "It was Paul's battle and certainly not one he wished to make public. He'd had issues with his sight for years, though things really began to deteriorate during the *Bachelor* shoot. Paul was determined that no one would find out, so we were forced to improvise. He relayed instructions through me to avoid direct communication with the rest of the crew."

"But why go to all that effort; why not just be open about it?"

"The last thing Paul Chekhov wanted was the world's sympathy," Clara sniffed. "We managed to get through *Bachelor* more or less intact. And, as usual, Paul wanted to sink his teeth straight into his next project, but by that point he couldn't even properly view location photographs, couldn't read a script, no matter how large we blew it up." She looked pained at the memory. "There's only so long you can fight these things."

Blondeau remembered the photos and the costumes he had discovered at the Ravenwood estate. Another Chekhov project lost to the world. Another tale he'd never be able to tell.

He said, "Then all that talk of intruders was just–"

"–the imagination of a blind man running away with him," Clara admitted. "He had a load of old standees – those big cardboard displays at cinemas – around his house, with characters from all his films over the years. I eventually put two and two together and realised that those were his 'intruders.'" She pursed her lips. "It's ironic, really, he'd become terrified of his own creations. Once I worked it out, I had them moved to storage to try to prove to him he had nothing to be afraid of."

Blondeau slammed his eyes shut with frustration. He remembered seeing them there, as he and Raikes had searched the stables, in the room with the costumed mannequins. He should have made the connection, there and then. Still, no one was perfect.

"And that's why he killed himself?" he asked. "The blindness?"

Clara nodded grudgingly. "He'd been warning me that he'd do it for years, as soon as he reached the point of being unable to work. Filmmaking was his entire life, always had been. He saw no point in continuing without it. And nothing I said could ever change his mind. I had my suspicions when he sent me off to New York for the *Bachelor* screening that he was trying to get me out the way to get it over with, but what could I do?"

Blondeau had no answer. Over time, the possibility that Chekhov had been murdered had built up in his mind like a snowball rolling downhill, to the point that it had become all he could see, but the more straightforward answer had always been there. The legendary director stripped of his sight. Unable to compose a shot, unable to read lines, his entire reason for being slowly tugged from his grasp. A control freak forced to rely on others for even the most basic of tasks. He could imagine how intolerable such a situation would have been for a man like Chekhov, how the barrel of his shotgun might have felt more appealing one cold lonely night in his rambling estate.

Clara sat watching him. Her hands were flat on the sofa; she looked poised to stand and show him to the door.

Unfortunately for her, he was only getting started...

"Tell me about the Shepherd Institute."

Her eyes widened. "I really have underestimated you." She glanced at the window. "Who else have you told?"

"No one." It wasn't technically true, but for practical purposes it might as well have been. Any evidence he'd ever had to prove his story was long gone by now. "And I hope to keep it that way. I'd just- well, I'd appreciate it if you could fill in the blanks for me, for my own understanding if nothing else." He knew there was the hint of a threat behind his words. He hoped it would be enough. Clara couldn't possibly know that hints were as far as he could ever go.

"Very well," Clara acquiesced. She drew a breath, looking as if she'd rather be discussing anything else in the world. "Paul was first contacted by the men from the Institute shortly after he moved to Ravenwood. They told him about their research. They told him they were working with troubled characters – repeat offenders, the mentally ill – finding new ways to help such people reintegrate into society. One of the things they were particularly interested in was the use of film as a part of the patients' therapy. Well, who better to ask?"

"And Chekhov accepted their offer?"

"Not straight away. He was initially set on moving forward with a film about Alexander the Great. He'd been planning it ever since he first picked up a camera. But after a year the project had gone nowhere. Paul had gotten bogged down, lost in the research." She shook her head sadly. "I always thought that somehow, subconsciously, he wanted it that way, rather than to have to head back into the outside world for another shoot, after what had happened in Peru. It had reached the point where he'd read practically all there was to read about the man, he'd run out of excuses. The offer from the Institute suddenly became more appealing.

"It wasn't just about occupying himself, though," she added. "Paul really did want to help those people. Or at least, he wanted to see if he could, if that was something that film could be a part of. He always like to push the envelope of the medium." She looked away from Blondeau, to the photo of Chekhov on the mantelpiece. Then she turned back, clasping her frail hands together.

"So it began. We..." She hesitated. "How should I say this? We 'encouraged' the rumour that Paul had suffered a breakdown shooting *Heart's Desire* as a way to explain his absence. That's not to say he didn't suffer out there, of course, just not quite to the extent we implied. You have to take advantage of these things, Mr. Blondeau."

"What did his work actually consist of?" he asked, eagerness in his voice.

"He spent the first few years trying to figure precisely that out. He had some research files from the British and American governments, but nothing that seemed to have been very successful. Initially, he spent a lot of time working with subliminal messaging. So, for example, he'd edit single frames of calming imagery – ocean waves, sunsets, birds in flight – into regular TV shows and films, and have patients with violent tendencies watch them. Or he'd play around with the audio. Adding in positive phrases under the main track, or played backwards, or just outside the frequency range of normal human hearing. He tried everything in other words, and none of it seemed to make a scrap of difference."

Blondeau wasn't surprised. He remembered looking up everything he could about subliminal messaging the previous year, at the height of his investigation. There'd been plenty of attempts, sure, but nothing that seemed to have produced any tangible results. Not even Paul Chekhov could work magic.

He asked, "At what point did they introduce the drugs?"

Clara frowned. "At some point you really are going to have to tell me how you know about all of this." She let out a deep breath. "They started all that when it became clear the subliminal work was getting them nowhere. The doctors came up with some concoction. I'm not sure Paul knew the details, nor wanted to. The purpose was twofold: to make the patients more open to suggestion, and to make it so they wouldn't remember what was being done to them." She shook her head grimly. "But it had no impact on the existing work whatsoever. That's when they decided on a less... subtle approach.

"They called it 'blasting,'" she explained. "Instead of splicing in single frames, Paul created entire films full of therapeutic imagery. Most was stock footage but some he shot himself, close to the estate. By this point he was engrossed in the project, desperate to make it work, he was working at a feverish pace. Criminals would be shown scenes of groups of people, sometimes animals, working together, to foster the idea of making a positive contribution to a wider community. He even did one for anorexics at one point, with shots of healthy athletes and models eating chocolate cakes and so forth." She shrugged. "Like I said, it wasn't subtle. There'd be messages overlaid, in text and audio. And it was all done with this godawful soundtrack, pulverising electronic beats that never let up."

Blondeau tried to imagine it. Being shot full of psychedelics, forced to sit through such films for hours at a time, over and over, for weeks, months, more. "Sounds like torture," he said.

"It's funny," Clara replied, "nowadays our youth pay good money to go and stand in the middle of nowhere and have similar experiences. But Paul had always had the belief that you could wear down people in such a manner. It's one of the reasons he did so many takes when filming. He believed you could slowly strip away an actor's defensive layers, until they were nothing more than a blank canvas that you could do as you pleased with." She grimaced. "I'm afraid that at the Shepherd Institute, he met some kindred souls in that belief. The treatment was like a sledgehammer, smashing its patients to pieces, all to allow them to be put back together, in a better way."

She paused, considering her words. "But you must understand, even at its worst, Paul always believed he was helping those people. His intentions were always good."

The road to hell is paved with good intentions. Once more Blondeau remembered the patient notes of Daniel Alushi: "There is no incontinence, there is no mutism, there is no retrograde amnesia." How much had Chekhov known about that aspect of his little experiments?

He asked: "What happened to Reginald DeLarge wasn't so good though, was it?"

Clara didn't react to the name. By now it seemed she had simply accepted that there were no limits to Blondeau's knowledge. "*That* was nothing to do with Paul," she said stiffly.

"Why should I believe you?" Blondeau sneered. "You don't think I've noticed that at every stage of this you're painting Chekhov in as positive a light as possible? I've seen Soviet propaganda films with better balance."

Clara bristled with indignation. "It's true. He barely interacted with the patients themselves, beyond occasional observation. When news of the shooting emerged and DeLarge's lawyer started spouting off about brainwashing, Paul became concerned. He got it in his head that he recognised DeLarge from the Institute. I'm not sure whether it was true or whether it was Paul's paranoia running away with him."

"Either way he was correct, though. Right?"

Clara measured her words: "Yes... and no. Paul began to investigate, asking round at the Institute, looking through old files." She sighed. "It's not what you think it is."

"No?"

"Reginald DeLarge *had* been treated at the Institute. He was a repeat offender with violent tendencies, in other words a perfect candidate. He took one of the standard treatments Paul had devised for such instances. What's more, he turned out to be one of their most successful cases. He was released back into society and, by all accounts, kept himself out of trouble. That's the thing, you see? DeLarge left the Institute years before he shot that politician. Paul had nothing to do with it."

For the first time since they had started talking, Blondeau was genuinely puzzled. “So what happened?”

“That’s when Paul discovered the truth about the Shepherd Institute. Without his knowledge, the methods he had developed had been inverted. Instead of using positive imagery to heal patients, they were doing the opposite, to instil anger and hatred. Paul’s techniques had become weaponised. Worst of all, they turned that weapon on their most successful cases. At their best, Paul’s films only worked on about one in ten patients. As these were the patients considered most receptive to the treatment, they were brought back to the Institute on some pretext or other and... *reconstructed* all over again.”

Blondeau was immediately sceptical. It all felt a little too convenient. “And that’s what happened to Reginald DeLarge?”

Clara nodded. “Paul never saw the films themselves, but it’s not hard to imagine. Images of the chosen target alongside those of disaster, destruction and misery. Make them the cause of all human suffering. Especially the patient’s. Make it so removing them from the world seems like the only reasonable thing to do. It must have simple beyond that. Give them a gun and let the scene play out.” She spread her hands theatrically.

“But why Philip Lakewell?”

“In regard to that I have nothing more than speculation. Paul had never been under any illusions that the Institute was connected to the British government. Lakewell must have made enemies in the wrong places.” She said it with disinterest, as if she considered the whole Lakewell business one step too far removed.

“Paul was drawn between natural curiosity,” she continued, “and a desire to protect his own hide. It’s funny, I think before *Heart’s Desire* the former would have won out. But it’s like I told you – the Paul Chekhov who came out of that jungle was a different man than the one who went in. He politely ended his relationship with the Institute and returned to making real films. His only hope was that whole business would never be spoken about again." She practically shuddered as she said it.

"And your hope as well?"

"Of course."

"It must have been tough for you, then," Blondeau said breezily, "when Chekhov changed his mind."

Clara narrowed her eyes. "Why would you say that?"

He shrugged. "Why else would you have cut those scenes out of the final version of *Bachelor*?"

And there it was at last. Straight away it felt as if the temperature in the room had dropped. Even the birds seemed to notice, quieting down, perching with their heads bowed.

"I think I have been fairly reasonable when confronted with your apparent omniscience," Clara said tightly, "but now I must protest. How on earth could you have possibly known that?"

Blondeau raised his eyebrows. "I didn't." *Until now.*

Clara screwed her eyes shut, defeated. She sucked in air through her teeth. "That was a rotten trick, Mr. Blondeau."

"Yes, well, don't expect an apology," Blondeau replied. "As soon as I realised you hadn't told me about Chekhov's blindness, I started to wonder what else you'd not been entirely honest about. Until then, I just had you down as a harmless little old lady."

Clara scowled. Blondeau wasn't sure whether it was from his description of her, or his realising how false it had been. Why hadn't he seen it before? Perhaps it was the birds that had distracted him on his first visit, keeping him on edge, and from seeing her for what she truly was. The birds were Clara's disguise.

Blondeau continued: "Then I thought it through. Victor Roache couldn't have done it, he never had the film before Constance took control of it. Now Constance, she could have, for sure, but she'd denied it so strenuously, I'd started to think I might actually believe her. Which left you. The only thing I don't understand is how you could have done it without Constance realising?"

Clara gave him a bemused look. "*That?* That was no trouble at all. I had a day at Ravenwood before she arrived. Once the police had gone, I was left there alone. Just myself and the film. I only needed a night."

"But who made the cuts?"

Clara sighed with frustration. "How is it that you still don't understand, even after all of this?" She didn't wait for an answer. "*I* made the cuts. Like I told you, Paul had me covering more and more of the responsibilities on *Bachelor* due to his declining sight. That included the editing. At that point he could still see the screen to know the right moment, but he didn't trust himself with the actual cutting itself, so I took over."

She sat up straight, shoulders arched, jaw tight. "In a just world, *Death of a Bachelor* would be a Paul Chekhov *and* Clara Davis film, instead of my name being two thirds of the way down the credits in a font so small you could barely make it out from the front row." She looked away. "But that's life, I suppose."

Blondeau tried to imagine how the whole thing had gone. Chekhov secretly handing over his responsibilities, one by one, as the shoot progressed. That old control freak had to have been one hell of a backseat driver. And Clara's increasing role in production must have been the reason the film felt so strangely disjointed. Unbeknown to the public, *Bachelor* was a film with two directors, two minds. No matter how close Chekhov and Clara's relationship had been over the years, no matter how hard she tried to emulate his methods, it had to have an impact.

"I worked right through that night cutting the film," Clara recalled, "sat in one of the buildings in the old stable block. Once the offending scenes had been removed, I put the reels back in the box only minutes before Constance arrived at the estate. She found me there sat beside them, half-asleep."

Blondeau nodded. It all added up. It worked.

Though there was still one thing he didn't understand...

"*Why?*"

Clara scoffed. "Isn't it obvious? If the truth had come out about what happened at that place, it would have forever tarnished how the world remembered Paul. Who now remembers Leni Riefenstahl or Elia Kazan for their talent, for the genius of their work? Someone needed to protect Paul's legacy." She gave a withering look. "Even from himself. He'd been acting like a damn fool getting that painting made up. I begged him to remove the scenes with it, but he wouldn't hear of it. I never knew whether it was simply mischief, or whether he truly wanted someone like you to pick the thread and unravel the whole affair. Well, either way, by killing himself, he lost his right to have a say in that matter as far as I'm concerned."

She looked straight into Blondeau's eyes. "I have no regrets and make no apologies for what I did. A man should not be defined by one mistake, especially one as great as Paul Chekhov."

Blondeau hadn't the slightest doubt she meant every word of it, that she'd do the same again if she had the chance. It rankled him. What right did she have to go against Chekhov's wishes, to decide that she knew best? Paul Chekhov had spent his career fighting with censors and studios to ensure his films were as true to his vision as possible. And yet, when it came to his own life, the world would only ever know the sanitised version. Paul Chekhov PG. It didn't sit right. It was a betrayal, no matter what justification Clara gave. Even Chekhov himself must not have thought her capable of such an act, or he'd have surely held out a little longer to ensure the film was released as intended.

He rose to his feet. There was really nothing more to be said.

Clara's eyes widened. "One moment, please," she said. She stood up and hurried off into the kitchen.

Blondeau waited. Not patiently. He'd never noticed before how airless the room felt. He wanted to get out of there, away from the murk of the past, the secrets and the lies.

Then Clara reappeared at the doorway. She held a knife in one hand, the tip pointed in his direction.

"I'm afraid I can't let you leave..."

Blondeau's eyes darted about the room for a weapon. There was a hardcover book on the coffee table, a ceramic table lamp that looked unwieldy. Perhaps he'd be better off just rushing her, or dashing for the exit. How fast could the old woman possibly be?

Clara raised the knife.

He was frozen with indecision. Why couldn't things ever end simply? *Why couldn't he have just left it all alone?*

Then Clara's other hand appeared in view, and the item it held.

"...without first having a piece of this carrot cake I baked earlier," she concluded, waving the plate in in his direction.

The harmless little old lady smiled. It was as if their entire conversation had never happened.

***

Stomach full, Blondeau left the house down the narrow stone path for what he hoped would be the last time. He walked through the courtyard and out onto the street. The California sunshine hit him like bleach. He let it wash over him, grateful for it.

So at last he had the truth.

Hadn't he?

It was a version of it, no doubt. Clara Davis was shrewd, but not enough to pull such details out of thin air. But as every unimaginative studio boss in L.A. knew, there was more than one way to tell the same story.

As he walked to his car he pictured another. One where Paul Chekhov knew full well what the Shepherd Institute were up to, where he was a willing participant in turning Reginald DeLarge and God knows how many others into walking bullets. In that version of events, perhaps the director had still felt some kind of guilt for what he'd done towards the end of his life. Or perhaps those scenes from *Death of a Bachelor*, now lost to the world forever, were nothing more than a homage to old colleagues.

Blondeau had got everything he wanted: the TV show, the respect – and jealousy – of his peers. But even after all this time, he was forced to admit: he still didn't know who the real Paul Chekhov was.

He had to check the address three times before he was certain of it. Not like that helped explain things. What possible reason could Constance Chekhov have for asking him to meet here – this drab two-floor brown-brick building in downtown L.A.?

He supposed there was only one way to find out. He walked to the entrance, squeezing past two idling workmen to make his way inside.

He entered a room with a reception desk with a high wooden counter and no one behind it. There was a stairway on the left, a pair of frosted glass doors to the right. Blondeau pushed through them, and that's when it started to make sense.

The room was long and austere. It had a jet-black wooden floor that reflected the spotlights above. There were three rows of glass cabinets of varying sizes running to the far end. The ones closest to him were empty. Halfway down the room, the last remaining Chekhov was talking to a younger woman with a clipboard.

Blondeau approached, his footsteps announcing his presence. The younger woman passed by with a hurried look. He was about to greet Constance when he glanced at the cabinet beside her and his words stuck in his mouth.

"Is that... one of the spacesuits from *Journey Beyond*?"

Constance smiled. "The very same."

Blondeau could hardly believe it. It was more than thirty years old yet looked pristine; the iconic bright orange hue hadn't faded at all. He could see his reflection in the visor.

Then he looked at the next cabinet. There was a mannequin wearing a diadem, dressed in a shade of deep, rich purple. He walked around Constance towards it.

"And this is–"

"Aurelian's toga from *Zenobia*," she answered patiently. "Apparently not entirely historically accurate, but you can't deny the sense of style."

Blondeau forced his eyes away from further cabinets back to her. "What's all this for?" he asked.

Constance narrowed her eyes. "You haven't heard?"

"I've haven't really kept up with Chekhov news for the past year or so, I'm afraid."

She seemed taken aback, and disappointed. "Well, *this* is my uncle's life work. Or at least it will be, once the other pieces arrive. We open to the public in a month's time, so they better hurry."

Blondeau turned back towards the entrance. "Interesting location for a museum."

"When the wind is right, you can almost taste Skid Row," she grinned. "I got offers from every film school in the city to house this stuff. And I nearly took them up; I can't deny it would have made life easier. Then I remembered how my uncle used to talk about such places. He'd come up the generation before Lucas, De Palma and the others, before those places existed, and it had always bugged him. He felt those guys had it easy, like they got given on a platter what he had to scrap for. 'If you want to learn filmmaking, get out of the classroom and go and make one,' he'd always say. And when I thought about that, suddenly it didn't feel right to stick all this behind the veil of academia. So I found this place." She waved her arms around. "The exterior needs a fresh paint job, but we're getting there."

Blondeau remembered why he had come. "I actually called you because I wanted to apologise. When we met last year, things got a bit full on. *I* got a bit full on, is what I mean to say. That wasn't entirely fair to you."

Constance scrutinised him. She gave a small nod, as if more for accepting his words were genuine than the apology itself. "If you want to make it up to me, you can write about this place in whatever publication you work for at the moment."

"I'm actually mainly on television these days," he said with attempted nonchalance.

"Even better," she replied, not even pretending to sound impressed. "Even a place like this is quite the investment in this city, so we need all the visitors we can get. And, of course, any and all profits will go to a good cause."

Blondeau laughed. The pygmy three-toed sloths of Panama had never had it so good. "I wouldn't have imagined it any other way."

He left her there to explore the rest of the room. *What treasures!* There was a scale model of the war-torn abbey of Monte Cassino, a fleet of miniature spacecraft and a rather disturbing array of human heads. There were Roman and Palmyrene swords and shields, World War II-era rifles, a jungle machete, a serial killer's dagger and a laser pistol from a future past. There were iron helmets and trilby hats and presidential suits and Elizabethan dresses and combat boots and stiletto heels and golden jewellery and casino chips.

The white walls were dotted with movie posters, photographs, storyboards and unrealised concept art. There was equipment, too – four decades of clapperboards, some of Chekhov's most beloved cameras and lenses, even a director's chair on a raised platform. He could already imagine some lard-arsed New Yorker reducing it to splinters.

He felt a particular jolt when coming face to face with Dr. Krauss's grotesque mask from *The Night Sessions*, thought back to that strange night when he had fought in the rain and the mud with a Hollywood A-lister, and then listened to his woes over a pint of bitter. It all felt like a dream.

Constance's arrival at his side returned him to the present. "There's something else I should show you."

She led him out of the main room and up the stairs on the left. There was a single door at the top. She opened it and waved him through.

Shelves full of cardboard boxes. That old story *again*.

Blondeau knew immediately what they were. He nearly blurted it out, before reminding himself which of his many secrets still mattered.

"These are from my uncle's estate in England," Constance said. "And there's plenty more to come. My uncle wrote everything down regarding the production of his films, and kept all of it. What you see downstairs – the costumes and the props – they might be the highlights of his career, but these boxes are the day-to-day reality of it."

She let out a short laugh. "You're not going to believe this, but when we started moving this stuff over from England, we found a homeless guy squatting at the estate."

"Unbelievable," Blondeau said, stern-faced.

"I know, right? We got the poor guy some help, but the truth is, if he'd known the true value of what was all around him, he could have really screwed things up for us." She winced at the thought of it.

She led Blondeau down the side of the room to an area with a small block of desks. "The plan is for downstairs to be open to all," she said, "but up here, all of this, you'll need to book ahead, this is for research."

Blondeau felt a sudden tightness in his chest. "You surely can't have read everything here," he said carefully. "What if someone finds out something they shouldn't? Something that doesn't reflect too well on your uncle?"

Constance shrugged. "What of it? My uncle was a great man; I never said he was a saint. If there's something in here that people should know, let them find it."

Blondeau admired her for it. More than she could possibly understand.

"Besides," she added, "how bad could it possibly be?"

He looked into her dark brown eyes. They were the only thing she shared with her uncle, yet at that moment, as they stood among the ocean of boxes that comprised his life, they were enough to make the resemblance clear.

I wouldn't know where to start.

He spent the rest of the morning there, leafing through but a small portion of Chekhov's letters, memos, contracts, plans, notes and general musings. If any of his secrets were hidden in those boxes, Blondeau didn't find them. Perhaps someone else would one day. Perhaps correspondences with the likes of Charles Chevalier or Leonard Blake would shine a light on another part of the most unfathomable of lives. Perhaps it would make the person who discovered them famous, wealthy and admired.

Blondeau was OK with that.

It was time for he and Paul Chekhov to part ways.

The California sun cast clear from a cloudless sky as he left the place. He drove to his hotel, picked up his suitcase and checked out.

He took a taxi to the airport and went home.

The End

A message from the author

Dear reader,
Thanks for taking the time to read this book, I hope you enjoyed it. If you have a few minutes spare, it would be great if you could leave a review on Amazon. It makes a huge difference in regards to helping this book be found by others, which is especially important for independently published authors such as myself.
Thanks again,
Robert

Also from this author…

THE ISLANDERS

ROBERT BELL

Roy Michaels ends his first day as president of the United States in a cell. His captors are happy to fill in the blanks. For decades, their organisation has replaced political leaders around the world with vat-grown doubles, who work at their behest to protect the public from the "whims and myopia of democracy." The real presidents, prime ministers and chancellors are held captive in a manor house on a remote island, though the comfort of their existence has led many to forget that fact.

Michaels arrives on the island, unwilling to surrender to his fate. To reunite with his family, he will need not only to find a method of escape, but also to navigate the strange social structures that have developed on this island of political titans. He must forge alliances and confront enemies, new and old.

Robert Bell's *The Islanders* is an imaginative satire which gently skewers politicians of all persuasions. Comic, thought-provoking and thrilling in equal measure, there's nothing quite like this...

Printed in Great Britain
by Amazon